Nightcaps at
The Beach House Hotel

by

Judith Keim

BOOKS BY JUDITH KEIM

THE HARTWELL WOMEN SERIES:

The Talking Tree – 1

Sweet Talk – 2

Straight Talk – 3

Baby Talk – 4

The Hartwell Women – Boxed Set

THE BEACH HOUSE HOTEL SERIES:

Breakfast at The Beach House Hotel – 1

Lunch at The Beach House Hotel – 2

Dinner at The Beach House Hotel – 3

Christmas at The Beach House Hotel – 4

Margaritas at The Beach House Hotel – 5

Dessert at The Beach House Hotel – 6

Coffee at The Beach House Hotel – 7

High Tea at The Beach House Hotel – 8

Nightcaps at The Beach House Hotel – 9

Bubbles at The Beach House Hotel – 10 (2025)

THE FAT FRIDAYS GROUP:

Fat Fridays – 1

Sassy Saturdays – 2

Secret Sundays – 3

THE SALTY KEY INN SERIES:

Finding Me – 1

Finding My Way – 2

Finding Love – 3

Finding Family – 4

The Salty Key Inn Series – Boxed Set

SEASHELL COTTAGE BOOKS:

A Christmas Star

Change of Heart

A Summer of Surprises

A Road Trip to Remember

The Beach Babes

THE CHANDLER HILL INN SERIES:

Going Home – 1

Coming Home – 2

Home at Last – 3

The Chandler Hill Inn Series – Boxed Set

THE DESERT SAGE INN SERIES:

The Desert Flowers – Rose – 1

The Desert Flowers – Lily – 2

The Desert Flowers – Willow – 3

The Desert Flowers – Mistletoe & Holly – 4

The Desert Sage Inn Series – Boxed Set

SOUL SISTERS AT CEDAR MOUNTAIN LODGE:

Christmas Sisters – Anthology

Christmas Kisses

Christmas Castles

Christmas Stories – Soul Sisters Anthology

Christmas Joy

The Christmas Joy Boxed Set

THE SANDERLING COVE INN SERIES:

Waves of Hope – 1

Sandy Wishes – 2

Salty Kisses – 3

THE LILAC LAKE INN SERIES

Love by Design – 1

Love Between the Lines – 2

Love Under the Stars – 3

LILAC LAKE BOOKS

Love's Cure – (2024)

Love's Home Run – (2025)

Love's Bloom – (2025)

Love's Harvest – (2025)

Love's Match – (2025)

OTHER BOOKS:

The ABCs of Living With a Dachshund

Winning BIG – a little love story for all ages

Holiday Hopes

The Winning Tickets

For more information: **www.judithkeim.com**

PRAISE FOR JUDITH KEIM'S NOVELS

THE BEACH HOUSE HOTEL SERIES – Books 1 – 10:

"Love the characters in this series. This series was my first introduction to Judith Keim. She is now one of my favorites. Looking forward to reading more of her books."

BREAKFAST AT THE BEACH HOUSE HOTEL – **"***An easy, delightful read that offers romance, family relationships, and strong women learning to be stronger. Real life situations filter through the pages. Enjoy!"*

LUNCH AT THE BEACH HOUSE HOTEL – **"***This series is such a joy to read. You feel you are actually living with them. Can't wait to read the latest one."*

DINNER AT THE BEACH HOUSE HOTEL – "*A Terrific Read! As usual, Judith Keim did it again. Enjoyed immensely. Continue writing such pleasantly reading books for all of us readers."*

CHRISTMAS AT THE BEACH HOUSE HOTEL – "*Not Just Another Christmas Novel. This is book number four in the series and my introduction to Judith Keim's writing. I wasn't disappointed. The characters are dimensional and engaging. The plot is well-crafted and advances at a pleasing pace.*

MARGARITAS AT THE BEACH HOUSE HOTEL – "*Overall, Margaritas at the Beach House Hotel is another wonderful addition to the series. Judith Keim takes the reader on a journey told through the voices of these amazing characters we have all come to love through the years!*

DESSERT AT THE BEACH HOUSE HOTEL – *"It is a heartwarming and beautiful women's fiction as only Judith Keim can do with her wonderful characters, amazing location. and family and friends whose daily lives circle around Ann and Rhonda and The Beach House Hotel.*

COFFEE AT THE BEACH HOUSE HOTEL – *"Great story and characters! A hard to put down book. Lots of things happening, including a kidnapping of a young boy. The beach house hotel is a wonderful hotel run by two women who are best friends. Highly recommend this book.*

HIGH TEA AT THE BEACH HOUSE HOTEL – *"What a lovely story! The Beach House Hotel series is a always a great read. Each book in the series brings a new aspect to the saga of Ann and Rhonda."*

THE HARTWELL WOMEN SERIES – Books 1 – 4:

"This was an EXCELLENT series. When I discovered Judith Keim, I read all of her books back to back. I thoroughly enjoyed the women Keim has written about. They are believable and you want to just jump into their lives and be their friends! I can't wait for any upcoming books!"

"I fell into Judith Keim's Hartwell Women series and have read & enjoyed all of her books in every series. Each centers around a strong & interesting woman character and their family interaction. Good reads that leave you wanting more."

THE FAT FRIDAYS GROUP – Books 1 – 3:

"Excellent story line for each character, and an insightful representation of situations which deal with some of the contemporary issues women are faced with today."

THE SALTY KEY INN SERIES – Books 1 – 4:

FINDING ME – *"The characters are endearing with the same struggles we all encounter. The setting makes me feel like I am a guest at The Salty Key Inn...relaxed, happy & light-hearted! The men are yummy and the women strong. You can't get better than that! Happy Reading!"*

FINDING MY WAY - *"Loved the family dynamics as well as uncertain emotions of dating and falling in love. Appreciated the morals and strength of parenting throughout. Just couldn't put this book down."*

FINDING LOVE – *"Judith Keim always puts substance into her books. This book was no different, I learned about PTSD, accepting oneself, there are always going to be problems but stick it out and make it work.*

FINDING FAMILY – *"Completing this series is like eating the last chip. Love Judith's writing and her female characters are always smart, strong, vulnerable to life and love experiences."*

"This was a refreshing book. Bringing the heart and soul of the family to us."

THE CHANDLER HILL INN SERIES – Books 1 – 3:

GOING HOME – *"I was completely immersed in this book, with the beautiful descriptive writing, and the author's way of bringing her characters to life. I felt like I was right inside her story."*

COMING HOME – *"Coming Home was such a wonderful story. The author has such a gift for getting the reader right to the heart of things."*

HOME AT LAST – *"In this wonderful conclusion, to a heartfelt and emotional trilogy set in Oregon's stunning wine country, Judith Keim has tied up the Chandler Hill series with the perfect bow."*

SEASHELL COTTAGE BOOKS:

A CHRISTMAS STAR – *"Love, laughter, sadness, great food, and hope for the future, all in one book. It doesn't get any better than this stunning read."*

CHANGE OF HEART – *"CHANGE OF HEART is the summer read we've all been waiting for. Judith Keim is a master at creating fascinating characters that are simply irresistible. Her stories leave you with a big smile on your face and a heart bursting with love."*
~Kellie Coates Gilbert, author of the popular Sun Valley Series

A SUMMER OF SURPRISES – *"Ms. Keim uses this book as an amazing platform to show that with hard emotional work, belief in yourself, and love, the scars of abuse can be conquered. It in no way preaches, it's a lovely story with a happy ending."*

A ROAD TRIP TO REMEMBER – *"The characters are so real that they jump off the page. Such a fun, HAPPY book at the perfect time. It will lift your spirits and even remind you of your own grandmother. Spirited and hopeful Aggie gets a second chance at love and she takes the steering wheel and drives straight for it."*

THE BEACH BABES – *"Another winner at the pen of Judith Keim. I love the characters and the book just flows. It feels as though you are at the beach with them and are a part of you.*

THE DESERT SAGE INN SERIES – Books 1 – 4:

THE DESERT FLOWERS – ROSE – *"The Desert Flowers - Rose, "In this first of a series, we see each woman come into her own and view new beginnings even as they must take this tearful journey as they slowly lose a dear friend.*

THE DESERT FLOWERS – LILY – *"The second book in the Desert Flowers series is just as wonderful as the first. Judith Keim is a brilliant storyteller. Her characters are truly lovely and people that you want to be friends with as soon as you start reading. Judith Keim is not afraid to weave real-life conflict and loss into her stories.*

THE DESERT FLOWERS – WILLOW – *"The feelings of love, joy, happiness, friendship, family, and the pain of loss are deeply felt by Willow Sanchez and her two cohorts Rose and Lily. The Desert Flowers met because of their deep feelings for Alec Thurston, a man who touched their lives in different ways."*

MISTLETOE AND HOLLY – *"As always, the author never ceases to amaze me. She's able to take characters and bring them to life in such a way that you think you're actually among family. It's a great holiday read. You won't be disappointed."*

THE SANDERLING COVE INN SERIES

WAVES OF HOPE – *"Such a wonderful story about several families in a beautiful location in Florida. A grandmother requests her three granddaughters to help her by running the family's inn for the summer. Other grandmothers in the area played a part in this plan to find happiness for their grandsons and granddaughters."*

SANDY WISHES – *"Three cousins needing a change and a few of the neighborhood boys from when they were young are back visiting their grandmothers. It is an adventure, a summer of discoveries, and embracing the person they are becoming."*

SALTY KISSES – "I love this story, as well as the entire series because it's about family, friendship, and love. The meddling grandmothers have only the best intentions and want to see their grandchildren find love and happiness. What grandparent wouldn't want that?"

THE LILAC LAKE INN SERIES – Books 1 – 3:

LOVE BY DESIGN –"Genie Wittner is planning on selling her beloved Lilac Inn B&B, and keeping a cottage for her three granddaughters, Whitney, the movie star, Dani an architect, and Taylor a writer. A little mystery, a possible ghost, and romance all make this a great read and the start of a new series."

LOVE BETWEEN THE LINES – "Taylor is one of 3 sisters who have inherited a cottage in Lilac Lake from their grandmother. She is an accomplished author who is having some issues getting inspired for her next book. Things only get worse when she receives an email from her new editor with a harsh critique of her last book. She's still fuming when Cooper shows up in town, determined to work together on getting the book ready."

LOVE UNDER THE STARS – "Love Under the Stars is the third book in The Lilac Lake Inn Series by author Judith Keim. Judith beautifully weaves together the final story in this amazing series about the Gilford sisters and their grandmother, GG."

Nightcaps at The Beach House Hotel

The Beach House Hotel Series – Book 9

Judith Keim

Wild Quail Publishing

Nightcaps at The Beach House Hotel is a work of fiction. Names, characters, places, public or private institutions, corporations, towns, and incidents are the product of the author's imagination or are used fictitiously. Any resemblance to actual events, locales, or persons, living or dead, is coincidental.

No part of *Nightcaps at The Beach House Hotel* may be reproduced or transmitted in any form or by any electronic or mechanical means, including information storage and retrieval systems, without permission in writing from the author, except by a reviewer who may quote brief passages in a review. This book may not be resold or uploaded for distribution to others. For permissions contact the author directly via electronic mail:

wildquail.pub@gmail.com
www.judithkeim.com

Published in the United States of America by:

Wild Quail Publishing
PO Box 171332
Boise, ID 83717-1332

ISBN# 978-1-965622-00-1
Copyright ©2024 Judith Keim
All rights reserved

Dedication

For fans of Ann and Rhonda,
who keep me writing about them!

CHAPTER ONE

I SAT WITH MY BUSINESS PARTNER, RHONDA DELMONTE Grayson, in our office at The Beach House Hotel on the Gulf Coast in sunny Sable, Florida, wondering if we were facing another problem that we'd have trouble solving.

"Who is this nighttime talk show host anyway?" Rhonda asked. "I've never heard of him. Of course, I can't stay up beyond nine o'clock. Besides, who wants to see a program where every famous star is talking about who is dating whom or telling us what their favorite thing to wear is, or what they like to eat? Who the fuck cares? I'm too tired working here at the hotel and taking care of kids and grandkids to want to bother with stuff like that."

I knew enough to wait until Rhonda caught her breath. She and I were as different as two people could be. I'd grown up with a strict grandmother in Boston where proper language and decorum were everything. It still amazed me that Rhonda and I had become best friends and business partners. But Rhonda had a heart as big as the diamonds she wore in her ears, on her fingers, and at her neck and wrists. And I'd never forget all she'd done for me.

"Before we decide to honor his request to stay here for several weeks, we need to view at least a couple of his shows to help us decide for ourselves if it could work," I said. "C'mon, it won't be so bad. We'll have a couple of nightcaps and snacks while we watch the show."

"Humph. I suppose we need to know who we're dealing with, especially because he's requesting the same dates as

Tina Marks," Rhonda said.

"The two of them would be staying in the hotel's two guesthouses apart from one another, so they should have the seclusion they require," I said. "But our loyalty goes to Tina." Tina Marks was like a daughter to us after we'd agreed to hide her at the hotel to lose some weight between movies. She'd been a tough brat when she'd first arrived but was now dear to us both.

"So, what's his name?" Rhonda asked me.

"Darryl Douglas," I replied. "He's fairly new in the business. He's had his show for only a couple of years. I looked him up online. He's got a nice smile."

"Already I don't trust him. I hate a person who smiles while they're gossiping," said Rhonda, and I knew this was a piece of baggage from Rhonda's childhood. She grew up in New Jersey in a rough neighborhood and had been teased for her size.

Now that she was happily married and financially secure after winning one hundred eighty-seven million dollars in the Florida lottery, people were much nicer to her. Still, Rhonda was a loyal person who saw through others who were not very kind. Maybe that's why our relationship worked. We'd both been betrayed by the men we'd first married.

"Let's look at a couple of his shows this week and see how we feel about his request after that," I said. "You can come to my house. Vaughn is away working on a movie in Canada, and Robbie will be in bed. We can enjoy our time together."

"Nightcaps, huh? With a few treats? Okay, but if I still don't like the guy, I don't care what kind of situation he's in, he's not staying at the hotel."

"As I understand it, Darryl's ex-wife is saying he owes her more money and there's some sort of problem at work. That's all his agent would tell me when he called to ask for the reservation. He did mention the vice-president had recommended the hotel."

Rhonda shook her head. "That does it. Every time Amelia Swanson recommends the hotel to someone, we get caught in a bad situation. I still haven't recovered from the kidnapping attempt."

"I admit that was scary, but it was a one-time thing. We've beefed up security at the hotel and have vetted our guests whenever we feel it's necessary."

"Let's take a walk on the beach. We do our best thinking there," said Rhonda.

I happily followed her through the back of the hotel, the pool area, and onto the sand. An onshore breeze ruffled the fronds of the palm trees on our property and, satisfied that all was well at the hotel, I took off my sandals and followed Rhonda onto the beach.

The smell of salt air loosened some of the tension in my body. I always felt more clearheaded watching the waves roll in, kiss the shore, and back away in a rhythm as old as time. I went to the water's frothy edge and dipped my toe into the cool wetness.

Seagulls and terns whirled above us, their cries echoing against the moving water. Down the beach, sandpipers and sanderlings trotted along the water's edge looking for food, leaving tiny footprints behind.

I took in a deep breath of fresh air and let out a sigh of happiness. Then I turned and studied the hotel.

Like a lazy flamingo stretched along the sand, the front of it hugged a wide expanse of beach while the rest of the building's image was softened by palm trees and the immaculate landscaping surrounding it.

"Look what we've done," said Rhonda, throwing an arm around my shoulder. "Our own special baby."

I laughed. We were surrounded by babies. Rhonda had three children and three grandchildren while I had my two kids and triplet grandchildren. But Rhonda was right. The Beach House Hotel was our special baby, born of the need to prove that two dumped women could make a new, better life on their own and with new men in their lives who truly loved them.

Rhonda and I took off, walking together on the sand, talking.

"We've always helped people," said Rhonda. "And I like that part of the business we've built. But we have to be careful. Remember, when we first started our privacy-for-guests policy, you worried we were going to be running a place where all kinds of hanky-panky would take place."

I couldn't help laughing. We'd started that policy when certain members of Congress had come to us needing an upscale place to meet in secret. Since then, the hotel had hosted numerous VIP guests and endured many unusual experiences. But we were known for being as upfront and straightforward as we could be. Our guests came back again and again.

"Has Tina decided to bring the kids when she comes to the hotel?" Rhonda asked me.

"She's leaving them at home with her nanny and bringing her personal trainer instead. She has to be ready to start filming in a month, and like her first time here, she needs to lose weight and get in shape. It must be hard to feel you have to be perfect to compete with younger actresses."

"It can be a nasty business." Rhonda grabbed my arm. "Speaking of nasty business, look who's headed our way. No chance I can run fast enough to get away."

"We'll say hi and keep walking," I said, hoping we could. Brock Goodwin was president of the neighborhood association and had been a thorn in our sides since the beginning when he'd tried to stop the hotel from opening. Though we'd succeeded in getting past those objections, he was always looking for a way to interfere. We detested him.

Tall, gray-haired, and in shape, Brock was sought-after by single women living in the area for his looks and suave manner which hid his true personality.

"Well, if it isn't the two biggest troublemakers in the neighborhood," said Brock.

"Hello, Brock," I said moving past him. "We can't stay to chat. We're talking business."

He ran to catch up to us. "Is there anything I should know about?"

"As you know, we keep business and our guests private," said Rhonda.

He studied her. "I can already tell you've got something going on, something you no doubt want to keep secret," he said in his presumptuous way. "You know I won't rest until I find out what it is. After all, as president of the neighborhood association, it's my duty to be well-informed."

"I hear someone is going to run against you for that position. Someone new in town," said Rhonda. "See ya later."

We kept on walking.

A few minutes later, I looked back. Brock was still standing there staring out at the water. I nudged Rhonda. "Good job. He's still wondering who might take his precious position away from him. You were kidding about it, right?"

"Yeah. Who wants to be president of a fuckin' neighborhood association? No one. That's who."

I started to chuckle, and soon we were both laughing hard. We'd do anything to get Brock off our backs. After tricking him into bidding on something he couldn't afford for a charity event, we'd made a special deal with him to stay away from the second guesthouse we were building on our property. It wasn't a bad idea. The house was constructed in record time with no problems from anyone. It was this house that Darryl wanted to stay in.

When we headed back to the hotel, Brock wasn't in sight. I decided to call our friend, Dorothy Stern, to tell her about Rhonda's remark to Brock. Dorothy was a retired businesswoman who'd help us out when we first opened the hotel by doing volunteer work sending out notices and invitations to our special events. At just over five feet tall, she was the one person who seemed able to stand up to Brock. She'd been known to put him in his place more than once. We adored her.

We headed into the kitchen for a morning cup of coffee and one of Consuela's cinnamon rolls. These treats had been helpful when trying to tempt early guests with reasons to stay at The Beach House Hotel. They had become a specialty of the hotel after a food critic from New York stayed at the hotel and mentioned it to all his fans.

Consuela greeted us with a smile. "*Buenos Dias!* You're just in time. A few minutes ago, I took a second batch of sweet rolls out of the oven."

"Good morning. Did you have a nice couple of days off?" I hugged her. Consuela and her husband, Manny, had been working for Rhonda before we opened the hotel. They stayed on and became the heart of the hotel family. The two of them were the parents I always wished I'd had.

"We did have a nice break, though you know Manny," said Consuela. "He doesn't like to leave the landscaping of the property in anyone else's hands for too long."

"Annie, I told you when we first met, he's my 'Manny around the house'," said Rhonda, giving me a wide grin.

Consuela and I glanced at one another and laughed.

At the time, Rhonda had also mentioned she had a beach house. I had no idea it was a seaside estate that had once been a small hotel.

"It's nice to have you and Manny back with us," I said, placing a warm sweet roll onto a plate.

"We couldn't run the place without you," said Rhonda giving Consuela a bosomy hug. "I'm going to take one more cinnamon roll to the office. Annie and I have to talk about an upcoming guest."

We took coffee and our treats to the office we shared.

I no sooner sat down at my desk than my cell phone rang. *Amelia Swanson.*

"Hello, Madame Vice President. I'm going to put you on speaker phone in our office so Rhonda can hear too. Okay?"

"Yes. I just wanted to check to see if you're going to be able to handle Darryl Douglas's request. His agent is a friend of mine and the president's too."

"We have the request, but I'm not sure we can accommodate him. We'll know more tomorrow. It would mean moving someone out of the guesthouse and into a room."

"And after the last time we did you a favor ..." Rhonda began.

"We'll be sure to let you know," I interrupted. I knew Rhonda was going to mention the kidnapping that took place, and I didn't want to get her riled up and then say something we'd both regret. We'd survived a couple of tricky situations satisfying Amelia's requests, and the thought of being forced to face the possibility of another traumatic one was worrisome.

"I've got to go," said Amelia. "I hope you understand the political importance of this for me. I may be needing people in the media in the future."

"We understand," I said, "but we must be able to take care of our guests properly."

"I'm aware," said Amelia. "You know how much I appreciate your help in the past. I can't think of a better place than your hotel to send people to."

I felt my lips curving. Amelia was an excellent politician.

"We'll have a decision tomorrow," I said.

"Okay, I'll hold you to it," said Amelia. "How's the weather? Any storms?"

"Nothing to report," I said, crossing my fingers. Early fall was a time for hurricanes to
visit.

"Nice to talk to you. I may be down to visit my sister soon and hope to stop in," said Amelia. "Thanks."

She ended the call, and Rhonda and I faced one another.

Rhonda made a face. "That woman always gets her way. No wonder she's close to the president. He couldn't do his job without her."

"That's not the way that position usually works, but I agree with you." I took a sip of coffee, my mind whirling. "Let's see what we can find out about Darryl online. First, I want to return these dishes to the kitchen and check the dining room. It's a bit of a slow time, and we need to know how the dining staff is doing."

We walked into the dining room and saw Dorothy Stern sitting at a table with three friends deep in conversation.

I waved, and Rhonda and I went over to her. "It's great to see you here. We have something to tell you in private. What are you ladies talking about?"

"Darryl Douglas. We think he's having some kind of breakdown and wants to leave the show," said Dorothy.

"It all started with that horrible ex-wife of his, Everly Jansen," said one of the other women. "She's greedy. She married him for his money."

"Yeah, it wasn't for his looks," said another woman. "I love the guy, but you have to admit he's not buff or drop-dead gorgeous like some of the stars he interviews."

"That's what makes him special. He has a quick wit, and the way he comes up with jokes is hilarious," said Dorothy. "We're all fans of his."

"And none of us wanted him to marry that woman. We knew she was bad news," said one of the women.

"I'm curious," said Rhonda. "Why do you care so much about Darryl Douglas and his career?"

"I'll tell you. As funny as he is, he doesn't tear down other people to make us laugh like a lot of other comedians." Dorothy glanced at the others for their approval. "I don't know. He's kind. Heaven knows we could use a lot more people like that."

The other women at the table nodded their agreement.

"But shows like his seem meaningless," countered Rhonda.

"You have to see his shows to believe us," said Dorothy.

"Right. That's why we're watching one tonight," I said shooting a look of determination to Rhonda. "But if what you say is right, it makes me like him already."

"Let me know what you both think," said Dorothy.

I gave her a thumbs up. Rhonda and I had to make that decision quickly, though we might regret it.

CHAPTER TWO

RHONDA AND I SAT ON THE COUCH IN MY LIVING ROOM facing the television. I'd fixed Irish coffee for each of us, and a plate of brownie bites sat on the table. Cindy, our black and tan short-haired dachshund, had been sent away from the food to Robbie's bedroom to sleep with him. He was eleven now and growing fast, but he was still young enough to want his dog at night.

Rhonda let out a long sigh. "This house seems very quiet. My kids would still be fighting sleep," she said, talking about her two children, Willow, eight, and Drew, six. Her oldest child, Angie, was in her late twenties like my daughter, Liz. They'd been college freshmen roommates, which is how Rhonda and I met. Now they were busy mothers of our collective six grandchildren. Hopefully, Liz and Angie would take over running the hotel, but that day seemed a long way off.

"Okay," I said lifting my cup of special coffee. "Here's to making a fair decision. Let's enjoy the show."

Rhonda raised her cup of coffee and took a sip. "Delicious. If nightcaps are the way to making a wise choice, I'm all for it. But, Annie, we gotta be sensible."

"I know. But, in truth, we need the business and Amelia's continued support. The hotel business is very competitive. Especially when we have others trying to emulate us."

The show's title, *Night Talk with Darryl Douglas*, came on screen with a musical introduction. I moved in my seat restlessly, hoping we could give Amelia the answer she wanted. Darryl's bio indicated he was the youngest of the family with four older sisters. I could only imagine how spoiled he must've been growing up.

At the sound of a certain drum roll, Darryl walked out on stage. He was of average height, a little overweight, and had a bright, easy smile as he waved to the studio audience.

"He looks like a cuddly Teddy Bear," I murmured, and beside me, Rhonda nodded.

"I bet those four sisters of his spoiled him like crazy," she said. "That or made his life miserable by dominating him."

"Maybe that's why he turned to comedy," I said, seeing him in a whole new light.

Darryl did a short monologue talking about teachers being back at school that had us both laughing. And then he walked behind his desk and announced who would be his guests for the evening.

A young actress who, no doubt, had had breast enhancement surgery was the first guest. Her perfect facial features and botoxed lips made her beautiful, but I'm sure she would've been perfectly fine without all the enhancements.

I could sense Rhonda grow tense beside me and knew she was irritated by the idea that some women had to meet certain standards of appearance to become successful. She hated the idea, and I understood. But that's what it often took to get noticed in the entertainment industry.

Darryl asked the actress about the role she was in and listened politely while she talked about how she'd fallen in love with her co-star, a sexy man known for fooling around. She smiled. "In making this movie, I've discovered what it's like to be with a man who knows how to truly make a woman satisfied. You know what I mean?"

She leaned forward, waiting for Darryl to answer.

Darryl grimaced and said, "Let's go to break time."

"Wow," said Rhonda. "He all but rolled his eyes. I don't blame him. I don't think the woman has a brain in her head. Do you think that's the problem with him doing the show?

'I'm not sure," I said. "I have a feeling we'll find out someday. I like Darryl. His jokes are funny. He has a great sense of humor. But he did seem embarrassed by his guests."

"I agree," said Rhonda, taking a brownie from the plate. "He seems like a nice guy. Let's give him the chance to stay here. It's for four weeks or so. Right?"

"That's what the request said. But we'd better verify that. I agree we give him the chance. He doesn't seem like the kind of guy who'd intrude on Tina's stay."

Rhonda waggled a finger at me. "I wouldn't trust him on that point. We'll just have to make sure they never meet. I don't think anyone would give up the chance to interview Tina Marks. She's usually very private."

"You're right. And the one person who can never know about either of them is Brock. Heaven knows what he'd do with information like that."

By the end of the program, Rhonda was snoring, and I was doing everything I could to stay awake. With Vaughn traveling from time to time, I sometimes read before going to sleep. But I never stayed up this late when I had to work the next day.

"Okay, Rhonda. Time to get up and go home," I said shaking her gently.

Her eyes flew open. "Is it the kids?"

"No, Rhonda, we were watching the Darryl Douglas show. Now it's over."

She yawned and stretched before standing. "Okay. Don't worry. I can make it home."

I walked her to the door, and after seeing her off, I locked the house and turned into my bedroom. The bed was empty without Vaughn. We'd talked earlier that evening, but words of love didn't compare to having him beside me.

The next morning, I awoke with a start, glanced at the clock, and hurried to wake Robbie.

He was stretched out, face down across the bed. Cindy nestled up beside him. She turned and looked at me, then moved as I called out to Robbie to wake up.

"Sorry. I overslept. Hurry. I'll fix breakfast for you while you get dressed." I studied the young man he was becoming and remembered the two-year-old toddler we'd adopted. He'd been orphaned by his parent's automobile accident. Robert, my ex, had dumped me for his voluptuous receptionist. Robbie was theirs, and now he was Vaughn's and mine.

He'd grown recently and I realized he'd be tall like his father.

I left him and hurried to let Cindy out before fixing breakfast for both. It was going to be a busy day at the hotel with a new group moving in for a small conference. As much as we relied on our regular guests, we needed a lot of group and wedding business. Rhonda and I always tried to give personal attention to them.

Robbie came into the kitchen. "Remember, I have a swim meet today. Are you coming?"

"I've got it marked down and will keep that time free. But emergencies do arise. I've heard from Stephanie. She and Randolph are planning on being there." Longtime guests at the hotel, the Willises had become substitute grandparents to Robbie. A pleasant situation for all.

"Great," said Robbie. "When is Dad coming back?"

"Not for a couple of weeks. The movie is taking longer than

they thought. But you know him. He's anxious to get home and get out on the water in the sailboat with you."

"I know," said Robbie. He quickly ate the cereal and drank the juice I'd set out for him.

I handed him some protein bars, and he tucked them into his backpack.

"Make sure you get a healthy lunch at school," I said snatching a kiss from him. I loved that he still let me kiss him.

"The coach makes sure we all eat well," Robbie said.

We got into the car, and I dropped him off at school before heading home again to get ready for work.

At the hotel, I slid into my seat in Bernhard Bruner's office just in time for his meeting. Bernie was a talented hotel general manager whom we trusted to run the hotel for us. Rhonda was already there, but she looked as if she'd stayed up past her bedtime, too.

Bernie asked us if we'd decided about having Darryl Douglas stay at the hotel. With a nod of approval from Rhonda, I said that we would agree to let him have the house for up to six weeks.

"Then I think that the guests assigned to the house for part of that time should be offered a stay in the Presidential Suite for the same price they would've paid for the house," said Bernie. "Is that agreeable to both of you?"

Rhonda and I quickly agreed. The Presidential Suite was beautiful. No guest would have reason to complain.

"The problem is that one of the guests we're talking about is someone who has been in verbal warfare with Darryl recently," said Bernie, giving us a worried look.

Rhonda's eyes widened. "Do you mean Darryl's ex-wife?"

"Yes," said Bernie. "I will suggest she come another time

when the house will be available, but if she refuses, there's nothing I can do about it. Just a heads up."

Rhonda and I exchanged glances. Tina, Darryl, and his ex-wife would all be staying at the hotel wanting confidentiality at the same time. Could we do it?

"Why don't we hire additional security to block anyone else from gaining access to either house?" said Bernie. "Having a guard protect the road leading to them is nothing new. No one would suspect a thing."

"Good idea," I said. "I just don't want trouble. Being exclusive and able to promise a certain degree of privacy is what has made The Beach House Hotel in such demand."

"We only have one person needing to be monitored round the clock," muttered Rhonda. "Brock Goodwin is such a pain in the ass."

"The staff is aware of the need to keep him out of that area," said Bernie. "But having a security guard by the road's entrance to the houses will be helpful."

"Okay, then, we've agreed on that. What else do we need to deal with?" I asked.

"This next weekend, we have the Gorman wedding. This is a social win for us," said Bernie. "Lorraine, why don't you fill us in on any special requirements."

Lorraine Grace ran Wedding Perfections for us. Married now to Angie's father-in-law, Arthur Smythe, she looked fabulous. We were lucky she still wanted to continue her business through the hotel. It seemed to work well that she was as busy as Arthur was with his financial consulting business.

"The Gorman's are a prominent family in New York and are well-known to Arthur. It was he who persuaded them to have the wedding here at the hotel. There will be lots of publicity both there and here in Florida, but I assure you it will be handled properly," Lorraine said.

"Are any of the guests staying on at the hotel?" I asked.

"A few of them may remain for an extra couple of days but nothing that would cause a problem, in my opinion," said Lorraine.

"We'd better tell the staff that they need to be careful what they say around the guests with all the VIPs inhouse," said Rhonda.

"Indeed. At the staff meeting, I intend to inform them they must be discreet," said Bernie. "Though they've already signed NDAs, even talking among themselves about either Tina or Darryl could become an issue if overheard."

We discussed several other items on the agenda, and then I rose. "Thank you, Bernie. Please let us know if there are any problems with Darryl's ex, Everly Jansen, over the new room arrangement."

"Will do," said Bernie. "I'll speak to the full staff this afternoon to review our policy and the upcoming wedding."

"Thanks," said Rhonda. She followed me out of his office. "I don't know about you, but I need some coffee."

"Me, too," I said. "I'm concerned about our upcoming situation with Darryl and his wife being here together, but we need both the money and Amelia's support."

"We've dealt with difficult guests since the beginning. There's no reason to think we can't do it again," said Rhonda. "There's no way I'm letting our hotel's reputation be ruined by a high-profile couple."

"But from what I've heard, there are also issues for Darryl at the studio. That makes his situation even worse."

"Let's see if there are any leftover sweet rolls," said Rhonda. "They always make me feel better."

We got coffee and treats and carried them to our office. Though it was September, we were reviewing holiday and high-season bookings.

"Lorraine is booked for weddings covering a lot of weekends," I said, "but we need to fill in weekdays. What about creating pampered packages?"

"We can use those for those slow days before and after the holidays," said Rhonda. "I like it. A Pampered Package including discounts in our spa, breakfast in bed, and a greeting basket with wine and snacks."

"Let's talk to Liz and Angie about doing some online advertising for it. We'll give them the details and available dates, and they can come up with a plan and graphics for social media," I said.

"Great idea," said Rhonda. "Anything to get them involved."

Liz and Angie managed to help us on their computers but didn't yet have the flexibility to work outside of their homes. Liz's triplets were three years old and very active. And while Angie's oldest, Evan, was eight, her youngest of the three was only two.

"I'll stop and talk to Liz on my way home," I said. "I haven't seen the 'T's' for a few days, and I need 'GeeGee' time with them." The "T's"—Olivia, Emily, and Noah—were adorable toddlers but exhausting. I loved them like crazy.

"I'm taking care of the two younger kids while Angie and Reggie go to a school program with Evan." Rhonda smiled. "It's important for him to have time with his parents without his sisters."

"He's a great older brother to them. Back to the hotel business. I like the idea of an additional security guard to protect the guesthouses, but do you think we need to hire even another one for the few days Darryl's wife is here?"

Rhonda shrugged. "Let's wait and see."

"Okay," I said. "Time to call Amelia. No matter what Everly

says about switching her room, we've agreed to accept Darryl as our guest for a six-week stay."

"You call her, Annie. Amelia knows I don't like her getting involved in our business."

"Okay," I said, remembering how angry Rhonda was after the kidnapping attempt we were dragged into. "This will be better than last time."

"You hope," said Rhonda, shaking her head.

Though I didn't like the situation, I was the numbers person and knew it was a wise decision financially. We'd have to make it work.

CHAPTER THREE

WHEN I ENTERED LIZ'S HOUSE, THE THREE LITTLE ONES rushed toward me shouting, "GeeGee!" My heart overflowed with love. All three were combinations of Liz and Chad with their varying shades of blond hair and blue eyes. Noah was the most physically active, but Olivia and Emily had been talking way before he began. But then, I could imagine it was hard for him to break into the constant chatter of his sisters.

"Hi, Mom! Glad to see you. What's up?" said Liz, coming into the playroom.

"Two things. I needed a grandma fix, and I want to talk to you about an idea Rhonda and I had for the hotel."

"Great. Chad and I are working on the hotel's website. Anything we need to add?"

"Yes. Something we want you and Angie to develop: A Pampered Package. We'll use this as a fall and holiday promotion for weekday stays."

"Hm-m-m sounds like fun. Do we get to stay at the hotel and test it?" asked Liz, giving me a teasing grin.

"Not exactly," I said. "But you know I'm willing to take care of the triplets overnight any time Vaughn is home. The two of us can handle them nicely."

Liz chuckled. "I get it. I don't know what I'd do without my part-time nanny. Want something cold to drink? Iced tea? Lemonade?"

"Lemonade sounds delicious," I said, laughing when Olivia tugged on my blouse and said, "I want up."

I lifted the little girl into my arms and nuzzled her neck. I'd wanted lots of children but had only been able to have Liz. And then, even with the unusual circumstances surrounding it, I now had the joy of being Robbie's mother. Still, there was something special about grandchildren—as if I had most of the fun and not all the work.

While we sipped our lemonade, Liz and I sat outside on her patio and watched the children run around the yard.

"Mom? You won't give up on Angie and me having a growing part in running the hotel, will you?"

I studied Liz's look of concern. "Absolutely not. I understand how frustrated you might be staying at home raising the kids. But we're already relying more and more on your handling of social media advertising and coming up with creative ideas. When you think about it, the hotel is almost as much a part of your lives as Rhonda's and mine."

"Thanks for understanding," said Liz. "I adore my children, but I want some outside stimulation."

"I get it, and, believe me, Rhonda and I will be anxious for you and Angie to take over for us when the time is right. Vaughn and I will reach the point where we'll need to settle down to a more normal life."

"Is he still working on the movie?" she asked.

"Yes, I miss him but know how important his work is to him."

Emily started crying and soon all three children were crying. Liz and I jumped to our feet to see what had happened. Olivia and Noah held big rubber balls.

"Where's your ball, Emily?" I asked, picking her up to soothe her.

Emily pointed to a bush by the fence. "In there."

"Why don't we help you get it, and you can stop crying," I said, giving her a loving squeeze before setting her down on the ground.

Moments later, with the three of them each holding a ball, Liz and I headed back to the patio. I checked my watch. "I've got to go. It's time for Robbie's swim meet."

"Wish him luck for me," said Liz, hugging me. "Thanks."

"Love you," I said, hugging her back, realizing how important it was for Liz to feel part of the hotel operation.

Sitting in the bleachers watching Robbie swim the American crawl, my heart burst with pride. He was an excellent swimmer who loved being active and part of a team. He'd been a toddler when he became ours, but I felt strongly that spending time with Vaughn had helped Robbie learn about going after challenges and being a sport when he didn't succeed. They spent hours together on Vaughn's sailboat. Time well spent. Vaughn's two children, Nell and Ty, had families of their own and lived elsewhere.

Stephanie Willis turned to me. "He won again!" She clapped a hand to her chest. "I'm so proud of him."

I gave her a quick hug. Stephanie and her husband Randolph were longtime guests of the hotel and had become close to my family. Observing Randolph clapping his approval, I was filled with satisfaction. Since Rhonda and I opened the hotel, we'd brought a lot of people into what I called "our hotel family." Maybe that's why many of our guests continued to come back year after year.

My thoughts turned to Darryl Douglas. He was due to arrive in two days.

Even though Darryl was going to be secreted away in one of our guesthouses, Rhonda and I stood at the top of the stairs at the front of the hotel ready to greet him.

At the sight of his limo driving through the gates of the

property, I nudged Rhonda. "Okay, here we go."

"For better or worse," she grumbled. Wearing a blue silk caftan, she made me think of a bluebird, my favorite, as her sleeves flapped as she hurried down the steps beside me. In a pale-blue linen dress, I felt plain beside her.

The white limousine pulled to a stop beside us.

We waited for the driver to come around the car and open the door for Darryl.

"Welcome to The Beach House Hotel," I said, as a man of average height and with more pounds than normal for a television star sat and stared at us from inside the car. He had engaging hazel eyes and thinning brown hair that may or may not be enhanced by a toupee on television.

"We hope you have a wonderful stay," Rhonda said.

"Now that you're here, we'll follow you and the limo to your house on the property. We'll have you check in there, so you won't be seen," I said. "We understand how important that is to you."

"Thank you," he said. "I don't want anyone to find out where I am. I need plenty of time to sort things out and to get some much-needed rest."

He closed the passenger door and his driver followed our directions to get to the road leading to the two houses.

Rhonda and I easily walked there, pleased to see that no other hotel guests had noticed Darryl. We could promise to do our best to see he was isolated, but that was all.

At the house, which was the one Tina had previously used, not the newer one, we ushered Darryl inside. We showed him around, explaining how certain things worked, and then had him review and sign the registration card and other agreements for his stay.

"You'll notice that included in the agreement is a special section requiring your signature to respect the confidentiality of other hotel guests," I said.

"The other house, just beyond here, is about to be occupied by someone who wants seclusion too," said Rhonda. "So, please stick to your property."

"Right," I said. "There's security assigned to both houses. Please respect him."

"Okay," said Darryl. "I figure I'll use the beach early in the morning when few people are around. Otherwise, I'll be here. I understand your chef, Jean-Luc Rodin, is exceptional. I'll be ordering room service unless I feel comfortable going incognito in the dining room."

"We understand," I said. "You aren't the only VIP requiring privacy who will be staying here."

"Yeah, we don't want you interviewing anyone here," said Rhonda. "We saw you on television, ya know."

Darryl bit his lip, and I realized he was shy.

Leaving the house with Rhonda, I mentioned that to her.

"Yes, I had a friend who could only get by in high school by telling jokes and making other kids laugh at him."

"Tina and her trainer arrive tonight. Hopefully, she can get settled in without Darryl seeing her. But if it does happen, I'm sure Tina will make him understand that they both need secrecy."

That evening, Tina arrived in a black Town Car and went straight to the house she was renting.

Rhonda and I were waiting for her there as pre-arranged. We'd already ordered a snack tray accompanied by a bottle of wine and sparkling water for all of us to share.

At the sound of the car approaching, Rhonda and I stepped

outside. With Tina, it was more a homecoming than greeting a beloved guest.

Tina got out of the car and hurried to greet us.

The three of us huddled for a group hug.

"It's very good to see you. You look terrific," I said to Tina.

"Not really," said Tina. "I've loved being home with the boys, but now it's time to get back to work. I have a wonderful role coming up, but it requires a lot of physical action. That's why I've brought Abbie with me. Meet my personal trainer, Abbie Hathaway."

As she and I shook hands, I was amused by Abbie's firm grip. Of average height, dark-haired and with luscious brown eyes, Abbie appeared to be in her 30s and was a perfect model of fitness with a buff, trim body I knew I could never achieve. For such a tough person, her manner was sweet, almost shy. I liked her immediately.

"Don't let her sweetness fool you," said Tina. "Abbie is a monster when it comes to training. I have no doubt I'll be ready for the movie when we get the signal it's a go."

"Why the delay?" asked Rhonda.

Tina shook her head. "I waited to get here before I told you. The hero of the movie is Sinclair Smith, who's recently married and is on his extended honeymoon. Guess who he married?"

The teasing look on Tina's face was perturbing as she stared at me.

I thought of a name and shook my head. It couldn't be, wouldn't be possible.

"Well?" said Tina.

"Are you talking about Lily Dorio?" I asked.

Rhonda burst into laughter. "No shit."

"Yes, it's her, the comeback kid. We can't seem to get rid of her. She's like a rubber ball bouncing in and out of our lives," said Tina.

I let out a long sigh. Lily Dorio was an actor who'd tried to interfere in the growing relationship I had with Vaughn and even afterward. "I'm sorry you have to deal with her, Tina. She's bound to cause trouble."

"Yes, I know," said Tina. "But I'm going to do my part and pray Sinclair will do his. As I mentioned, I like the script which is why I'm willing to work hard to get in shape."

"You can't let her ruin it for you," said Rhonda. "Somehow Karma is going to get back at Lily. Just do your own thing."

"Yes, I agree," said Tina. "Let's get settled, and then I'll have a glass of wine ... uh, make that water with you. Abbie can have my wine."

Abbie gave Tina a satisfied look. "I'm glad to do the honors." She turned to us. "I've heard a whole lot about the two of you. I can't wait to get to know you better."

I smiled in return and wondered what the next couple of weeks would bring.

It being a school night, Rhonda and I didn't stay long. But even after I returned home to be with Robbie, my heart was happy from seeing Tina again. She'd always be the young girl who I'd helped to heal from a terrible childhood. She'd had an overly ambitious mother who would offer her to execs to get new roles in movies.

After getting Robbie and Cindy settled for the night, I got ready for bed, climbed in, and sat beneath a light blanket with a new book.

My cell phone rang. *Vaughn.*

Smiling at the fluttering of my pulse, I answered. "Hi! How are you?"

"Fine. Missing you. Are you in bed?" His low voice, familiar to fans of his, made me smile even wider.

"Yes, I am," I answered. "It is empty without you."

"I'm more than ready to come home. 'Sure you don't want to travel to Toronto to see me?"

I let out a deep sigh. I loved knowing he wanted me there, but the truth was, he'd be busy, and I was needed in Sable. "I wish I could, but we have a tricky situation at the hotel, and I wouldn't feel right leaving Rhonda to deal with it alone."

"Don't tell me it's another request of Amelia Swanson's," Vaughn said. "You promised you'd be careful going forward. Almost losing you in that kidnapping scheme was something I never want to repeat."

"The only person in trouble is Darryl Douglas," I said. "Rhonda and I watched his show a couple of nights ago, and he seemed okay."

"Darryl Douglas the nighttime talk show host?" Vaughn said. "I hear he's having more than one problem. Why is he at the hotel?"

"I'm not sure," I said. "But, believe me, he just wants a quiet, private time here."

"Guess what? I heard some very interesting news. Sinclair Smith married Lily Dorio. Poor guy."

"They're honeymooning. That's why Tina was able to get away for a few weeks to get herself in shape for the movie she's starring in with him."

"There's always trouble surrounding Lily," said Vaughn with an edge of bitterness.

I didn't blame him. She'd pretended to be his pregnant girlfriend. Told everyone he was the father to hide an affair with a producer. Vaughn was a straight-up guy who was infuriated by her lies.

"Well, hopefully, we won't have to deal with her again," I said, mentally crossing my fingers. "How much longer are you going to be away?"

"I'm hoping to come home in a week or so. Tell Robbie to have the boat ready. "

"I will."

"Ann? Do you have any idea how much I love you? Having you waiting for me at home with our family means the world to me. You're the anchor I need."

"And you're the wind I need," I said, meaning it with my entire being. I hadn't known real love until I met and married him.

He chuckled softly. "How about a private cruise on the boat so we can make love under the stars."

"You know I love stargazing," I said, teasing him.

We laughed together and then after catching him up on family news, we said goodnight.

I couldn't wait for him to come home.

CHAPTER FOUR

ONE DAY, AFTER DROPPING ROBBIE OFF AT SCHOOL FOR an early morning swim practice, I decided to go to the hotel and check on things there. Darryl had mentioned walking on the beach, and I wanted to see if he'd been able to do that. The exercise might do him good, provided he had the isolation he needed.

It was quiet at the hotel. I walked through it and out to the beach. I saw a couple holding hands walking together, an older woman looking for shells, and in the distance, a man I thought might be Darryl walking towards me.

I headed in his direction. Before he reached me, I noticed Abbie Hathaway jog by him. She stopped beside me as Darryl approached us.

"Good morning," I said and waited to see how they'd react to each other. I couldn't introduce them to each other and keep to a privacy policy.

"Nice to see you here, Ann," said Abbie. She turned to Darryl. "You, too. I'm Abbie Hathaway, a personal trainer."

Darryl smiled shyly. "Really? I could use one. Do you have any free time?"

Abbie studied him, and I noticed Darryl tighten his stomach. "Yes, I do have some free time."

"Okay, great," he said. "I'm Darryl, and I'm staying in one of the houses on the property. Maybe we could discuss setting up a schedule."

"Fine. I'm staying in the other house. A little later, I'll walk over to talk to you."

"Okay, we'll meet there." Darryl walked away from us.

Abbie looked at me. "I didn't dare tell him I knew who he was. I almost didn't recognize him in that baseball cap. But Darryl Douglas is so well known that he's going to have trouble going unnoticed."

"Maybe after working with him, he won't be as recognizable," I said, not unkindly. "Where's Tina?"

"I can be a tough trainer but even I know the importance of Tina getting rest. We start training at nine. And she can be stubborn. But I guess you know that. She told me all about her first stay here at the hotel."

"It was touch and go for a while, but Tina settled down after we were able to trust one another. She was one of our first guests to require complete seclusion, but we've had a lot since then."

Abbie indicated the space around us. "This is beautiful. No wonder everyone talks about The Beach House Hotel being very special."

"Thanks. Rhonda and I try to keep that feeling going by insisting on a great staff eager to please. Bernhard Bruner manages the hotel for us, and he has a stellar reputation. We're lucky to have him."

"Guess I'd better go and get ready to work out with Tina," said Abbie.

"Will it be a problem working with both Tina and Darryl?" I asked.

Abbie grinned. "I think it's going to be a lot of fun." She trotted away, and I thought maybe she wasn't as shy as I'd first thought.

When Rhonda arrived at the hotel, I filled her in on my meeting with Darryl and Abbie on the beach.

"Good thing 'you know who' didn't see you," said Rhonda.

"It was too early even for Brock," I said. "I'm curious though to find out more about Abbie."

"She must have a website. Let's look her up," said Rhonda after taking a sip of coffee. She typed in her name and came up with a website. "Here it is. *Abbie Hathaway, personal trainer to the stars.* And look, Annie, she's the youngest in her family, with four older brothers. That's the reverse of Darryl. There's potential here." Her smile widened as she rubbed her hands together.

"Oh, no! You're not going to try any of your matchmaking skills with her and Darryl, are you?" The thought of Rhonda trying to put the two of them together made my stomach flip.

"I admit it's a little early to think of how to make it work, but I like the idea," said Rhonda.

"We don't know either of them very well. It might backfire," I protested. Rhonda was convinced she was an excellent matchmaker when, in truth, nature, not she, paired people up.

"I'll know as time passes if I'm right, but there's no reason for me not to try," said Rhonda. "Just take a look at Lorraine and Arthur. I've never seen them this happy."

I couldn't deny it. The two of them acted like young lovers. "What else does the website say?" I asked, looking over Rhonda's shoulder.

A list of clients included Sinclair Smith. I checked out Abbie's training and was very impressed by her education. No wonder she could charge such high fees. The woman knew what she was doing.

"We'd better get to our Christmas campaign ideas," I said to her. "We need to announce that it's not too early to book rooms and dining facilities for Christmas parties. I don't want to get caught turning away people like we had to do last year."

"Yeah, that was a mess," Rhonda agreed.

"Even though it's a few months away, we need to talk to Bernie about bonuses for people who sign up to work Christmas and New Year's Day."

"It was great to be able to offer them something extra on top of their Christmas bonus. It helped a lot of families celebrate the holiday." Rhonda grinned. "You know I love Christmas."

"Oh yes," I replied. Our first Christmas together was loads of fun for us and our girls. A far different experience from mine growing up when it was just a dutiful, cold grandmother and me.

We were working on holiday bookings when Dorothy appeared. Short and stocky and with short gray hair, she was a bundle of energy for someone her age. Her thick glasses made her eyes look large behind them, and one got the feeling she didn't miss much.

"Hi, Dorothy," I said. "Nice to see you. What brings you here today? You're scheduled for tomorrow."

"I couldn't wait to tell you the latest news about Brock," she said. "He's now trying to get the Neighborhood Association to pass a new rule that the president be notified of any VIP guests arriving in the neighborhood."

"That's bullshit. He's just mad because we won't tell him or anyone else who's staying here at the hotel," said Rhonda.

"Even if such a crazy rule passed, we're under no obligation to abide by it," I said, unable to hold back a chuckle. "I think the man is losing it."

"He's become a joke among us, but he does a remarkable job in trying to build his self-importance," said Dorothy. "At any rate, I thought you should be warned. He's going to try to make a point of finding out who's here at the hotel."

"Just what we need," grumped Rhonda. "We're talking about the Christmas holiday. Are you willing to help us with our employee Christmas party like you did last year?"

"I'd be honored," said Dorothy. "And with the Hanukkah and Kwanzaa celebrations too. That makes my holiday complete."

"It's months away but we want to be better prepared this year, so we can spend time with our own families. The triplets should be a lot of fun this Christmas."

"It's very exciting for me to see all the changes with both the hotel and your families in the past several years," said Dorothy. "I feel a part of it."

Rhonda got up out of her chair and hugged Dorothy. "You were our first volunteer. We'll always be grateful."

Back when we started, Dorothy had helped with mailings and worked with me in setting up various business files. A successful businesswoman herself, she was very capable.

"I'd better go. I'll see you tomorrow," said Dorothy.

After Dorothy left, Rhonda turned to me. "Brock is a real jackass. But we'd better be careful."

"Let's walk over to the houses and talk to Darryl, Tina, and Abbie," I said. "They have a right to know what we're up against."

Rhonda and I knocked on the door to the house Darryl was staying in.

Darryl appeared wearing swim trunks, a T-shirt, and sneakers. He'd shaved his head, giving him a different but appealing look. Maybe it was the thought of him with four older sisters that made me feel as if he was someone to cuddle.

"Hi," he said. "Can I help you with something?"

"We've had some distressing news," I said. "A neighbor, a truly irksome guy who thinks he's important because he's the president of the Neighborhood Association, feels he should know who's staying at our hotel. We promised you security, but you must be alert to the situation."

"Yeah," said Rhonda. "You want to be careful when speaking to others, especially when you're on the beach."

"I know you like to walk there in the early morning," I said.

"You'd better talk to Abbie too. She's here with me now. She's going to be training me." He turned and called out, "Abbie, there's something you need to hear."

Rhonda nudged me so hard I almost stumbled. I could see her mind working on a way to bring these two together romantically.

Abbie came up behind Darryl. "What's going on?"

Rhonda and I filled her in on the situation.

"Oh, yes," said Abbie. "I think I met him after you left the beach, Ann. His name is Brock something. Right?"

"That's the bastard," said Rhonda. "What did he want?"

"He asked who I was and where I was staying. I didn't give him any information, I merely said I wasn't interested."

Rhonda and I exchanged amused glances.

"Guess he was surprised when you told him that, huh?" I said.

Abbie shook her head. "Working where I do, I meet a lot of people with big egos. His was humongous."

Darryl stood by listening to the exchange with a thoughtful expression.

"Both of you need to be careful," I repeated.

"We will," said Darryl. "Thanks for letting us know."

Rhonda and I left the house and headed to Tina next door.

Rhonda turned to me. "What did I tell you? I sensed something possible between them right away. Now, all they need is a little push from me."

"That's exactly what they don't need. Let them work together on training and keep out of the rest," I said.

"We'll see," said Rhonda, and I knew she wouldn't let it go.

Tina greeted us with excitement. "Hey, are you here for a little girl gab?"

"Sort of," I said. "Brock Goodwin is at it again. He's trying to find a way to discover who's staying at the hotel. We wanted to warn you to be careful."

Tina clucked her tongue. "Does he ever stop annoying people?"

"Not if he can help it," joked Rhonda. "We've already told Darryl and Annie." Her face lit up with a smile. "What's going on between them? I think there's a chance for a long-term commitment there. I'm working on it."

Tina glanced at me and laughed before facing Rhonda. "I wouldn't bet money on it. Abbie is used to working with some very handsome, successful men who make a play for her. She told me she was not interested in anyone. Certainly not one in the entertainment industry. But I've met Darryl and he seems very nice."

"I tried to tell her," I said, feeling helpless.

"Don't worry about Abbie. She can take care of herself," said Tina, and we let the issue drop.

CHAPTER FIVE

LATER IN THE WEEK, I CAME HOME FROM THE HOTEL AND found the house quiet. Not even Cindy greeted me at the door. My heart raced. Maybe, if I was lucky, I'd find Robbie with Vaughn down at the boat.

I hurried out to the lanai and grinned at the sight of them working on *Zephyr*, Vaughn's thirty-six-foot Pearson sailboat. I went through the lanai and was walking down to the dock when Cindy raced up to greet me. She was wearing a yellow life jacket, letting me know Vaughn was getting the boat ready to sail.

Vaughn looked up at me and waved. The sexy smile that all his fans loved lit his dark eyes. He dropped the line he was holding and strode toward me as I ran into his arms. We hugged tightly, and then I lifted my face. He kissed me, sending frissons of delight through me. Even though we'd been married for some years, we were still experiencing an exciting romance.

"Will you two stop kissing? I want to go sailing," said Robbie, making a silly face.

Vaughn and I exchanged amused glances and then Vaughn tousled Robbie's hair. "Someday you'll find a girl you want to kiss as much as I want to do with your mother."

Robbie shrugged. "Bethany isn't interested in me. She likes Brett."

"You have plenty of time ahead of you to find the right person," said Vaughn, trying not to show his amusement.

"What's for dinner?" I asked.

"I ordered a picnic from the Sable Café so you wouldn't have to do any work. Get changed, and we'll have time for a quick sail before it gets too dark," said Vaughn. "I've supplied the boat with drinks."

"Perfect. I'll be right back." I hurried inside the house to get ready. Time seemed to come alive when Vaughn was home.

A few minutes later, I sat in the cockpit of the boat while Robbie stood at the wheel and Vaughn tossed the docking line onto the boat and hopped in. It seemed like yesterday that Robbie, barely older than a toddler, sat with me in the cockpit watching Vaughn's every move at the wheel.

It was a beautiful evening as Robbie guided the boat from our inlet into a larger waterway out to the open waters of the Gulf of Mexico. There, Vaughn raised the mainsail, and I unfurled the jib to catch as much wind as possible.

"Look! There's a dolphin!" I cried as Robbie turned off the engine. The wind filled our sails, sending us forward. As the bow of the boat cut through the water, a pleasant hissing sound told of our speed.

I looked at a couple of dolphins following us playfully, jumping through the water. I was lucky to be in this place with people I loved.

Vaughn seemed to know what I was feeling and winked at me.

The sun was lowering in the sky, and I hoped this time I would see the green flash everyone talked about. If the atmosphere was just right as the sun dipped below the horizon, a green flash could appear. I'd met people who swore they saw it, but for most of us, looking for it was a fun part of the process of moving into the night.

Vaughn looked up at me from the galley. "How does a glass of wine sound?"

"Like the perfect end to a busy, worrisome day."

Vaughn handed me a glass of red wine and sat beside me in the cockpit.

I snuggled up against him. "Why were you able to get home a little early? Good news, I hope."

"I told them I'd been away long enough and needed a few days at home while they do some editing on the film."

"I'm glad you're here." Thinking of the Gorman wedding, I frowned. "I'll work out a deal with Rhonda to handle a wedding this weekend. Lorraine is in charge, but Rhonda and I always try to be present for part of the festivities. It makes a difference to the wedding party and future business."

"Let's not think of that. Let's simply enjoy the evening and ... time together," Vaughn said, giving me a sexy grin. "I don't know when I'll be called back."

"Perfect." I observed Robbie handling the boat, and pride filled me. He was becoming a very capable sailor.

The wind lifted my hair and swirled it around my face. Laughing, I brushed it away. The salt air filled my nostrils, and I watched seagulls and terns whirl above us, crying out in their shrill voices. Sitting here with two of the people I loved most, my life seemed perfect.

Vaughn clasped my hand and squeezed it. I studied him, seeing his love for me, and my breath caught. I'd never thought I'd be this lucky.

After a night of lovemaking, I awoke to find Vaughn staring at me. "Hello, sweetheart. What shall we do today?"

I reached for him and hugged him tightly. "Let me get things settled with Rhonda, and then we can plan something."

We kissed, and I got out of bed determined to take advantage of Vaughn being home.

In the kitchen, I fixed a cup of coffee and took it and my

cell phone out to the lanai. I knew it was early, but Rhonda's husband, Will, was an early riser, and with the kids in school, I figured Rhonda would be up.

She answered on the second ring. "Hi, there. What's up?"

"Vaughn's home for a couple of days, and I'm wondering if you'll handle the Gorman wedding. I'm sure Lorraine has everything organized, and Laura Young is scheduled to help."

"Sure, I'll help. But, Annie, I must warn you Willow and Drew are both fighting the flu, and I'm not feeling great after taking care of them."

"Oh, I'm sorry to hear that. Let me know how your day goes. I'll go to the hotel this morning, but I'd like this afternoon and the rest of the weekend off." I seldom asked for time off, but with Vaughn's erratic schedule, this was important.

I finished my coffee and went into the kitchen where Vaughn had fixed breakfast for Robbie. He looked up at me. "Well? Did you get the time off?"

Feeling conflicted, I shrugged. "It's complicated, but I think I have this afternoon off. Rhonda's kids are sick, and she isn't feeling great."

I could see the disappointment on his face, but we supported one another in our jobs, and I knew he wouldn't make a big issue of it. Still, I was as disappointed as he was.

"We can look for a new dinghy," said Robbie to his dad.

Vaughn's face brightened. "Yes, we do need one."

I smiled at the two of them. Boys and toys.

A short while later, I arrived at the hotel and went directly to Lorraine Grace's office, which served as the coordination center for weddings. Laura was there looking frazzled. A woman in her late twenties, she'd been helping Lorraine parttime with weddings doing a lot of the administrative work while Lorraine planned and executed wedding functions.

"What's wrong?" I asked Laura, a pretty, brown-haired woman with dark brown eyes, who was normally calm.

"Lorraine called me. She and Arthur are both sick. Apparently, there is some kind of flu going around. I told her not to worry that you, Rhonda, and I would handle the Gorman wedding."

"Oh, dear. I'm afraid it's going to be just you and me. Rhonda isn't feeling well, and if she's getting the flu, we don't want her at the hotel."

"Most of the wedding guests are arriving this afternoon. The Rehearsal Dinner is here tonight. The groom's family specifically requested the dinner be held here, so Jean-Luc could prepare duck a'l'orange. They're regular hotel guests and had it here previously."

"What are we talking about in numbers for that meal?" It worried me to have a fancy, time-consuming meal for a lot of people in addition to serving our regular guests.

Laura looked through the notebook Lorraine had set up for the wedding. "It looks like there are only two bridesmaids and three groomsmen. And with the other guests listed the total is twenty-four."

"What about the wedding dinner? How many people and what is the menu for that?"

"That's a little easier. They are expecting forty people and are offering a choice of surf and turf or poached salmon for those who don't eat red meat. Jean-Luc can easily handle that."

Though this was an important wedding for PR purposes, it sounded like a tasteful, small gathering. But that meant that each detail had to be perfect. "Do we have the gift baskets ready?"

Laura checked another section of the notebook. "Yes. Dorothy Stern and two friends packed them up yesterday." She smiled. "Dorothy loves to do this. She says it reminds her of getting ready for her wedding years ago."

"Nice. Will you see that they get delivered to the proper rooms? I assume housekeeping has been notified."

"Yes. It's checked here."

"What time is the cocktail reception?" I asked. "I'll arrange to be here to welcome everyone, but will you oversee dinner and make sure all is going well? Vaughn is home for only a couple of days and, if possible, I'd like to have the evening with him."

"Okay, I'll handle it today, but tomorrow I'm leaving for New York to attend a family celebration. I'd already cleared it with Lorraine."

I let out a long breath. "No problem." After Rhonda and I first opened the hotel, I knew that our time would never be ours alone. The hotel, the biggest baby of all, would come first.

I left Laura and went to find Bernie to inform him of how I planned to handle things.

"Good thing you're on it. Annette is all set to handle service for both dinners." Bernie's wife, Annette, had turned out to be a wonderful addition to our staff acting as hostess to special dinners and quietly overseeing the service staff.

Feeling better about things, I headed home. I planned to be back in plenty of time before the cocktail service to make sure the wedding guests were well looked after.

I arrived home to find a note from Vaughn sitting on the kitchen counter. *"I've gone on errands. Be back in time for a late lunch."*

After checking my watch, I made a quick phone call to Hair

Styles. Malinda was always gracious about finding room for me to have my hair trimmed and nails painted. I crossed my fingers. Like it or not, I'd be on display this weekend and needed help.

Malinda told me to come right away, that she could fit me in for the next twenty minutes, and she'd ask the manicurist to quickly do my fingernails.

Grateful for the friendship I'd developed with her over the past several years, I headed into town.

A little over an hour later, I emerged from the salon looking and feeling better. I kept my dark hair in a simple cut just above my shoulders, where it curled under in a smooth style. I wanted to look nice to greet Elise Gorman, mother of the bride, and her friend, Janelle Cummings. Both were well-known in New York City social circles for their charity work. Through them, we hoped to get more business.

Before I could make it home, Vaughn called me on my cell.

"How about meeting me at The Wharf for lunch?" he said. "I have a feeling that might be the only time we get to share a meal today."

"Perfect. I'm afraid you're right. The Gorman wedding is important to us, and Lorraine is out sick. I'm helping Laura handle things but will have to be around this evening for sure. Rhonda texted me that she was too sick to come in."

"Guess that's the hotel business," said Vaughn. "Meet me at the restaurant, and we'll have a nice lunch."

The Wharf was a rustic restaurant on the waterfront north of downtown. It was known for its water views and excellent seafood. The large bar was for casual dining, but the restaurant had a more formal dining room where Vaughn and I liked to sit to enjoy quiet discussions.

I pulled up in the parking lot as Vaughn was heading inside.

Seeing me, he waved and waited.

"Hi," he said, bending down to kiss me.

A couple walking by recognized Vaughn and stopped, but we ignored them and then went inside to the dining room. The receptionist led us to a table in the corner where we could talk quietly.

"Thanks for making the reservation. I don't feel like sharing you with your fans," I said, giving him a teasing smile.

He chuckled. "You're probably more famous in town than I am."

I shook my head. "No way. What are you going to have to eat? I want to eat heartily because I think you're right, I may not be able to have another real meal today."

"I know what I'm going to order. I've been thinking about it all morning. Key Lime Grouper with a blue crab cake," said Vaughn.

"I'm going to start with some fresh oysters and then have the Florida Louis Salad with extra shrimp." With Vaughn gone, it wasn't often that I went out to restaurants.

"Sounds great." He signaled a waitress over and placed our orders.

Sipping our iced water, we chatted about the filming. I watched Vaughn's face as he talked about his character. It was clear that he loved his work. After years of being in a soap opera, *The Sins of the Children*, he loved being able to choose what scripts and roles he wanted.

I was happy for him.

Our food came to the table, and we were quiet as we dug in. I appreciated that neither of us felt as if we had to talk all the time. It made the conversation between us more interesting.

After we finished eating, Vaughn focused his dark-eyed

gaze on me. "Let's go back to the house and have some time to ourselves before Robbie comes home and you have to go to work."

I knew exactly what he wanted and rose.

We walked out of the restaurant together, holding hands.

CHAPTER SIX

I TOOK A LAST LOOK AT MYSELF IN THE MIRROR. SATISFIED I could do no better, I turned and went into the kitchen to say goodbye to Vaughn and Robbie.

"You look nice, Mom," said Robbie, earning a hug from me.

"Gorgeous," Vaughn said, sweeping me into his embrace.

Laughing, I said, "Have fun, you two. I shouldn't be too late. There's plenty of food choices in the freezer."

"We're ordering pizza. Dad said we could," said Robbie.

"Okay, enjoy!" I bent to rub Cindy's ears and left the house, my thoughts already turning to duties at the hotel.

I arrived there to see a lot of activity at the registration desk.

"What's going on?" I asked Laura.

"The bride's parents hired a bus to drive many of the guests from the airport in Tampa to here. Now, there's a line to get everyone checked in."

"Let's offer those guests waiting in line some lemon water," I said. "Where's Elise Gorman?"

Laura indicated a tall, regal-looking blonde who was standing aside talking to people. As I approached, I could hear her say, "I'm sorry check-in is taking so much time."

I walked up to her. "Welcome to The Beach House Hotel. I'm Ann Sanders, one of the owners. I'm sorry we were never made aware of the transportation arrangements. We have a reception table set up in the lobby with ice-cold water, hot coffee, and fresh lemonade. Perhaps those waiting in line would like some refreshments."

Elise smiled. "Yes, that would be helpful. I should've told Lorraine we'd be arriving in a big bunch."

"It's a beautiful day and an exciting time for you. No reason to worry. The staff will take care of everyone as soon as they can," I said, pleased Elise wasn't making a fuss. Maybe this wedding would be easier to handle than some.

With people standing around the refreshment table in the lobby, the atmosphere changed. No longer were guests disgruntled over the wait time.

Elise introduced me to her husband, Corwin, an older man with pleasant features and thin gray hair who obviously adored his younger, attractive wife.

"Is Arthur Smythe around?" Corwin asked me.

"I'm afraid both he and his wife, Lorraine, are sick with the flu, but I know he's anxious to see you. Hopefully, this illness is just a 24-hour thing."

Elise frowned. "But Lorraine is supposed to handle all the details."

I waved Laura over. "This is Lorraine's reliable assistant, Laura Young. She and I will be taking care of the details. If there's anything we can do for you, anything at all, please let us know."

"Thank you," said Elise.

A short redhead woman approached us.

Elisa greeted her with a hug. "Janelle, this is Ann Sanders, one of the owners, and Laura Young, Lorraine's assistant. They are going to help us with the wedding."

Janelle held out her right hand. A large diamond flashed on the other one. "Hi, I'm Janelle Cummings. We're excited to be here. Lorraine has been wonderful to work with. I'm sure you will be, too."

I liked Janelle immediately and vowed to do my best to make the weekend go smoothly.

Janelle waved a middle-aged man over. "Wilbur, I want you to meet Ann Sanders, one of the owners, and Laura Young, Lorraine's assistant. They will be making sure everything will run smoothly for the wedding. The Rehearsal Dinner is here this evening and should be fantastic."

Wilbur Cumming had butterscotch hair and hazel eyes set in a handsome face. His trim figure indicated a healthy lifestyle. I wondered what he'd think of the dinner Janelle had ordered and then told myself not to judge. But I wasn't surprised when Wilbur asked what exercise facilities we offered.

I gave the four of them a quick review of our services and Laura handed them a wedding itinerary she'd printed for each guest. "There will be information in each room, along with a welcome basket requested by Alyssa and Burr."

"Wonderful," said Elise. "This is going to be a much smaller wedding than either Janelle or I wanted, but I want it to be perfect."

"Right," Janelle readily agreed. "The kids wouldn't wait for a big New York wedding and opted for this instead. Because we love them so much, Elise and I agreed. The wedding is something she and I have wanted for years."

Elise chuckled. "Since the kids met in a New Hampshire camp as counselors. I assume they're already here."

I turned to Laura.

She nodded. "They arrived a couple of hours ago."

Bernie approached us and introduced himself. "I believe we're ready for you at the registration desk. My apologies for the slight delay."

I could tell he was unhappy about the overwhelming rush, but he was his usual calm, somewhat aristocratic self.

I made the introductions and left them to take a walk through the hotel. First, I went into the private dining room to check on the progress for the Rehearsal Dinner. The bride had chosen a color theme of peach and blush, which worked with the bolder-colored flowers from Tropical Fleurs and the peach linen tablecloths on the six tables for four. As usual, Lorraine had planned well.

I left that room to go outside to make sure the pool area was ready for an onslaught of guests. A small bar had been set up at the end of the pool deck.

Leaving the hotel behind, I walked down to the beach where we'd set up a sunset-watching deck where guests could come to observe the daily event that had become a must for visitors looking for the green flash.

A hotel staff member was working behind the bar getting ready. A young man was sitting at the edge of the empty deck, dangling his legs over it, allowing his feet to rest in the sand. When he looked up at me, I knew who he was. He looked exactly like his father.

"Hi, you must be Burr Cummings, the groom of the weekend," I said, smiling at him.

He stood and offered me his hand. Closer to him now, I noticed how much more relaxed he was than his father who'd seemed a little uptight to me.

"Hi," he said.

"I'm Ann Sanders, one of the owners. Welcome to The Beach House Hotel. I hope the wedding is everything you and Alyssa want."

Burr puffed out a long sigh. "We just want this over with. We're doing this for our mothers who've compromised by coming here for a smaller wedding than the one they've been planning for years."

"Well, I hope you take the time to enjoy this one here," I said. "It's something that's supposed to happen only once."

"That's the problem," said Burr. "We're already married,

but our parents don't know. We eloped as soon as we found out Alyssa was pregnant. We wanted to tell them right away, but our mothers were so involved in planning a big wedding we didn't know how to do it. Instead, we were able to have a wedding more to our liking here at the hotel. It's beautiful."

"Thanks." I studied him. "How can we help?"

"It seems like you already have. Both moms are pleased with the hotel and all that you're doing. That's a major accomplishment. As I said, we're doing this wedding for them. We want it to be perfect, want them to have wonderful memories of it. They're not going to like the fact that Alyssa is already pregnant. She had plans to go to law school. But now she isn't going to start that program. Neither of us wants that to happen."

I was wondering what to say when I felt someone behind me. I turned to find a young woman with blond hair pulled back into a ponytail smiling at me.

Burr wrapped an arm around her. "This is Alyssa." He kissed her and said, "Ann Sanders is one of the owners of the hotel. I was telling her the truth about our wedding."

A worried look crossed Alyssa's pretty face and dulled her blue eyes. "You won't say anything, will you? My mother is going to be very unhappy when she learns I won't be going to law school. She has such high hopes for me becoming an important woman."

I remembered all the times I'd miscarried, had wanted more children, and I caught my breath. Nothing was more important than being a loving mother.

A hopeful expression filled Alyssa's face. "I'm looking forward to being a mother to Burr's baby. I don't need to be a lawyer. Do you agree?"

I told her how hard I'd tried to have more children and how important mothers were. "There are lots of ways you can do both – be a good parent and still give to society in some way through work or volunteer opportunities."

Alyssa threw her arms around me and hugged me tight. "Thank you." She lifted her face, and her eyes were shiny with tears. "Sorry. I'm very emotional."

"When is the baby due?" I asked. Alyssa barely showed.

"Not until next year. I'm only three months pregnant." She turned to Burr who returned her smile with such love, I felt sure it would work out.

"Well, let's make this occasion one the family will remember with great joy," I said. "Please come to me or speak to Laura Young about any of your needs. I'm sure she left her information with you in your rooms?"

Alyssa nodded. "She explained she'll be on call anytime."

"Great. See you two later at the cocktail party Burr's parents are hosting." I turned and walked away. Weddings were always full of surprises.

As I approached the hotel, I saw Elise coming off the beach. I waved and went over to her. "Did you have a nice walk?"

"Yes, until a nosy neighbor kept asking me questions. He specifically wanted to know if I was staying in one of the houses on the property or knew anyone who was." Elise shook her head. "I must say, I didn't like the man. He said he was the president of the Neighborhood Association as if I was supposed to be impressed."

"I know exactly who he was. Brock Goodwin is his name. I'd advise you and your guests to stay away from him and tell him nothing. He's a nuisance."

"Such a shame. But then I'm not going to let anything ruin my daughter's wedding," said Elise.

"Of course not," I quickly agreed, wishing Rhonda was going to be around for moral support.

CHAPTER SEVEN

I MET ANNETTE IN THE BACK KITCHEN, DELIGHTED TO SEE her. She'd oversee the cocktail party and the dinner for us. Annette was a quieter, gentler version of her husband, Bernie's, aristocratic manner. The staff respected her and learned from her how to be better servers and attendants.

I went with her to the private dining room to make sure that the small group had enough space to stand around the bar talking to one another.

Annette and I agreed the room would work, and I went to see how Jean Luc's prep for dinner was going. However, protocol didn't allow anyone to simply walk in on the chef. I checked with the sous-chef who told me all was in order.

I decided to go into my office to wait for the cocktail party to begin. Then, if everything was running smoothly, I'd be free to go home and be on call from there.

A short while later, I stood at the entrance to the dining room with Annette, smiling and talking to guests as they arrived. After knowing the story behind the wedding couple, I was relieved to observe the camaraderie among the guests. Burr's brother, Adam, was a real party boy but hopefully would respect Burr's wishes to have a nice weekend without trouble.

"It's a lovely group," murmured Annette to me. "I read about the work Elise and Janelle have done with a program for underprivileged children in New York City. They've accomplished a lot together."

"They seem very nice. Two mothers wanting their children happily married," I said. Alyssa was worried about her mother's reaction to the news of a baby, and now I think I understood why. Elise was a powerful person and sounded like a woman who wouldn't appreciate someone who wasn't doing her share to help a cause outside the home.

"Do you have everything under control?" I asked Annette. "Okay if I go home? Vaughn is here for a couple of days."

Annette grinned at me. "No problem. Off you go. If anything serious arises, I'll call. But not unless I absolutely must."

"You're a doll," I said, giving her a quick hug. "Laura and I will oversee breakfast in the dining room and then we have until four o'clock to get ready for the wedding at five."

"Fine. I'll meet you here then to make sure dinner is ready. The schedule says cocktails are on the pool deck."

"Yes," I said. "It should be a beautiful evening."

Vaughn was sitting on the lanai reading when I arrived home. Cindy was nestled by his side. Both jumped up when I said, "Hello."

"You're home nice and early. Robbie and I had dinner, but can I fix you something?" Vaughn asked.

"If you have left over pizza, I'll heat a slice of that. That will be sufficient. And a glass of wine to go with it."

Vaughn got up and kissed me. "A bit of a stressful day?"

I followed him into the kitchen. "After all these years of running the hotel, I wouldn't think I'd stress like this, wanting everything to be perfect. It never is. And you won't guess what the situation is this time. The bride and groom are already secretly married because she's pregnant. They didn't want to disappoint their mothers by having no ceremony at all. They all agreed to a small wedding here instead of a big, fancier one in New York. I hope no trouble comes of it."

"As long as the hotel provides good service, you shouldn't have to worry at all," said Vaughn pouring me a glass of wine while I heated a slice of pizza.

"True. I just wish I didn't have a nagging worry about it," I said, accepting the wine from him. "Secrets are bound to backfire. Both families seem very nice, very proper."

"Let's sit and relax," said Vaughn, heading onto the lanai. "I'm enjoying being home away from the grind of hurry and wait while making a movie."

I sat on the couch with Vaughn and leaned back against the cushions. I'd just finished my slice of pizza when my cell rang. *Annette.*

My heart thumped with concern. "Hello? What's up?"

"I'm sorry to disturb you, but I think you'd better come to the hotel. Bernie's here, but I think one of you owners should be too. A huge fight has broken out among members of the wedding party. I'll fill you in when you get here."

"Okay. No problem. I'm on my way. Is anyone hurt?"

"No. Some clothes may be ruined from being thrown in the pool but that's it," said Annette. "But now the party wants to cancel the wedding."

"That can't happen," I said, wondering what in the world was going on.

I arrived at the hotel to find the pool area closed. Bernie was talking to Burr and his brother. Both gave him sheepish looks.

Standing aside both Elise and Janelle were looking furious.

"Hello, everyone," I said, approaching them.

Elise and Janelle came over to me and each grabbed one of my arms and marched me away from Bernie and the boys. Only then did I notice Alyssa sitting on one of the lobby couches, surrounded by her two bridesmaids, crying.

"I'm furious with my boys," said Janelle. "They should know better. The evening, everything is ruined."

"I can't believe Alyssa did this to me," Elise said, trying not to cry. "This whole wedding is a fake. I'm not going through with it."

"Let's go to one of the private meeting rooms and talk this over," I said calmly, though my mind was whirling as it put together a believable scenario.

We walked into a small boardroom and pulled chairs into a circle. Janelle handed Elise a tissue from her evening purse.

'Okay, tell me exactly what happened," I said.

Elise turned to Janelle and Janelle cleared her throat. "After dinner, we were serving nightcaps on the pool deck. I don't know what my son, Adam, said to Burr, but Burr warned him to be quiet and when Adam shouted something about a baby, Burr pushed him into the pool. Adam grabbed him and soon several in the wedding party jumped into the pool, thinking it was some sort of game." She twisted her hands. "I'm sorry."

"That's just part of the story," said Elise. "When we questioned Burr, he confessed that he and Alyssa are already married because she's pregnant." Tears streamed down her cheeks. "She should've told me. We could've done things differently. Now, this whole wedding is fake, just like someone said."

Elise wiped her face while Janelle, looking ill, reached over and took hold of her hand.

"May I be honest with the two of you?" I asked. "I found out this afternoon from Burr that he and Alyssa were already married. I was shocked until I realized that they both wanted to give their mothers a beautiful wedding to remember, a wedding like you'd always wanted, but smaller."

Elise bit her lip.

"For a young couple to have such love for their parents is very touching," I continued. "Certainly, there are places in the world where a private ceremony occurs before one with family and friends. Why don't you consider this an opportunity to celebrate not only a marriage but the birth of your first grandchild?"

Elise and Janelle remained quiet.

"We've had many weddings here at the hotel, but your wedding has stood out to us because there is such love and affection between both families. Use this time to make happy memories. I'm sure Burr was only trying to protect Alyssa. How sweet is that?"

Elise and Janelle gazed at one another.

"We have lovely plans going forward. The wedding is going to be beautiful, and the Sunday brunch for you and your guests will be delicious with the hotel's famous cinnamon rolls."

"I would love it if you'd say yes, Elise," said Janelle. "We've wanted Burr and Alyssa together for a long time. And now we have a baby to think about?"

"It's all happened so fast, but it wouldn't do any good to cancel the wedding." Elise's breath hitched. "The fake wedding."

"In simply talking to Burr and meeting Alyssa, I don't believe it's fair to call it a fake wedding. They are adorably in love." I smiled at the two of them, unable to keep a tear from blurring my vision. "It's a sweet story."

Janelle opened her arms and Elise went into them. "Let's go talk to the kids. Are you ready?"

Elise nodded, and they rose and left the room.

I sat for a moment, collecting my thoughts. Everything I told them was true. I felt it to my bones.

Later, I discussed the situation with Annette and Bernie. "There will be no changes to the wedding as Lorraine and Laura have planned it. When you think about it, it's a sweet story of kids not wanting to upset their parents."

"It's fortunate that we had the private party sign posted for the pool area. No one got hurt. We're lucky about that. The fewer people involved, the better," said Bernie.

"I'll keep an eye on Adam and the other young people at dinner tomorrow night," said Annette. "Adam had too much to drink at the dinner."

"That's a very tricky position to place yourself in," said Bernie. "But we'll mention it to the staff and ask for them to be aware of such things."

"If you don't mind, I'm going home," I said, rising. "I promised Laura I'd be present for breakfast."

"Thank you, Ann, for coming here and being part of the resolution," said Bernie somewhat formally.

I smiled. "Thank you, Bernie." We were very lucky to have him looking out for us. He'd made sure no claims would be filed against the hotel.

All the way home, I imagined cuddling with Vaughn.

CHAPTER EIGHT

RHONDA CALLED IN THE MORNING TO CHECK ON THE situation. "I think I've stopped throwing up, but I'm too weak to come into the hotel today."

"Until you feel better, stay away. The last thing we need is for everyone at the hotel to get sick."

"How's the wedding shaping up?" she asked, and I filled her in.

"Glad we could keep the booking and everything turned out right," said Rhonda.

"Me, too. The bride and groom are very sweet. I think everything will be fine. As far as weddings go, it's one of the more pleasant groups. I hated the thought of losing them and creating bad news about the hotel. No one was hurt, and the wedding is going forward. Laura is doing an excellent job."

"I talked to Lorraine yesterday," said Rhonda. "She and Arthur both have the same type of flu. I suspect she'll be able to help on Sunday and give you more time with Vaughn."

"That would be nice. He's busy with Robbie today, but tomorrow I'd like to go sailing with him." We hung up, and I headed over to the hotel to walk on the beach. I was anxious to see how things were going with Darryl, Tina, and Abbie.

On my way, I realized I'd forgotten to tell Rhonda about Brock meeting Elise on the beach and how she hadn't liked his interrogation. Rhonda would be furious.

I parked the car at the hotel and made my way to the beach,

easily bypassing a few guests who were up at this early hour.

Kicking off my sandals, I wiggled my toes in the cool sand and headed to the water.

As always, the salty air, the rhythmic sound of the waves, and the cries of birds above me filled me with thankfulness to be alive and well.

I turned and walked away from the hotel toward a more private area of the beach in front of the houses on the property. When I looked up, I saw Darryl and Abbie running toward me. Darryl kept up with Abbie's long-legged stride, but he looked winded. When he got closer, I could see the sweat pouring off his face. Wearing swimming trunks, he was in a little better shape than he'd been just a few days ago.

"Hi," I said.

They came to a stop beside me and bent over to catch their breath.

"I guess Abbie is working you hard," I said to Darryl.

He straightened, glanced at her, then turned to me. "I've had more exercise in the time spent here than I have in a long while. It's painful, but I like it."

Abbie laughed. "We're just getting started, if we're going to accomplish what you wanted."

He grinned at her. "You're a health dictator."

"And you are going to obey," Abbie said playfully. The electricity between them was enough to send shivers across my skin. Rhonda would claim she knew all along, but these two seemed a perfect match for each other.

When Darryl took off his baseball cap to wipe his brow, I observed his shaved head. The effect was dramatic and handsome. His body still made me want to cuddle him, but I could see the beginning of some changes in him. Best of all, there was a new sparkle in his eye.

Abbie was as gorgeous as ever but had a more relaxed

manner. Hopefully, being at The Beach House Hotel had something to do with it.

"I'll leave you two alone. I'm just checking to make sure that Brock Goodwin hasn't been trying to ask you more questions."

"Whenever we see him, we jog on by, so he doesn't see us go onto the trail to the houses," said Abbie. "Believe me, I've met his kind before. Bad news."

"Okay, then, I'll see you around. I'm going to help with breakfast at the hotel." I left and headed inside the hotel, making a stop in the kitchen. A cup of coffee was just what I needed.

Consuela handled most breakfasts at the hotel with help from the kitchen staff. It was a lot less complicated than lunch and dinners under Jean-Luc's direction. She was there, supervising the orders when I arrived. I blew her a kiss, grabbed a cup of coffee, and headed to my office to see what was happening. The special bridal breakfast wasn't due to start for another half-hour, leaving plenty of time after breakfast for guests to relax, sightsee, play some golf, or go shopping. Alyssa, her mother, Janelle, and her two bridesmaids were due for hair appointments and manicures this afternoon.

In the office, I checked for emergency actions to take and looked at the financials from last night's events hosted by Janelle and Wilbur Cummings. They'd spent a lot of money. I was glad the rest of the wedding plans were going through.

I went to the private dining room to check on the breakfast buffet set up for the bridal party. The staff was just setting up. I knew one of the offerings was crepes rolled around a fresh strawberry mixture. I'd had them before, and they were delicious.

Laura arrived as I was talking to one of the servers. I

walked over to her.

"Hi, Ann," she said. "I've just come from Bernie's office. He told me about the fiasco last night. I'm glad it's all been handled. I wanted to check in before I left for the airport for my New York trip. I'm sorry to leave you like this, but Annette has promised to cover for me."

"Don't worry," I said. "Family is important, and you've had this on your schedule for a long time. I think the worst is over. Plans are moving forward with the wedding."

"Okay, then. Good luck. I talked to Lorraine. She's confident she can take over tomorrow." Laura waved and left.

I watched her go thinking how lucky we were to find someone young who was reliable and loved her job. My thoughts flew to Liz, who was anxious to be part of running the hotel. Her time would come. In the meantime, I intended to enjoy my grandbabies who were growing much too fast.

I hung around the dining room waiting for Elise to show up. She and Corwin arrived with friends, and I was able to talk to her privately.

"Everything is as you ordered. Is there anything else we can do for you?" I asked.

She gave me a quick hug. "Thanks for talking to Janelle and me last night. It helped put things in perspective. I'm going to simply enjoy the time here, wedding baby and all."

"I'm glad," I said. "We want you to enjoy it. You've certainly lucked out on the weather."

"Yes. We were concerned about an October wedding, but we've had plenty of sunshine and no rain."

I was well aware that the same wouldn't be true for later in the week. But I wasn't about to worry about that now. Vaughn was home.

I left the dining room content things were running well and went to find Bernie.

We talked over the day's activities and plans for tomorrow, and then I went home. Vaughn and Robbie had gone on errands looking for a dinghy and had plans to catch a movie Robbie wanted to see. I loved the idea of their spending time together and decided to go see the triplets. For years, even before my divorce, I'd had a close relationship with Liz. Now, as a mother herself, Liz relied on me to give her advice about the children. I treasured these moments with her.

I called to see if it was a good time to come over, and Liz said, "It's perfect. Can I talk you into watching the T's? Chad wants to take me to lunch?"

"Sure," I said. "You tell me what I need to do, and I'll take over."

I hung up both excited and a little concerned about handling the three active toddlers. Two children were easy compared to three children of the same age, all bent into getting into predicaments, mostly from curiosity. But the toddlers were agreeable about following directions. Unless one of them decided to cry. Thinking of it now, I couldn't help chuckling. Things went from calm to pandemonium in the blink of an eye.

Knowing I had limited time before I'd have to get ready for the wedding, I headed over to Liz's house.

As soon as I saw the excitement on the children's faces at seeing me, I couldn't stop a sting of tears. Though a significant part of my time was spent working, it was these treasured moments that were the best. Looking back, they were what I'd most remember.

"Hi, GeeGee," said Olivia, the boldest of the three, running up to me. Emma and Noah weren't far behind. I scooped them into my arms. It was a hot day, and their little bodies were sweaty. Maybe I'd let them go into the pool before naptime.

"Me up," said Noah.

"No, me!" cried Emma.

Olivia said, "Me! Me!"

Laughing, I hugged each of them.

Liz and Chad appeared at the entrance to the playroom looking relaxed and happy.

"Thanks for watching the T's," said Chad. Tall with strawberry-blond hair, he was a computer whiz and had his own consulting company. That was a factor in buying their house. Space above the garage was turned into his office. And though he was often away on calls, it was nice to have him nearby.

"We appreciate it," said Liz, looking adorable in a sleeveless, flowered dress that showed off her toned arms. "We're going to grab lunch and then look for a new car for me. It's time."

"Have fun. Remember, I must leave here no later than three because I have a VIP wedding at the hotel. Rhonda and Lorraine have been sick, so Laura, Annette, and I are handling it together."

"No problem," said Liz. "Have fun with the kids."

"Is it okay if I allow them to use the splash pool? That might tire them out before naptime."

"Sounds like a wise idea," said Chad. He left and returned with the kids' swimsuits.

After putting fresh water in the pool, Liz hugged each child, said goodbye, and left with Chad.

I sat on the carpet with the kids and played with them. They loved to build blocks into towers and then knock them down. Soon though, squabbling began over ownership of the blocks, and I decided it was time for them to go outside into the splash pool.

I helped them strip down and then got them into their swimsuits.

Feeling like a mother duck, I led them into the kitchen and out the sliding door onto the covered patio where the plastic pool sat.

They ran over to the pool.

Noah was the first to step into it and sit down in the water. Not to be outdone, Emma and Olivia quickly followed, squealing with joy. Such a simple pleasure, I thought, reminding myself to enjoy the rest of the day.

"GeeGee, I want the ball!' said Emma, indicating the rubber ball lying in the grass not far away.

I retrieved the ball along with two other pool toys. "Here you go. What do you say, everyone?"

A sweet chorus of "Thank you!" followed.

Not caring if I got wet, I sat in a chair beside them, watching them play. As always, I was interested in the interaction between them. They each had moments when they seemed to be in charge either by action or by word. I hoped they always remained as close and loving as they were.

When the children grew tired, I got them out of the pool, stripped off their bathing suits to deal with later, and went inside to get them dressed for their naps. At three, they still needed a nap in the afternoon.

Liz had toilet-trained the children, but I made sure each one went to the bathroom before I tucked them into their cribs. Liz had talked about the cute beds they had for children, and I'd quickly dissuaded her from moving too fast to get them into beds.

Now, as I gazed down at each sleepy child, my heart filled with gratitude for the children Liz thought she might never have. I, too, had struggled to have children and knew what a blessing each one was.

I kissed them and left to go to the patio to take care of the bathing suits and straighten up. No wonder Liz was exhausted every night. I told myself I could remain charming and helpful to the wedding guests and hoped I was right.

I arrived home to find Vaughn and Robbie down at the dock with what looked like a new dinghy. I hurried down the hill to check in with them before changing to go to the hotel.

"Success," said Vaughn. "Robbie chose a great new dinghy for *Zephyr*.

"It's a beauty," said Robbie, sounding and acting so grownup that it caught me off-guard after spending time with the triplets.

"It looks great. I'm off to the hotel to work a wedding, but I'll be home as soon as I can."

Vaughn came over to me and drew me into his arms. "Remember our wedding?"

"I certainly do. A reason I love seeing other people happily married. And though this couple has some problems to get past, I think they're going to be fine."

Vaughn lowered his lips to mine, and I felt like a bride all over again. When he stepped away from me, Vaughn winked. "To be continued."

I laughed and waved to Robbie who was cleaning out the dinghy, and I headed to the house to get ready for work.

In my bedroom, I took a quick shower and dressed in a simple black sheath and comfortable, low heels.

Rhonda and I always dressed nicely for work and especially for weddings. But we'd quickly learned the importance of comfortable clothing and shoes. One never knew what was going to happen at affairs like these.

For luck, I added the gold necklace Vaughn had given to me before we were married. The Initials A and V were brought together and crossed over with a bar holding three diamonds which had indicated our three children. Now, the three diamonds also symbolized the triplets.

CHAPTER NINE

AT THE HOTEL, I WENT DIRECTLY TO THE SIDE GARDEN where Alyssa and Burr were to be married. Manny was supervising a small crew lining up chairs in the grass. Annette followed behind slipping white covers over the backs of the chairs. Two people from Tropical Fleurs were tying flowers to the chairs closest to the aisle between the two sections of chairs. A huge basket of flowers would be placed on the altar at the last minute and then used indoors in the dining room set aside for the bridal party.

Alyssa's theme of blush and peach worked well, and I couldn't wait to see the bridesmaids' dresses. I was standing there looking over the garden when I felt someone come up behind me.

I turned to see Rhonda smiling at me. "You know I love weddings. I couldn't miss this one."

"How are you feeling?"

"I'm fine. It was one of those twenty-four-hour cases of flu. Everyone at our house is back to normal. I'm sorry I left you and Laura to do the bulk of the work."

"No problem. But as soon as I can, I'm leaving to go home to Vaughn and Robbie. You know how it is, I'm never quite sure of Vaughn's schedule."

"That's why I'm here. Love the colors," said Rhonda. "How's everything else going? Any bad news from Brock?"

"Not yet. You know it's coming. It's just a matter of when," I said, feeling my blood pressure rise. It amazed me that one man could cause us so much trouble. But we knew what kind of person he was and did our best to stop his nosing around.

"Have you checked the dining room?" Rhonda asked.

"No, let's do that now. I'm satisfied with the way things are going here," I said. "Annette should be overseeing the work there."

When we investigated the private dining room, the tables were set with white linen and light blush-colored linen napkins. The silver rims on the plates matched the sparkling silverware and crystal water and wine glasses standing at each place. In the middle of the tables sat a thick white electric candle placed inside a ring of fresh flowers in the bride's colors. The effect was understated loveliness.

"It's beautiful," said Rhonda to Annette who'd walked over to us.

"I think so, too," said Annette. "Mrs. Gorman is a pleasure to work with. She knows what she wants and isn't too demanding."

"You're lucky," said Rhonda. "I remember other weddings that weren't as easy." She glanced at me. Weddings brought out the best and the worst in people.

Rhonda and I went to the lobby to see if the minister and the guitar player had arrived.

The minister of the Unitarian Church was often called upon to handle weddings for different couples who'd opted for a destination wedding. She was a lovely, older woman who related easily to people with a quick smile and open mind.

The guitar player, a young man who played in a local classical music quartet, was another wedding regular at the hotel. Professional and eager for the work, he was reliable. Even now, he stood ready with his equipment talking to Bernie.

Rhonda and I went over to talk to him just as the minister arrived. After we'd greeted them both, we led them to the side garden to show them how it was set up.

They stopped a moment at the entrance to the garden to take in the sight, and I could see from their looks of pleasure that they were as satisfied as I was. The garden, with its palm trees, tropical landscaping, and flowers, was Manny's domain, and he took great pride in his work. On occasions like this, his dedication made all the difference between ordinary and something very special.

The minister walked up to the simple white altar on which two candles sat, waiting for the centerpiece to be placed between them. She took out the bible she'd brought with her.

The guitar player sat in a nearby chair and took out his guitar.

The staff member from Tropical Fleurs carried the centerpiece in and set it up on the altar.

Rhonda grinned at me. "Looks like we're set to go."

I stood aside with her as Burr arrived with Adam and the other groomsman. Burr stood at the front beside the altar as people were ushered to their chairs. Then, in what seemed no time, Janelle and her husband were seated in front. And then it was Elise's turn to be seated. She looked gorgeous in a peach-colored, tea-length dress.

One bridesmaid, then another came down the aisle and stood by the altar. They were young and lovely in sleeveless dresses, one in a blush color, the other in a very dark peach - colored dress.

The guitar player strummed the familiar sounds of Mendelssohn's Wedding March, and everyone stood as Alyssa and her father arrived.

My breath caught as I gazed at Alyssa. She was a striking bride and had that special glow that some pregnant women get. Her blond hair was pulled back into a French twist, and white orchids were woven into the braid which I thought was more effective than a crown of flowers.

From the look on Burr's face when he saw Alyssa, I felt comfortable that the two of them would make their marriage work.

Rhonda and I stood quietly on the sideline making sure everything was going smoothly. This was the part of working a wedding that we loved most, hearing the vows, and seeing our guests happy and hopeful.

Listening to these vows, I felt my eyes water. Beside me, Rhonda was blowing her nose as tears streamed down her cheeks. I'd learned to be sure to have plenty of tissues with me if Rhonda was present. She couldn't hold anything back.

When the minister said, "You may now kiss your bride," Rhonda and I gave each other a subtle high-five. We'd made it through another wedding. Now the real work would begin, making sure there would be no problems with the following celebrations. I noticed that Adam seemed subdued after almost ruining the wedding.

At the cocktail reception in the dining room, Rhonda and I had the opportunity to congratulate the bride and groom.

"You look gorgeous, Alyssa," I said.

"I hear we have you to thank for talking our mothers into being reasonable," said Burr.

"I'd like to think this is a perfect opportunity to celebrate both the wedding and the upcoming first grandchild," said Elise joining us.

Burr and Alyssa looked at one another and beamed.

"I'm very happy for the two of you," said Rhonda. "I'm excellent at matchmaking, and I would've put the two of you together right away. You're perfect together."

As we walked away, I shook my head. If Darryl and Abbie continued to show interest in one another, I was sure Rhonda would take all the credit.

###

With Rhonda's and Annette's blessings, I left the hotel to go home to Vaughn. As I'd mentioned to Rhonda, I never knew what his schedule would be. Maybe that's why we tried so hard to take advantage of every opportunity we had to enjoy one another.

At home, Robbie was on the couch on the lanai with Cindy watching television. I saw Vaughn down by the dock sitting on the boat. Even though it was getting dark, he sometimes liked just resting there.

"I'm going to change my clothes and go sit with Dad for a while," I said to Robbie.

I left him and went to my room, slipping out of my work clothes and putting on a pair of jeans and a knit top. Then, not wanting to waste a minute, I hurried down to the boat. *Zephyr* was a beautiful sloop and Vaughn's pride and joy.

He looked up from his seat in the cockpit and smiled. "I was hoping you'd get back soon. It's a beautiful night and the stars are already coming out. How did the wedding go?"

"It was charming. The couple is very special. Hopefully, after a Bridal Brunch, it will be another one over and done with."

"Great, because I just got a call from the producer. I have to leave on Monday morning. I was lucky to have a few days off, so I'm not complaining. But I always hate to leave here. After we wrap up the last few scenes, I'm going to check on my condo in New York City. Want to meet me there?"

"I might be able to. Thanks. Let me know when the dates are, and we'll take it from there," I said, suddenly excited to be in New York. And if that didn't work out, maybe something else would.

"Care for a nightcap to celebrate being together?" he asked.

"I'd love to celebrate us with you." Starring in the soap

opera, Vaughn had spoken many romantic lines in his role as mayor of a small town. It had taken me a while to realize that not all heartwarming lines were from the show. He had a natural, romantic way about him.

He poured me a drink from a container he had and handed it to me as I settled on the bench next to him. We gazed up at the stars that had sprung to life above us in the darkening sky. The moon was a glowing round orb above us, shedding silver light on top of the gentle waves lapping on the shore of the inlet and against the dock's pilings. A deep sense of peace filled my soul. Nature and Vaughn's love did that for me.

I turned to him, and his lips met mine, gently at first and then with growing passion.

When we pulled apart, Vaughn smiled at me. "And people ask why I always want to come home."

We chuckled together. I hoped that as the years passed, we'd always have these special moments.

Sunday morning, while Vaughn was reading a script for his agent and Robbie was next door at his friend, Brett's house, I slipped away to the hotel. The Bridal Brunch was about to end, and I couldn't stay away.

When I arrived at the private dining room, Rhonda and Annette were there. Annette was, as usual, doing a fabulous job of overseeing the celebrations. Rhonda was greeting the guests as they rose to get ready to leave the hotel.

Elise called me over to her. "I want to thank you and Rhonda for a wonderful wedding. We got off to a shaky start with the kids, but it has turned out to be a very special occasion thanks to your encouragement. I know many of my friends will be having children wanting to get married. I'll be sure to let them know about The Beach House Hotel."

We both looked up as Lorraine came hurrying over to us. "Elise, I'm delighted to meet you. I apologize for being too sick to be here sooner."

As Elise and Lorraine shook hands, I was impressed that Lorraine had done her homework on her clients and knew exactly who Elise was.

"Thank you for your enthusiasm," I said, leaving Elise with Lorraine, who'd make sure she got the names of those friends Elise talked about.

Janelle and Rhonda were talking, and I went over to them. "Such a beautiful wedding, Janelle. It's always nice to see such a delightful couple together."

"All's well that ends well," said Janelle smiling. "We adore Alyssa, and I'm thrilled we're going to have a grandchild, even if the timing is off."

We continued to chat with the wedding guests until the last one left the room.

Rhonda turned to me. "This is one of the better weddings we've had. Why do I have the feeling there's trouble ahead?"

"Hush," I said. "We don't want any problems sent our way."

"You're right, Annie. But in all the years we've run this hotel, we've always had something to deal with because we're working with people. Do you remember, dear Wilkins Jones? That was our initiation into the hotel business."

We'd been horrified when a magazine reporter had expired when making love with a woman who wasn't his wife. There hadn't been any other deaths since that time, and we certainly didn't want one. But it had been a wake-up call to both of us that anything can happen at a hotel.

CHAPTER TEN

MONDAY MORNING, AFTER SEEING ROBBIE OFF TO school and taking Vaughn to the airport for his flight to Canada, I raced to get to the hotel in time for Bernie's staff meeting.

Thankfully, Rhonda was already there as I slid into my seat a few minutes late. Bernie was used to the idea that as mothers and grandmothers, Rhonda and I had other responsibilities and with us, family came first unless there was an emergency.

Bernie was speaking. "The wedding over the weekend was according to everything I've heard a success with staff stepping in to help with Lorraine's absence. Does anyone have any comments or suggestions?"

"I'd like to say that Annette did an outstanding job of handling the details. I recommend she be included on the wedding planner's staff as a part-timer," I said, turning to Lorraine.

"I would very much like that," Lorraine said. "Laura is a wonderful employee, but we need more help. As we all know, weddings here at the hotel are very special because of the service we provide."

"Our wedding clients seem willing to pay for the extras we offer them," I added.

"Since she's your wife, Bernie, I'll speak to Annette today and make her an offer," said Lorraine.

Bernie nodded his approval. "And how are we doing with our VIP guests in the two houses?" He turned to Ines Salinas, our new VIP coordinator.

"So far, it seems to be working out well. Tina Marks and Darryl Douglas are satisfied with the arrangements. We've been providing food service along with the usual maid service. And Manny has assigned reliable groundskeepers to those properties. The guards haven't had any real problems with access to the guesthouses except with Brock Goodwin. But they quickly took care of it."

"What an ass," Rhonda murmured.

"Any requests for either of them to leave the houses on the property?" Bernie asked Ines.

She shook her head. "Not that I know of."

"We've had a new problem arise. Darryl's ex-wife, Everly Jansen, who was scheduled to stay in the Presidential Suite next week is now arriving a week early," said Bernie. "We need to make sure she has no inkling that Darryl is with us. And we certainly don't want any bad publicity for the hotel."

"But she's a woman who seeks attention," I said. "The publicity about her isn't favorable."

"Yeah, she's making up all kinds of things about Darryl hoping to get more money out of him," said Rhonda. "She thinks he cheated her out of a fair divorce settlement. At least that's what *Hollywood News* says."

"Well, I don't depend on news from Hollywood to tell me how to run a hotel," said Bernie in his stern way. "We'll carry on as we usually do."

I glanced at Rhonda.

"You're right, Bernie," she said.

"We must be careful with her, keep the press out, maintain the sense of security we're known for," said Bernie.

"I agree. If anyone should hear anything about our private houseguests or any others, I suggest they report it to both Bernie and Ines," I said.

"Yes," said Bernie. "All of our guests deserve privacy."

We went on to other topics, but my thoughts returned to Everly Jansen. As soon as the meeting was over, I wanted to do further investigation on her.

Bernie ended the meeting.

As Rhonda and I headed to our office, I said, "Let's find out a little more about Everly Jansen."

"Okay. And then we'd better inform Darryl about her presence here at the hotel."

We huddled in front of my computer while I clicked on several online articles about her. She'd worked at the ACBE network which is where she met Darryl. Darryl, in his early forties, was a single guy popular on television and with a lot of money. Some claimed that's why Everly, twelve years younger, sought him out. After a whirlwind courtship, they had an extravagant wedding in Hawaii. There were photos of the enormous diamond engagement ring he'd given her. Wedding photos showed pictures of the voluptuous blond looking triumphant and Darryl's four sisters looking on with uncertain smiles. It was clear they were not happy with his choice. Darryl looked dazed.

Remembering how shy I thought he was, I pointed this out to Rhonda.

"A little gold digger," said Rhonda. "Like the kind my Sal got involved with after he lost his mind and left me. Thank God he didn't marry any of them."

We checked for more information. It turned out Everly's job had been given to her by a friend of the family, and as soon as she married Darryl, she quit. To do what, the article didn't say.

I stopped reading. "There's no sense in continuing. I'm sure Everly must have some nice qualities, but I'm not going to try to read about them. She's a very disliked person."

"A frickin' shame Darryl got mixed up with her," said

Rhonda. "I'm hoping I can do my magic and help him find a better love."

I rolled my eyes and stood. "Let's go tell him about Everly's visit." Normally, we'd keep quiet about our guests, but this was an emergency, and he had a right to know.

On the walk over to Darryl's house, we had a chance to study the grounds of the hotel. We were very fortunate to have Manny head a team of workers who kept the lawn, landscaping, and grounds pristine. It was essential to maintain an upscale look as part of what guests could expect when coming to the hotel.

By using the private back path to the houses, we quickly arrived at our destination.

We stopped at Darryl's house first. We went to the front door and knocked.

"Come in," said a male voice.

Rhonda and I entered the house to find Darryl doing exercises out on the pool deck.

He stood when he saw us. As he came over to greet us, I saw the change in him. He was a healthy tanned, trimmer, and more muscular person than the man he'd been when he'd arrived.

"Wow!" said Rhonda. "Look what happened to you."

"That's all due to Abbie," he said and indicated Abbie behind him. She was wearing short shorts and a tank top that showed the shape of her trim, defined body.

I could feel the energy between them and glanced at Rhonda who wore a satisfied smile. There was nothing I could do to stop her from saying. "You two are great together. Just like I thought."

A look passed between Darryl and Abbie, and then she said,

"It's time for me to train with Tina. We're making progress."

"And progress here, I'm glad to see," said Rhonda, and I knew she wasn't talking about the training.

I held up my hand to stop Abbie from leaving. "We're here to give you both some news. We'll be talking to Tina too. Normally, we don't speak about other guests staying at the hotel, but, in this case, we must, because it may affect all three of you in the houses if she gets the opportunity to find out you're here."

"Yes, we want you to know that Darryl's ex, Everly Jansen, will be staying in the Presidential Suite for the next week or so," said Rhonda. "We already provide you with security and seclusion, but you'll need to be extra careful about being seen."

"We don't allow uninvited news cameras in the hotel, but from what we've read, Everly doesn't mind publicity," I said, hoping I was being tactful enough.

"She's a real piece of work," said Rhonda.

So much for being tactful.

Darryl let out a long sigh. "I'm here to get away from all the publicity about my wanting to cancel my contract on the show. There's another matter I'm dealing with too. The last thing I want to do is meet my ex-wife here."

"We'd arranged for her to stay here next week, not knowing how long you'd be staying," I explained.

"This has been a productive visit for me," said Darryl, glancing at Abbie. "I want to extend my stay to six weeks. Maybe longer."

"We'll work that out," said Rhonda. "This is important. The two of you are getting along so well."

Rhonda ignored the "cease and desist" look I was giving her and smiled happily at the two of them.

"Thanks for the tip about Everly," said Darryl. "Believe me,

I have no intention of either seeing my ex or having anything to do with the press for any reason."

"That's a relief to hear," I said. "Now, we're going to talk to Tina. We want to ensure that Everly's presence does nothing to expose Tina."

Rhonda and I left Darryl's house and walked down the road to the most recent house we'd built. It was as attractive as the original house which had been mine until I sold it to the hotel.

As I knew she would, Rhonda nudged me. "Those two are very sweet together. I hardly have any work to do with this one."

I shook my head at Rhonda's idea of being a matchmaker, but I returned her smile. It made her happy.

Tina answered the door wearing workout shorts and a tank top. "Hi, I'm glad to see you. We haven't had any time together recently, and I've missed it."

"We've had some people out sick with the flu, but I think everyone's healthy again," I said. "We didn't want to expose anyone to it."

"We need to talk to you," said Rhonda.

"Come on in. I've been meaning to call you. I'm going to return to California for a couple of days and come right back here. Abbie will stay in the house while I'm gone."

"What do you think of Abbie and Darryl as a couple?" asked Rhonda. "I think they're perfect together."

Tina stopped and put her hands on her hips. "Are you trying to be a matchmaker again?"

The three of us looked at one another and burst out laughing as Rhonda's cheeks grew pink. "You know I'm excellent at it," Rhonda said, defending herself.

"I must admit you've been right a couple of times," said

Tina, continuing to tease Rhonda.

I stood by, enjoying all of it.

"What's taking you away from here?" I asked Tina.

"Victor has a school play he has a big part in, and I promised him I'd see it. That, some medical appointments, and a chance to have my hair cut and styled with Antonio. But, as I said, I'll return. It's going to be a fast in-and-out situation because I'm still not ready for the role."

I couldn't resist hugging her. "You're beautiful, Tina. You always will be to me."

"Cameras can be horribly cruel. Once the movie is over, I'll relax a bit." She frowned. "What did you want to talk to me about?" She indicated for us to have a seat on one of the chairs surrounding the kitchen table.

"Normally, we wouldn't discuss anyone who's staying in the hotel with any other guests," I said. "But we feel you have a right to know that Darryl's ex-wife is going to be staying in the Presidential Suite."

"According to what we've read, she could cause both Darryl and you trouble if she somehow made it to the guesthouses or heard about you," said Rhonda.

"We had to move her out of a stay in a house to accommodate Darryl's longer one," I said. "If Everly found out, it could be a problem because she's already out to confront him on other issues."

"I certainly don't want to be part of that mess," said Tina. "I appreciate your telling me this. How long is Everly staying here?"

"She's booked in the Suite for two weeks," Rhonda said. "We don't know if she'll stay that long. She's changed her arrival."

"I've spent some time with Darryl, of course, through training times together. He's a very nice man," said Tina.

"And, Rhonda, I think you're right. Abbie is starting to fall for him. She's very accustomed to working with high-profile people, but she says he's different, very genuine."

"We heard that Abbie has four older brothers. I bet she's a little spoiled," Rhonda said.

Tina shook her head. "Abbie's tough physically and mentally, but she's a sweet person. It's very interesting, now that you've mentioned it. Both Abbie and Darryl are the youngest of five siblings, four of which are the opposite sex. Maybe that's why they get along well. It's certainly happened fast."

I held back a chuckle at the glow of success on Rhonda's face. If she beat the odds and things did work out between Darryl and Abbie, she'd never let us forget it.

We talked about Tina's boys, Vincent and his younger brother, Tyler, and then Abbie arrived.

After greeting us, Abbie said to Tina, "Ready to begin?"

Tina groaned and got to her feet. "Guess I have no choice."

"You're doing very well," said Abbie. "A couple more weeks and you'll be glad you listened to me."

Rhonda and I stood.

"Safe trip home," I said to Tina. "Please let us know when you return. We want to make sure our security team will assist you."

Tina gave each of us goodbye hugs. "I'll talk to you later."

On the walk back to the hotel, Rhonda said, "I wish I didn't have a bad feeling about Everly coming here."

CHAPTER ELEVEN

AS WE OFTEN DID TO GREET GUESTS, RHONDA AND I stood at the top of the stairs waiting for Everly to arrive. Bernie had spoken to the valets and front desk staff about the need for confidentiality and had informed them newspeople were not allowed to trail after Everly on the property. She loved to be photographed for any reason. Even now, Everly or someone who worked for her must have called the local television station because a cameraman and reporter were waiting for her arrival just inside the hotel's gates.

"I'm tellin' ya, Annie, this guest spells trouble before she even gets here. Look, there's Terri Thomas, from the Sable Newspaper. And now more local television crews. What are we going to do?"

"They can't get beyond the front lawn. We'll have to trust our security people will do their job." I tried to sound as convincing as I could, but I was furious that Everly or her staff had arranged this. Was she going to make her stay at The Beach House Hotel all about her? It looked that way.

A white limousine pulled inside the gates and stopped. One of the back windows rolled down and an arm extended from it, eagerly waving a hand.

Rhonda and I started down the stairs.

The limo pulled up in front of us, and we waited for the driver to open the passenger door. A sandaled foot and thin leg emerged before the gaunt figure of Everly Jansen came into view. We'd seen photos of Everly before, but nothing prepared me for the sight of a woman who'd once been beautiful and now looked ... well, used.

"Welcome to The Beach House Hotel," said Rhonda, in a tone that wasn't very warm. No doubt because she, like I, was very worried about this guest.

"Hello," I said. "Why don't you come this way and we'll get you registered into the hotel and comfortably settled in your suite."

"Oh, no. Not yet. My supporters know I'm here, and I want to thank them for the help and encouragement they give me." Smiling, she turned and waved to the cameras. "Hello, dear fans, I want you to know how much I appreciate you. After all the horrible things that have been said about me by my ex-husband's lawyers, I needed to have a rest before I continue to carry on the fight for what is mine."

"You already have a divorce settlement. Why do you think you can open a case against that?" asked one reporter.

"The cost of living has gone up in the last two years. I've discovered I can't get by comfortably on what the settlement provided. It's only fair for me to get more money."

"Are you doing this because of your ex's possible lucrative new contract with ACBE?" asked another reporter.

"I'm going to let my lawyer sort all of that out. I just want what is due to me," Everly said. "If it wasn't for me, Darryl Douglas might still be working at some nightclubs on the road."

"But you didn't have much success at being known at ACBE before marrying Darryl," said one of the reporters. "I think it's the other way around."

Everly shot the newsman such a look of fury, he inched closer hoping for more information.

Regaining her composure and smiling broadly again, Everly waved and blew a kiss to the cameras.

We walked beside Everly as she climbed the front steps of

the hotel.

Once inside, she turned to us. "I'm not going to bother to register. I want to go directly to The Presidential Suite. Flying today is so unpleasant."

"We'll show you to your suite and send someone from the Front Desk up to your room to take care of your registration," I said, warning Rhonda with a look to keep quiet. Rhonda was, as she would say, totally pissed to have Everly treat us and our procedures that way.

We led Everly to a winding staircase in the corner of the lobby to what once was Rhonda's private headquarters. Now it served as The Presidential Suite, worthy of any hotel.

We opened the carved wooden door of the suite and motioned Everly inside. From the front entrance, one faced the living room. A large Oriental carpet in greens, blues, and deep red covered most of the wooden floor. It was offset by white couches and subtly patterned chairs in complementary colors.

The dining room was next to the kitchen, which wasn't large but was well laid out. Outside, between the kitchen and living room, a large balcony held a table and chairs and overlooked the side garden. In contrast, the master bedroom offered a perfect view of the beach and Gulf water. The master bath was everyone's favorite space. The shiny brass fixtures added to the marbled interior which had an enormous shower that Rhonda had once told me was her "playpen."

Another bedroom, full bath, and powder room were part of the suite.

Everly followed us around but did not comment until she saw the gift basket left for her. "I hope it's a good wine. I'm ready for some," she said, lifting the bottle of pinot noir from the basket.

"Anything you need, just call the front desk," said Rhonda.

"Have a wonderful stay. We'll send someone up from the front desk to get the information we need. Thank you," I said, backing away from her toward the front entrance, fighting the awful feeling that something bad was about to happen.

Rhonda closed the door behind us and shook her head. "She's on something. Did you see the way her hands were shaking?"

"I didn't, but I'm afraid you're right. It was more than being hungover or travel fatigue."

We went to the front desk and told one of the clerks what we wanted him to do.

Bernie came over to us. "How did things go? Sorry, I was busy with a call and didn't make it out to the lobby to greet Everly Jansen."

"We've just sent someone up to her room to get her registration information. She refused to go to the front desk and do it even though no one else was there," I said.

"She's a pain in the ass already," said Rhonda.

"Don't worry, the staff and I will take over from here," said Bernie in what was a soothing tone for him—crisp and clear.

"Okay, thanks," I said. "I see we have a VIP private dinner tonight. I assume Annette is handling that, but I'll be on hand to greet them and help Annette."

Bernie bobbed his head and walked away to see about the commotion outside in front of the hotel.

Rhonda and I followed but hung back as Bernie approached the group of photographers and news reporters. "Ladies and gentlemen, I'm asking you to please leave. The Beach House Hotel is known for offering our guests the privacy they deserve. Any requests for information need to come through my office as manager of the hotel. Thank you."

I couldn't help smiling. The more serious Bernie became, the thicker his German accent.

Rhonda and I headed to our office. There were other things we needed to take care of.

We were discussing plans for Thanksgiving, Christmas, and New Year's celebrations when I received a call from the front desk.

"Hello, Ms. Sanders. I want you and Ms. Grayson to know that the charge card Ms. Jansen used for her deposit didn't go through. Neither did a second card."

I thanked the clerk and turned to Rhonda. "Problem already. Everly's charge cards didn't go through."

"Surprise, surprise," grumped Rhonda. "Let Bernie handle it. I'm already too annoyed to be polite."

I blinked in surprise. Rhonda must be really upset to admit she couldn't deal with the situation. Normally, she would've been on her feet, ready to confront Everly with some spicy language. She hated deceit.

"Are you alright, Rhonda?" I asked, giving her a steady look.

Rhonda sighed and shook her head. "I'm worried about Will. Ever since Reggie's father, Arthur, married Lorraine and came to live in Sabal, he and Reggie have been working overtime to finish work and to try to get new clients. It's as if they're trying to compete with Arthur who brought many of his high-profile clients with him to Florida. It's really like comparing apples and oranges."

"Have you talked to him about it? He's at an age when he should be thinking about slowing down."

"He doesn't want to listen to me. It's as if he must prove he's as successful as Arthur. He's every bit as successful as Arthur, but he's handling a different kind of client." Rhonda sighed. "I don't know what I can do."

"Do you want to go on vacation? Maybe go over to the Palm Island Club? That's one of Vaughn's favorite nearby spots for relaxation. It might help."

Rhonda's eyes widened. "I've tried talking to him about going away with no success. Maybe he'd consider somewhere closer. We'll see. I'm doing my best not to let it affect my attitude, but I don't need much to set me off. It's just that I feel worried and helpless. Know what I mean?"

"I do," I said. We loved our husbands and when they were worried or depressed, it affected us.

"Why don't you go ahead and call the Palm Island Club and see what dates they have open for one of their cottages?"

Rhonda drew a deep breath. "Okay. But, Annie, how can I leave you alone with the hotel when we have a guest who's a problem and both houses are occupied?"

"That's why we have Bernie. It's his job to manage the hotel. We're here to manage the hotel's reputation and growth."

"You're right. This isn't the first troublemaking guest we've had to deal with. Everyone from VIPs to fake royalty. I'm going to call the Palm Island Club now."

I headed out to the beach for some fresh air and a chance to collect my thoughts. Everly Jansen spelled trouble. I knew it. But I also knew we'd have to deal with it. The chance for public relations to go wrong was part of our worry.

As luck would have it, I saw Brock Goodwin talking to a group of women down the beach. It surprised me that many of the single women in the neighborhood found him attractive and a nice addition to social gatherings. But then I'd had the chance to see what kind of man he was when I foolishly went on a date with him and discovered he was a pig in disguise.

I headed away from the group and walked slowly among the frothy edges of the water. Holding my sandals in my hand, I stood in the water ankle-deep and loved the feeling of the sand shifting beneath my feet as the water came into shore and pulled away. It made me feel part of nature.

"Hello, Ann," said Brock coming up to me. "I saw all the commotion at the hotel with the arrival of Everly Jansen. I hope she isn't going to become a nuisance for the neighborhood with all the paparazzi following her. We don't want television trucks parked on the streets, making it impossible to get by."

"Rhonda and I don't care for the publicity either," I said, surprising him with my agreement. "We've asked them to leave the property. What Everly and her following do outside our gates is not our problem."

Brock's face wrinkled as he frowned. "See? That's just the kind of thing I expect from you and Rhonda. No cooperation with the neighborhood."

"You know that's not true. But realistically there's nothing we can do about this."

"Well, then, I'll have to come talk to Everly myself," said Brock, drawing himself up straight.

"You'll have to get her permission to visit her. You can't just walk into the hotel demanding to see her."

"I know. But when she knows who I am, she'll want to talk to me," said Brock, his ego in overdrive.

"See you later," I said, wondering why the beach, the place I loved, was always ruined by his presence.

CHAPTER TWELVE

WHEN I GOT BACK TO THE OFFICE, RHONDA WAS JUST ending a call. "I've got the reservation for this weekend. Will has agreed to go for the three days. Now all I need is a new swimsuit. Will you go shopping with me? You know it's going to be a traumatic event."

"Sure. Finding a swimsuit is as difficult as finding a comfortable bra or the right shade of lipstick. I never seem to get it just right."

"It's been a while since I've gone shopping, and I trust you to tell me what works and what doesn't. I want something sexy. Great sex helps, and I intend to make this time away count." Rhonda grinned and wiggled her eyebrows with exaggeration.

I laughed. She and Will had a great relationship. They were immediately smitten when they first met, and that feeling had remained even through normal family trauma.

Rhonda bit her lip. "You know, if Will is comparing himself to Arthur, there's no way I'd do well comparing myself to Lorraine. She's attractive and very put-together. A real lady."

"Whoa! Where is this coming from? We're not going to make any comparisons to anyone else. Okay?"

Rhonda sighed. "You're right. With me, what you see is what you get. I just wish it wasn't quite so much of me."

"I understand. I've learned not to compare myself to the actresses Vaughn works with. It wouldn't be wise." I put my arm around Rhonda. "We all love you just the way you are."

Rhonda was quiet, and then she slowly nodded. "Okay, let's

do it. But if I ask you to hold my hand, promise you will."

I laughed. While it might seem silly to others, many women felt as we did, that we couldn't measure up to the images we were constantly shown on television, in the movies, and in publications.

"C'mon, let's go," said Rhonda.

We drove to the Seashell Swim Shop in the center of town and headed inside. I was thankful it was mid-afternoon when the lunch crowd normally headed back to their lodgings for relaxation.

The young woman manning the store was helpful and politely suggested certain suits for Rhonda, who told her that she was looking for sexy, not a conservative suit for a middle-aged woman.

The store clerk hung several bathing suits in a changing room and left. "Let me know if I can bring you other sizes or colors."

"Thanks," said Rhonda.

I sat in a chair outside the dressing room. "I'm right here. Show me what you like."

"Okay, here goes," Rhonda said, closing the door behind her.

Several minutes later, Rhonda opened the door. "What do you think?"

I studied her. She'd chosen a two-piece suit in a bright blue. "How about that style in the bold print we saw?"

"I tried it on but I'm not sure. Oh, Annie, what am I doing here? I should be wearing a blanket to cover me up."

"No, we're not going there," I said firmly, even as I noticed Rhonda's lower lip trembling. "Show me the print suit."

After a few minutes, Rhonda stepped outside the dressing

room. "There. Do you like it?"

"Yes, that's the one. It looks great on you. I think Will is going to like it."

"Really?" Rhonda sounded excited. "Okay, then. I'll get it."

I laughed when Rhonda gave me a big squeeze. "You're the best, Annie. Remember that awful black suit you wore when I first met you?"

"Yes, I do." I'd never forget how she told me I looked as if I was going to a beach funeral.

"Your taste has gotten better," Rhonda said. "Thanks for coming with me."

Rhonda had helped me loosen up and discard many of the demands my grandmother had made of me to be quiet, ladylike, and not stand out but to become my own person.

We left the shop and I drove home to talk to my nanny, Liana Sousa, about putting in more hours while Rhonda was away. Though I'd told Rhonda not to worry, I wanted to make sure I had the flexibility I might need if any trouble came up.

Robbie and Liana were in the kitchen when I arrived. Robbie was eating an after-school snack, and Cindy was sitting on the floor next to him waiting for any crumbs to drop.

I loved seeing the three of them comfortable like this. Liana was a bright young woman who was taking courses at the local Community College and would eventually need to leave us. In the meantime, I treasured her.

I changed my clothes, eager to have time with Robbie. He was growing fast, and I sometimes felt as if I was missing out on being part of his life. Vaughn assured me that though Robbie and I didn't chat about things like I used to do with Liz growing up, Robbie was still close to me. Just much quieter and far less talkative.

Liana and I sat in the kitchen discussing her classes and setting a schedule for the next couple of weeks. Then we said goodbye.

I went to check on Robbie. He was in his room playing video games when I went in to talk to him.

"How's it going?" I asked. "You don't have a swim meet for a while. What are you going to do to keep busy after your schoolwork?"

Robbie grinned and pointed to his video game.

"Are you interested in playing other sports?" I sat down on his bed.

"No, thanks. I'm happy doing just the swimming," said Robbie. "And I want to keep sailing with Dad whenever he's home."

"Everything is going fine at school?" I asked.

Robbie looked at me. "I'm fine, Mom. The teacher says I'm doing a great job."

I could see he was getting impatient, and I stood.

Robbie noticed my disappointment and said, "Love you, Mom."

"I love you too, honey." I leaned over and kissed him. Pretty soon, I supposed the time would come when he wouldn't want me to do that. But I'd continue until he told me so.

In the kitchen, I poured myself a glass of lemonade and picked up my cell to call Liz.

"Hi," she said. "How are you? I can't wait to tell you what the T's did today."

I smiled and sat down to listen. I loved both my children.

The next morning, after dropping Robbie off at school, I headed to work. I'd tossed and turned all night missing Vaughn. Our job as parents was to give our children independence, but without Vaughn, it could feel very lonely.

I checked into my office, saw there were no emergencies, and headed out to the beach. A cold front had moved in, and it was cooler than normal as I took off my shoes and walked onto the beach. The sun had warmed the sand, but the onshore breeze held a bit of a chill. To keep myself warm, I walked at a brisk pace.

The salty air, the cries of the birds whirling in the wind above me, and the sight of people looking for seashells settled me. At times like this, I felt lucky to be here in the moment and remembered cold wintry days in Boston. Being divorced had upended my life. As painful as the process was, it was the best thing that could've happened to me. Working with Rhonda, and loving the hotel as we did, my life was very rewarding. And then, finding Vaughn, a man I loved with all my heart, and having Robbie join our family completed me in a way I hadn't thought possible when it was just Liz and me facing the world.

I was so lost in thought as I walked along that when I looked up, I saw Brock striding toward me.

"Good morning, Ann. I want you to know that Everly Jansen has agreed to see me. I told her I was president of the Neighborhood Association and wanted to welcome her officially. I'm having drinks with her this afternoon."

"I'm sure she was delighted to hear from you," I said, not holding back on the sarcasm. Thank goodness, Rhonda wasn't here to tell him exactly what she thought. I'm sure it would have included at least one f-bomb.

"I'm just being a good neighbor and letting you know," he said, waving to someone further down the beach.

As he left, I decided to take advantage of the time to say goodbye to Tina. Her flight to California was later today.

I started toward the houses and stopped when I saw a

commotion on the beach in front of the hotel.

Everly was posing for photographers in the sand wearing a flesh-colored bikini that exposed most of her.

I wondered what was going on in that brain of hers. She was suing Darryl for more money, but she didn't appear to be suffering any hardships. She wore huge diamond earrings and held up a pair of expensive sandals as she beamed at the photographers. But then I remembered the two declined credit cards.

I watched as Brock went right over to her and put an arm around her. "As president of the Neighborhood Association, I'm welcoming Everly to the neighborhood." He smiled at the camera as Everly cleverly danced away from him.

Rhonda came onto the sand and stood beside me as the group moved down the beach, following every prancing step Everly made.

"What in hell is going on?" Rhonda said. "And Brock is part of it."

"Everly is putting on a show for everyone. I'm not sure why. Brock has arranged to meet with Everly this afternoon. He claims it's to welcome her to the neighborhood."

"What a crock," said Rhonda. "Are you sure you don't mind if Will and I take a short break? We can always cancel."

"Will's health and your need for a break are more important than anything else," I said. "I was about to say goodbye to Tina. Why don't you come with me? She'll want to see you."

"Okay. I'm excited about our mini-vacation. I love this hotel, but sometimes it feels like it's a crying, grumpy baby. Ya know?"

"Oh, yes. It would be easier if we didn't have a certain person interfering all the time."

Rhonda glared at Brock in the distance. "I'm tellin' ya, I'm going to wring his effin' neck one day, and it honestly won't be my fault, if I do."

I laughed. Rhonda and Brock would never get along.

While we were saying goodbye to Tina, Abbie entered the house. "I'm giving Darryl a break to deal with his agent. The man keeps calling. asking him to shut Everly up. But it's not his job, is it? He's been working hard to lose weight, and he's toughening up, but the pressure for him to go back to work is also building."

"I'm sorry," said Tina. "But you'll honor your contract with me and stay here while I make a quick trip home and back, won't you?"

"Sure. I'll continue to honor my contract with Darryl, too, though he might not be as accessible. What was all the commotion on the beach a little earlier? I couldn't see it, but I could hear it."

"It was Everly posing for photographs," I said.

"And the worst person I know, Brock Goodwin, was trying to butt in," said Rhonda. "If he ever starts to approach you, walk away. He's nothing but trouble."

"That's the truth," said Tina.

"Come back as soon as you can," I said, giving Tina a big hug. "And please hug those boys for me. Tell them Auntie Ann misses them."

"And Aunt Rhonda, too," she said, hugging Tina goodbye.

As we walked away from the houses, Rhonda said, "If you want me to stay, please tell me. Will and I will take a vacation another time."

I shook my head. "I meant what I said earlier. You both need some time off. Things are bound to calm down."

She glanced at me. Neither one of us believed it.

CHAPTER THIRTEEN

THE NEXT DAY, RHONDA AND I WERE WORKING IN OUR office when Everly came to see us.

"Hi, Everly. Is everything all right?" I asked.

"I'm here on a scouting mission for my friend, Brock. He told me he'd pay me money if I could find out who's staying in the private houses. I'm going to take him up on his offer. He's helping me with some issues, and I'll help him."

"As cute and friendly as all that is," said Rhonda, "we have as little to do with Brock as possible."

"And it's company policy that our guests have a right to seclusion." I stood, hoping to end the conversation.

"We know that doesn't interest you, but most of our guests appreciate that," said Rhonda. "Those houses are off-limits for Brock and for you. Get it?"

Everly frowned. "Who are you to talk to me that way? I'll do what I damn well please."

I herded Everly in the direction of the door and walked her out of the office. "If I were you, I'd be careful about any deals with Brock Goodwin. Just a word of warning. You've signed an NDA promising you'd respect the privacy of others. I expect you to honor it. Understand?"

Without responding, she turned and walked away.

When I returned, Rhonda was just hanging up the phone. "I've canceled my trip."

"Wait! Don't do that. Everything will settle down. It's just been a bad morning," I said.

"It's going to get worse if Everly finds out Darryl is staying here. We have to do something about it," said Rhonda grimly. "You know how it is when I get a funny feeling about things."

I gave her a thoughtful nod. It was true. She seemed to know ahead of time when trouble was about to happen. "What do you think we should do?"

"We need to get Darryl and Abbie off the property to a safe place," she said, giving me a steady look. "Thank goodness, Tina won't be an issue."

"Okay, you're right. Darryl and Abbie can stay at my house. Heaven knows they won't be bothered there."

"I don't dare have them at my place with my kids, who'd be more than ready to tell anyone about it," said Rhonda. "But Robbie is older and won't have to deal with neighbors asking."

"You're right. Let's go talk to Darryl now before any news gets out about his stay here," I said. "I don't trust Everly to honor her agreement to protect our guests' privacy."

Full of resolve, we started to walk over to the house where Darryl was staying.

"Our hotel's reputation can't be destroyed by a selfish, promo-seeking bitch," said Rhonda. "We've worked too hard to let that happen."

"I agree. I wish there was a way to get rid of Everly, but Bernie thinks it would create unwelcome attention."

"Yeah, talk about ruining our reputation," said Rhonda.

Once again, Rhonda and I slipped away from the hotel and took a secluded path to the houses. We walked with purpose.

"Why is it that every time there's a problem at the hotel, Brock is somehow involved?" said Rhonda with unmistakable anger. "I'm sick to death of his interference. I'm going to find a way to get back at him."

I slung my arm around Rhonda. "I wouldn't worry about it.

He always ends up in trouble. How he gets away with it is another issue."

When we got to Darryl's house, he was swimming in the pool. We rang the bell and waited for him to answer the door.

He arrived at the door wet and with a towel wrapped around his waist. Seeing him like this, I was amazed by his trimmer, healthier self. His shaved head had in some strange way made his eyes look bigger. Though not handsome like a movie star, his appearance was very appealing and as before, made me want to hug him like a sister would.

"Hello, what brings you here?" he said, indicating for us to come inside.

"We think it's going to be better for you to spend some time away from the hotel," I said. "You and Abbie are both welcome to spend a few days at my house until we can be sure Everly won't discover you're staying here."

"She's been talking to Brock Goodwin, and together, they're determined to learn who's staying in the houses," said Rhonda.

"We told Everly that guests have a right to their privacy," I said.

Darryl made a face. "You won't get far with that. I was very mistaken about her, completely fooled. And now, I'm pretty sure, she's involved with drug use, which is why she wants more money even though she got a more-than-fair settlement."

"What do you say? Are you willing to move until things calm down?" said Rhonda. "We're going to try to get her to leave the hotel. But we must be careful because of the hotel's reputation."

"I promise you comfortable surroundings," I said, trying to encourage him.

"Okay," he said. "The last thing I want is for Everly to

discover I'm here. This has been a wonderful stay for me. Especially with Abbie's help."

"Abbie is going to go with you," said Rhonda with satisfaction.

"When are we leaving?" he asked.

"As soon as possible," I said. "We'll get someone from security to drive you over. I'm going to my house right after we talk to Abbie."

"And I'll stay here and see that you both get off safely," said Rhonda. "We're all going to feel better when this happens."

"Definitely," said Darryl.

"Be sure and bring your swim trunks, I've got a nice pool," I said, waving goodbye to him.

We walked along another private path to the house where Abbie was staying. Tina should've already left for her flight.

Abbie answered the door looking relaxed in a pair of shorts and a T-shirt. She smiled when she saw us, lighting her dark brown eyes, giving them a sense of mystery.

We explained the situation to her. "Okay. I know what kind of pressure Darryl is under and I want to help in any way I can. When are we leaving?"

"As soon as you can pack up," said Rhonda.

What we couldn't say was that we didn't want a battle to break out between Darryl and Everly here at the hotel where Everly would use any method she could to get publicity out of it. Publicity that might hurt the hotel. We'd never had a situation quite like this.

When I arrived home, I saw Liana's car in the driveway and realized it was time for her to pick up Robbie at school.

I went inside. Cindy greeted me with happy wiggles as Liana said, "You're home early. Do you want me to leave?"

"No, I'm here because we're going to have guests staying with us for a few days. Guests that we're hiding for a while."

Liana's lips curved. "A little bit of intrigue, huh?"

"You could say that. I do ask that you don't mention it to anyone. You'll see why when you meet them."

Liana held up her palm. "I promise. Want me to pick up Robbie?"

"Yes, please. I want to make sure our two guest rooms are ready. Thanks."

After Liana left, I went to the guest wing of the house, which branched off just beyond Robbie's room. We had not one but two guest rooms for Vaughn's children and their families. It worked well. Adults in one room and children in another. Both had ensuite bathrooms, which made it easy to have two different groups at once.

Rhonda called to say that a security car had left the hotel carrying Darryl and Abbie. "I'll follow as soon as I talk to Bernie about how we want to get rid of Everly."

"Okay. I know you're upset with her, but let's be careful about how we handle it," I said.

"I will," Rhonda said.

Moments later, I heard a car pull into the driveway and walked out the front door to greet my guests.

Darryl and Abbie emerged from the car and stood gazing around.

"Beautiful property," said Darryl. "And lots of isolation here."

"We have just a few neighbors and none of them close to us, which makes it nice. My husband enjoys being able to do his own thing here."

I led them inside and showed them to their rooms.

"This is very nice, Ann," said Abbie. "It's no hardship to be here."

I chuckled. "The food might not be as tasty. But we can order meals from the hotel anytime. It shouldn't upset your schedule too much."

"The food at the hotel has been outstanding," said Abbie. "Darryl has been eating well but losing weight, which helps me do my part of his health routine."

"Are you talking about me?" asked Darryl, coming into the room.

"Saying only good things," said Abbie returning his grin.

"Thanks for having us here," said Darryl. "The more I've thought about it, the more I realize what harm Everly could do to all of us. One of the security people told me he saw her on television with the guy you don't like."

"Brock Goodwin?" I asked.

He nodded. "There's something about the two of them together that makes me uneasy. They look as if they're up to no good. At least, that's the feeling I get."

"You're probably right. Let me show you the rest of the house. I want you to be comfortable here."

I introduced them to Cindy and walked with them throughout the house. "Feel free to use the kitchen anytime and help yourself to anything you want."

Outside, I showed them the pool and spa. They're heated and are available anytime. The sailboat you see is Vaughn's beloved *Zephyr*. If you stay long enough, he'll be more than willing to take you out on it. He should be home soon."

"I'd like that," said Darryl.

"I'll call Vaughn and check with him to see when he's coming home. He just left town, but I never know when his schedule might change."

Rhonda arrived with a message that we would meet with

Bernie in a half-hour, and while she was sitting with Darryl and Abbie on the lanai, I quickly called Vaughn.

He answered right away. "Hey, I was about to call you. We've got enough sick cast members that shooting has been postponed for a week while other work is being done on the film."

"Great! Does that mean you'll come home?" I said, thrilled to hear the news.

"Yes, I'll fly out tomorrow. I'll let you know when. It's chaotic here."

Vaughn ended the call, and I let out a sigh of relief. Having Vaughn act as host would make things much easier.

I went out to the lanai.

Cindy, who'd been sitting with Darryl suddenly barked and leapt off the couch.

"Oh, that must be my son, Robbie, coming home from school," I said.

We all looked up as Robbie walked onto the lanai. He gazed at our guests curiously but addressed Rhonda. "Hi, Aunt Rhonda. Willow and Drew didn't come with you?"

"Not this time," said Rhonda, motioning him forward. As he neared her, she wrapped an arm around him, pulled him close, and quickly kissed him on the cheek.

He stepped back, and though I knew he was embarrassed, he smiled. He loved Rhonda. Both of my children did.

Liana came into the room, and I introduced her before walking both Robbie and her to the kitchen.

I ruffled Robbie's hair and turned to Liana. "Rhonda and I are going to leave for the hotel shortly. I want to make sure Darryl and Abbie are comfortable before we do."

"Yes, I understand," said Liana, and I thought how lucky I was to have her help.

CHAPTER FOURTEEN

AFTER MAKING SURE THAT DARRYL AND ABBIE WERE comfortable with their plans to swim in the pool and relax at my house, Rhonda and I headed back to the hotel.

"It's a PR nightmare," said Rhonda, filling me in on the way. "A Miami television newsperson wants to set up an interview with Everly. Everly said it was fine, but the woman calling wanted to make sure it was okay with the hotel to do the interview here."

"And what did Bernie say?" I asked.

"He said he would send them an agreement stating what was allowed and what wasn't. He told her it would have to be signed before they could set a time and date for any interview at the hotel."

"Good for him," I said. "Hopefully, it will become a non-issue, but we have to find a way to get Everly to leave."

At the hotel, we joined Bernie in his office.

"Any word from the Miami newsperson?" Rhonda asked after we'd taken our seats.

"I have the signed agreement in my hands," said Bernie. "It was just sent to me. Now we need to figure out a time and place."

"I think we should hold off as long as we can," I said.

"An hour or so ago, Everly called down to the Front Desk wanting to know when she could give her interview. They're paying her quite a bit of money for an exclusive, and she wants it set up right away." Bernie shook his head. "Her words were slurred and full of foul language."

"Why don't Rhonda and I talk to her to see if she's going to be reasonable about respecting our rules," I suggested.

"Let's give her a while to collect herself, and then we'll go visit her," said Rhonda. "I need some time to think about how we want to approach her. I still want her gone from the hotel. Maybe we can work that in somehow."

"That sounds reasonable," said Bernie. "Darryl and Abbie are comfortable at your house, Annie?"

"Yes, they're grateful to be away from the hotel until things have calmed down here," I said.

Bernie stood. "Okay, then, we have a plan for Everly. I'll see to the VIP group meeting in the library."

"Let's go sit on the sunset deck," I said. "Being in the sea breeze always clears my mind."

"Okay," said Rhonda. "It's been quite a day. After we visit Everly, I'll treat you to a margarita. I think we've earned one."

I grinned. "Okay, and then I'm going to pick up dinner at the hotel and take it home. I want to make sure it's all food Abbie approves of. Darryl is making a lot of progress."

"He's looking good, really good," said Rhonda. "Do you think Everly is putting on this show of hers to try and get him back?"

"If so, she doesn't understand the man at all," I said. "He's not someone who constantly seeks attention. He's funny and charming on television but a rather quiet person away from it."

Outside, we'd just taken our seats on the deck when we saw a figure walking toward us.

"Run, Annie!" said Rhonda, getting to her feet.

I pulled her back into her chair. "Stop. We can't let Brock keep us from enjoying our own property."

"But just seeing him makes me want to smack that smirk off his face," Rhonda said, twitching in her seat.

"Let's see what he has to say this time. Bet it's about that photograph," I murmured as he came closer.

"' Afternoon, ladies," said Brock. "Guess you saw my picture in the paper. It made front-page news. But then, I think Everly likes me. I've helped her get acquainted with the neighborhood. In fact, I'm going to visit her later on."

When neither Rhonda nor I spoke, he shrugged. "Guess I beat you this time."

"See you later," I said before Rhonda could tell him off. If it kept him from the houses on the property, I was glad to let Brock think he was ahead of the game he was constantly playing with us.

As Brock walked away, his chest puffed out with self-importance.

Before she could follow him, I took hold of Rhonda's arm. "Forget it."

"Someday I won't," she said, giving me a challenging look. "And not even you, with all your sweet ways, will be able to stop me from wringing his fuckin' neck."

I laughed. I couldn't help it.

Rhonda joined in. "Honestly, that man drives me crazy."

"Me, too," I said. "Now, let's go take care of another annoying person."

As we prepared to head back to the hotel, I paused for a moment, gazing at the building we loved like a child. We couldn't let anyone harm it. We'd made it such a classy, beloved place for people to enjoy.

"Our baby, huh?" said Rhonda.

I smiled and nodded. "Let's keep it safe."

###

We went inside the hotel and climbed the stairway to The Presidential Suite.

At the top, we faced the thick, carved wooden door of the suite. I was about to knock when I noticed the door wasn't closed properly.

"Hello?" I called and waited for an answer.

"Maybe she's gone," said Rhonda. "We'd better check."

We stepped inside to the front entrance, and I called out again.

"The living room is a mess," grumbled Rhonda as we began to check out all the rooms, looking for her.

"The kitchen is a disaster," I said, passing through it.

We went to the master bedroom and let out gasps of horror.

Everly lay on the floor motionless, oddly sprawled atop the carpet, as if she'd fallen.

Rhonda gripped my arm. "Maybe she's drunk. Bernie made it sound as if she'd been drinking."

I stared at the still body, studying it, my heart sinking. "I don't think she's drunk. I'm pretty sure she's dead."

I walked over to her and held my hand in front of her nose and mouth. There was no breath. Her lips were blue and her skin ... I couldn't look any longer. Feeling sick, I turned away. I'd seen death before.

"Oh, my God, Annie, what are we going to do?" Rhonda said.

"We need to call 911 and let Bernie know what's happened."

Rhonda grabbed hold of the door frame on her way out of the room. "Oh, God! I think I'm going to throw up."

I stumbled out of the room behind her.

In the living room, while Rhonda called 911, I called our security office and then called Bernie. In a fog, I told them what we'd found. I had the sense to make sure they wouldn't make a commotion when they came to see. We didn't want our other guests to be aware. I could hear Rhonda telling people the same thing on her call.

We both ended our calls and faced one another.

"We've had only one other guest die in the hotel," I said, still in shock.

"I can't believe it. Everly sure knows how to shake things up," said Rhonda. "I can't go back in that room."

Bernie and a member of our security team arrived together. They went to check out the scene and returned to the living room.

"We found needles in the bathroom," said Bernie. "We're not touching anything. We'll wait for the police to arrive."

"I'm going to go down to the lobby to talk to the front desk staff and explain the need for discretion," I said.

"I'm leaving with you," said Rhonda. "I'll talk to others in our reception staff, tell them what has happened."

"Thanks," said Bernie. "I'll wait here with the body. I'm sure the police will want to talk to you about this. I'll meet you in your office as soon as I can. We'll want to release some sort of statement."

Rhonda and I went downstairs together. I couldn't stop shivering. "Is this the result of the bad feeling you had?"

Rhonda sighed. "Something like it. I knew I shouldn't leave for vacation, but I didn't think it would be because someone died here."

"We've gotten through a lot of traumatic situations. I know we can do it again," I said, trying to reassure myself along with her. "As soon as possible, I'll go home and talk to Darryl. He won't want to be anywhere near the hotel. As soon as word gets out, newspeople will be everywhere trying to get what scraps of information they can."

"Let's make sure Bernie schedules more security," said Rhonda.

"It's going to be a bit tricky to balance things out," I said. "We want to make a good impression of the hotel for being an elegant place to stay, and a hotel that truly does respect the privacy of their guests."

"Everly's family will need to be notified. How are we going to find out who they are?" said Rhonda. "Darryl?"

"We can ask him for information about who to call. I imagine funeral arrangements will be taken care of someplace else. There's no reason for any ceremony here at the hotel," I said, becoming angry that Everly had caused more headaches for us. Yet, a part of me felt devastated to know that she'd died alone, away from home.

"It's sad," said Rhonda. "I've already talked to my kids about the danger of drugs. They don't understand all about the deaths because of their ages; they simply know it's bad for them."

"Robbie's at an age where we talk seriously about drugs killing people. His school is aware of any problems and is quick to report them." After seeing what had happened to Everly, I wanted to cry at the thought of anyone in my family being caught up in addiction. Whether Everly killed herself on purpose or it happened because of her use, it was such a terrible, terrible waste.

CHAPTER FIFTEEN

A POLICE CAR ROLLED THROUGH THE GATES.

I walked down the front stairs to greet the two officers inside. Living in a small town like Sabal, most policemen were known to us. Today was no exception. I spoke to Becka Santos and recognized her partner, Joe Bennett.

"Thank you both for coming quickly. The deceased person is in the Presidential Suite. Rhonda and I ask you to please not make a commotion when you go inside the hotel. We don't want our other guests to know what's going on."

"I understand, Ann. We'll park the car, and you can lead us to the person," said Becka. "Who is it?"

"Everly Jansen. As sorry as we are for this to happen to her, we need to be careful about the hotel's reputation. You know how she loved publicity."

While they parked their car, I waited for them to join me. Drug use at the hotel hadn't been much of an issue. We'd certainly never had anyone die from an overdose on the property.

Becka and Joe followed me into the hotel, and we walked quickly to the set of stairs leading to the Presidential Suite. A security guard stood at the bottom of the stairway and moved aside as we came closer.

When we got to the suite, Bernie greeted us at the entrance. "The medical examiner is on his way. Nothing has been touched."

The officers went to the master bedroom where a security guard stood by.

"I need to go home and tell Darryl what has happened," I said to Bernie, as Rhonda joined us.

"I'm sure you'll be free to go after the officers take a statement from you," said Bernie. "It's a good thing Darryl is staying at your house, away from here. Maybe he can help us. We need to notify the family."

"That's another reason I need to talk to Darryl. He may know who to call," I said.

"I'll speak to Becka to see how they want to handle this," said Bernie.

He left Rhonda and me alone.

"This is such a freakin' mess," said Rhonda. "Hopefully, they'll wait to remove the body until most of our guests are busy at dinner."

Becka and Joe returned.

"Things seem to be in order here," said Becka. "We've put a call into our DVD officer. Drugs and Vice Division. In the meantime, we can take notes from you about what you saw when you arrived here."

"The drug officer may also want to talk to you, too," said Joe. "But we can get as many of the facts as we can right now."

"Let's sit in the living room," I said. "We'll be more comfortable."

Rhonda and I took seats on one couch while Becka and Joe sat on another, facing us.

"Okay, start at the beginning," said Becka.

Rhonda and I took turns telling about our arrival at the Suite and each moment following the discovery of Everly's body, assuring them we'd touched nothing.

"I did lean over to place my hand in front of Everly's nose and mouth but there was no breath and it looked like there wouldn't be any," I said, hunching my shoulders as a shiver traveled down my back. I'd never forget what I saw. It was an ugly death.

"Did you go into the bathroom?" asked Joe.

Rhonda shook her head. "Neither of us did. But Bernie and a security guard did. Annie and I just wanted to get out of there."

"Can you tell us who Everly had been seeing?" Becka asked.

"No. She certainly liked publicity, but I don't recall any visitors," I said.

Rhonda and I looked at one another as we both realized something.

"What is it?" asked Becka.

"Brock Goodwin mentioned that he was going to see Everly today," I said.

"He made a big deal out of being photographed with her," said Rhonda. "He told us they were helping one another. He's such a liar that it's hard to know what's real with him."

"We both saw his photograph with Everly in the newspaper," Joe said to Becka.

"We'll inform the DVD officer, and he can take it from there," said Becka.

"Is it possible for me to go home?" I asked. "I have guests staying with me." For now, I'd keep Darryl's whereabouts private. But if one of the officers needed to talk to him, I'd let them know.

"You're free to go. I think we have all the information we need for now," said Becka. "I'm sure you have things to take care of."

I went to find Bernie to tell him I was leaving, and a DVD officer was arriving. After giving him a complete update, I headed home. Rhonda would stay behind with Bernie.

When I arrived home, Darryl and Abbie were sitting on the

lanai reading while Robbie sprawled on the floor, playing a video game on his iPad. Liana had left for her college class.

"Hi, Mom! Liana made us stuff for a taco dinner like she usually does on class night," said Robbie.

"Perfect," I said, relieved I wouldn't have to worry about that. When Vaughn was home tomorrow, he'd be glad to grill some steaks.

"That sounds wonderful," said Abbie. "Something different."

"Liana uses her grandmother's recipes, and her food is delicious." I grew somber as I said to Darryl, "I need to speak to you in private. Will you join me in the living room?"

"Sure. Is everything all right?" he said, getting to his feet.

"No," I managed to say and held back a sob.

We walked into the living room, and I indicated Darryl should sit on the couch.

I took a seat nearby and faced him. "I have some terrible news. We found Everly dead in her hotel room. She apparently died from a drug overdose. It's being investigated now."

Darryl closed his eyes and let out a long breath. "What a damn waste. I'm sorry it came to this. I can't say I'm surprised though. It was one reason we broke up. She liked to party, and I didn't. Still don't. Not with drugs."

I shook my head sadly. "I'm sorry. I really am. I hope this doesn't bring you more trouble."

He gave me an unhappy look. "Thank you."

"I'm offering you a place here for as long as you'd like," I said. "You certainly don't want to be at the hotel."

"Thanks. I appreciate that." Darryl's eyes filled. "It's all unnecessary. She wouldn't get help."

"Do you know who should be notified?" I asked him.

"Everly's sister, Veronika, lives in New York City. We've stayed in touch. I'll call her," said Darryl. "You can give the number to whoever needs it."

"I'm sure newspeople will want to get a statement from you."

"Okay. I'll call my agent and have him make a statement for me. I don't want him or anyone else to know where I'm staying."

"I think it's best. Now, let's go speak to Abbie. She's welcome to stay here until Tina returns." I couldn't help smiling. "Things seem to be going well with your training sessions."

He returned my smile. "I can't say enough good things about it. Abbie's a taskmaster, but I've never been happier to do the work."

"It's certainly paying off," I said. "You must feel great about that."

"I do. I've never felt better," Darryl said, rising. "Abbie's agreed to continue working with me after her contract is over with Tina."

"That's nice," I said, forcing myself not to overreact. Maybe Rhonda would have reason to celebrate their relationship sooner than we thought. That conversation would come at a later time. Now, we had to deal with Everly.

When we got to the lanai, I said to Robbie, "Please come here. I need to talk to you about something, and then we'll give Darryl and Abbie some time alone."

Robbie glanced at Darryl and got to his feet.

Cindy followed us into Robbie's room.

I explained that a friend of Darryl's had died and that while he was staying with us, we had to give him privacy.

Robbie nodded. "Okay."

I hugged him. He was such a good kid.

Rhonda called on my cell. "How's it going there?"

"Okay. I told Darryl, and he wasn't surprised. Saddened,

though. He's going to call Everly's sister in New York and tell her what's happened. He'll be staying at my house for the foreseeable future. And he doesn't want anyone to know that."

"I agree he should remain out of sight. I met with the drugs officer. He may want to talk to us tomorrow. He was very interested to learn about Brock's interaction with Everly. I couldn't think of anyone else who may have had contact with her. The housekeeping staff and front desk people will be interviewed and anyone else who might've seen anything."

"Are you going home?" I asked her.

"Yes. I'm on my way. This has been one effing day. Thank God, Will has already fed the children. I need to relax with him and talk about rescheduling our vacation."

"I don't think it'll take long for this situation to calm down," I said. "It's pretty obvious what happened. Where Everly got the drugs is a mystery that might be difficult to trace. Where does that leave Brock?"

"Hanging by his balls," said Rhonda gleefully. She let out a hearty laugh. Thinking of all the rotten things Brock had tried to do to us in the past, I couldn't help joining in. Maybe this time, he'd learn a lesson or two.

CHAPTER SIXTEEN

AFTER A QUICK EASY DINNER OF TACOS AND ALL THE trimmings, including a rice and bean casserole that Robbie liked, I made sure that Robbie finished his homework. Then, I went out to the lanai to join Darryl and Abbie. I'd be glad to have Vaughn home so we could be on his boat, which was an easy way to entertain guests.

"How are you doing, Darryl?" I asked.

"Okay," he said. "I've talked to my agent, informed Veronika, and told my producer that I would not be coming back to the studio."

"That's a lot to handle," I said, commiserating with him.

"There's a lot for me to think about," he admitted. "As much as Everly liked publicity, her sister is adamant about having a small, private service for Everly without any press."

"And I'll be here for him," said Abbie. "Friends support friends."

Darryl smiled at her, and I wondered why Abbie didn't realize the look he gave her was about a lot more than being friends. Still, I wouldn't say anything. This wasn't the time or place.

"It's dark outside, but if you two want to take a walk around the neighborhood, I think it's safe to do so. It's very private and people do respect one another."

"That's a great idea. We splurged with food at dinner and need to work some of it off," said Abbie. She jumped to her feet and tugged Darryl up out of his seat.

"I need the exercise," he said and then winked at me. "Who

would've believed I'd say something like this a couple of weeks ago?"

I grinned. "I don't want you to feel imprisoned here."

"Thanks again for letting us stay," said Darryl. "When things calm down, I want to return to the hotel for as long as you'll have me. I'm working on some new plans. "

"All good ones," said Abbie, smiling at him.

The next morning, I arose and after seeing that Darryl and Abbie were set for the day, I dropped Robbie off at school and headed to the hotel.

I was eager to see how the situation with Everly's death had been handled.

Bernie and Rhonda were in his office when I arrived.

"I'm glad you both are here so I can give you an update," said Bernie. "The body was removed discreetly just before the busy dinner hour last night. The coroner's initial report arrived this morning. The police have determined that all evidence has been collected."

He held up papers for us to see. "Later this morning, after a final check, they will release the room to us. I've arranged for a crew to replace the carpet and furnishing in the master bedroom, and the housekeeping department will give the entire suite a deep cleaning. There will be no sign of what happened there, and we want to keep all talk about it under control. I've sent a message to all department heads. We're meeting this morning to go over the importance of speaking to all staff members about our protocol."

"It seems as if it's a pretty straightforward case," I said.

"Yes, the police officer handling it is now concerned about where Everly might have gotten the drugs. The alcohol came from the hotel, of course."

"Does the police detective need to talk to Annie and me again?" asked Rhonda.

Bernie shook his head. "The information he gave me said he was focused on anyone Everly might have met with. Unfortunately for Brock Goodwin, that includes him."

"He'd be in the clear if he wasn't such an egotistical bastard," said Rhonda. "I hope he wasn't stupid enough to help her find the drugs."

"What was it? Fentanyl?" I asked.

"Probably. That and alcohol," Bernie said. "I have no idea what drugs she took."

"Thank you for handling this so well," I said.

"Yes, we appreciate all you've done," said Rhonda. "It's a tragic situation."

"I told Darryl about it," I said. "He was upset to learn Everly's life had ended this way, but he wasn't surprised. It seems she liked to party a lot, which is one reason he filed for divorce. He called Everly's sister in New York."

"Thanks for that information," said Bernie. "I think we've handled the situation the best we could. As I'll tell our department heads, the way to approach this is to simply not allow any talk about it. The media is going to want to make a big deal over it. There's nothing we can do about it except to keep our stance that all guests are due privacy, including her."

"Absolutely," I said.

"What are we going to do about Brock, if anything?" asked Rhonda.

"I'm afraid it's out of our hands," said Bernie. He held up the old newspaper with Brock's picture with Everly on the front page. "He needs to explain a lot."

"That might help us by keeping the focus on the drug source and away from the hotel," I said optimistically.

"Humph, if Brock is doing us a favor, it'll be the first time," said Rhonda.

Bernie held up a finger. "He's calling me now."

Rhonda and I sat quietly while Bernie carried on a brief conversation with Brock.

"No, indeed," said Bernie into the phone. "We've done nothing of the sort, merely answered questions for the officers involved in the case. If you'll excuse me, I have a hotel to run."

Bernie ended the call and faced us shaking his head. "Brock is furious that someone mentioned that he was going to visit Everly yesterday. He's blaming us for the suspicion placed upon him for providing Everly with the drugs."

"I'll wait until the situation has eased, and then I'll speak to him," I said. "Rhonda and I can't jeopardize our reputation by not cooperating with the police. It wasn't done out of spite."

"But now that I think of it, I like the idea he's caught in this mess because of his ego," said Rhonda.

"Agreed," said Bernie. "Let's carry on like we normally do."

Rhonda and I left his office and went to the kitchen for a strong cup of coffee and something sweet. We were facing a couple of tense days.

Later that morning, Rhonda and I were sitting in our office when Dorothy Stern arrived. "I'm glad you're both here. I assume you've seen the paper this morning or heard the news online or on television. The neighborhood is abuzz to think that Brock is somehow involved with Everly Jansen's death. One gentleman is calling for Brock Goodwin to resign as president of the Neighborhood Association."

Dorothy stopped talking and collapsed in a chair. "I got here as soon as I could to give you the news. Will you represent the hotel with a vote against Brock?"

Though Rhonda was grinning, she turned to me.

"I'd love to, but I know we can't get involved. There's an investigation taking place and it involves the hotel. It's best if we stay out of it."

Rhonda sighed. "You're right, Annie. God knows I'd love to help vote him out, but we must protect the hotel."

I reached over and clasped Dorothy's hand. "I hope you understand."

"I do. From a business point of view, it's the right decision. Brock is scared. As gratifying as it is to see him like that, I want his removal done in such a way that nothing can change it," said Dorothy.

"He won't go down without a fight. Be careful," I said. I remembered the times I'd had to represent the hotel in neighborhood meetings and how nasty Brock could be.

"Yes, we'll be careful," said Dorothy. "I was hoping to make you feel better. I know it must be upsetting to have a death at the hotel."

"An overdose is so senseless," I said. "I knew she was a troubled woman, but I had no idea she'd resort to drugs to end her life if that's what she did. Maybe it was accidental."

"She was too egotistical to kill herself," said Rhonda.

"You're smart to stay out of it and say as little as possible," said Dorothy. "I love you women and all you've done to show others you can succeed."

I rose and hugged Dorothy. From the very beginning, she'd been a wonderful supporter of ours.

Rhonda was next to embrace the tiny but spunky woman. She and Dorothy had done charitable work together before she even had the idea of a hotel. Women helping women.

My heart raced as I headed to the airport to pick up Vaughn. Even though he could've paid for an Uber, he loved it when I came to pick him up. And though he'd been gone for only a short time, it still felt like an exciting homecoming.

I pulled up to the curb and waited for just a moment before he emerged from the baggage claim area. When he saw me, he waved, and I was sent back to the time I first met him as a cast member of *The Sins of the Children*, the soap opera in which he starred as mayor of a small town. Even now, my pulse raced at the sight of him, and I could hardly believe that we'd ended up together. He was as different from my ex as he could be. Which made it all the sweeter.

A few people recognized him and headed his way. Vaughn swiftly tossed his bag into the back of the car and slid into the passenger seat.

"Welcome home," I said, accepting his kiss. "A lot is going on at the hotel."

"I read about it online. You'll have to fill me in on the details. I think it's wise for Darryl and Abbie to stay at our house. The press isn't going to let go of this for a while. Brock Goodwin's name is being mentioned as the last person who may have seen Everly alive."

"Brock's blaming Rhonda and me, of course, but we did nothing but answer the officer's questions. We can't and won't jeopardize the reputation of the hotel."

"I agree," said Vaughn. "He's made this happen to himself. Now tell me a bit about Darryl and Abbie."

"You'll like them both. Darryl is shy and quiet. He has a lot on his mind right now, so it seems natural. Abbie is a firecracker who keeps him doing all his exercises and watches what he eats. In a short amount of time, it's made a huge difference. I think Darryl's in love with Abbie, though she doesn't seem to realize it."

"Are you and Rhonda trying to make it seem more than friendly-like?" Vaughn asked, sending me a piercing look.

"Well, I think a growing relationship is inevitable, but I won't claim responsibility for it. Rhonda is a different story."

"Don't I know it. But even so, fate and Rhonda have brought people together and they're happy," admitted Vaughn.

I chuckled. "I hope you're up to taking all of us out in the boat for supper. The weather is cooperating, and it's such a wonderful way to make friends."

"You know how much I love doing it," said Vaughn. He leaned back in his seat and closed his eyes. "It feels great to be home. It's getting chilly for filming in Canada."

When we arrived at the house, Cindy greeted us, followed by Abbie.

"Your watch dog alerted me," said Abbie smiling down at the Dachshund.

"Abbie, meet my husband, Vaughn Sanders," I said. "Vaughn, this is Abbie Hathaway."

Darryl approached us, and I made more introductions.

"We're in luck," I said. "Vaughn has agreed to an evening sail. I'm going to order a picnic from the hotel. Any requests?"

Darryl looked at Abbie.

"How about an assortment of salads?" Abbie said.

"That sounds great. Steak salad, lobster salad, and chicken and fruit salad. That, with French bread. Okay?"

All three adults nodded enthusiastically.

"I'll see if Robbie would rather stay with his friend, Brett," I said, turning away from the group.

"Everyone will need a sweater or a windbreaker," said Vaughn. "When the sun goes down, it's cold on the water."

In a short time, I'd dropped Robbie off at Brett's house and picked up the dinner from the hotel. Being an owner of the hotel had the benefit of being able to order food from the kitchen if it didn't disrupt Jean-Luc.

"Is everyone ready?" said Vaughn. "Darryl, have you done any sailing?"

"A few times out on Long Island Sound," he said.

"Okay. I'm making you my First Mate," said Vaughn, and I was amused by the sense of pride that flashed on Darryl's face.

Abbie and I exchanged smiles. "I've sailed with one of my brothers."

We climbed aboard the boat, and while I stowed food in the galley, Vaughn showed various features of the boat to Abbie and Darryl. "When I say, 'coming about', it means I'm turning the boat around and you need to watch for the main boom to swing around. In other words, 'duck'!"

Vaughn got the motor running and turned to Darryl. "Untie the lines from the dock's bollards, toss the bow line onto the boat, and then throw the stern line into the boat and quickly jump aboard."

"Aye, aye, Captain!" said Darryl, going on the dock to take care of the lines. He was grinning like a schoolboy at being given this task.

I glanced at Vaughn, and he winked at me. He liked making other people comfortable on the boat and building camaraderie with the men he hosted.

With both lines and Darryl aboard, Vaughn began easing the boat out of the inlet in back of our house.

"It's beautiful," murmured Abbie. "I love California, but I must admit, I'm enjoying Florida more. It's not as crowded and is more tropical in feel."

"Nights like this are special," I said. "Lean back and enjoy the ride. It's very peaceful."

We gazed at the beautiful houses lining the inlet and the homes along the passage to open water.

As soon as we were out on the Gulf, Vaughn told Darryl about the next steps of raising the mainsail and the jib. Then he said, "Darryl, I'm going to give you the wheel, and I'll raise the sails. Keep the boat on a steady course."

After Darryl stepped behind the wheel, Vaughn made sure the boat was head to wind and then he quickly moved to raise the mainsail before cutting off the engine.

The boat immediately responded and heeled a bit.

"Ease off," Vaughn told Darryl. "I'll get the jib."

I was relieved Vaughn was handling the sails. The wind was a steady breeze and once underway, we'd be moving fast.

"It's going to be a great sail," I said to Abbie. "What can I get you to drink? We have everything from water to red wine."

"I'd love some red wine," said Abbie. She looked to Darryl. "What are you going to have to drink?"

"I'll take a beer," said Darryl and gave a thumbs up to Abbie.

Watching the interplay between them, I was charmed.

I went below and fixed a plate of cheese and crackers, added some chilled green grapes to the platter, and handed it up to Abbie. Then I handed drinks up to the others, including a beer for Vaughn.

It was a quiet time of day with the sun descending.

"Look for the green flash," I said and explained to them when that might happen if all conditions were right.

I climbed into the cockpit and sat with a glass of wine, feeling the tension leave my body.

"Here's to us!" I said, raising my plastic glass.

Everyone joined in with a cheer, and I leaned back against a cushion and listened to the hiss of the water as the hull of the boat sliced through it. I knew Vaughn's eyes were on me and swiveled to return his smile. Sailing always seemed to bring us close.

"Tell me a bit about you," I said to Abbie. "I know you have four older brothers. Where did you go to school? Did you always want to work as a trainer?"

"Before anyone can tease me, yes, I was the spoiled daughter with older brothers," said Abbie. "But those very brothers teased and heckled me and forced me to be tough. I guess that's why I don't have any problem being tough on my clients."

"I can vouch for that," said Darryl flexing his arms.

Amid the laughter, Abbie continued. "I decided against sports medicine and studied instead to become a physical therapist and trainer. Believe me, I studied premed classes and have a solid background for the work I do."

"It's obvious you love the work," I said.

"I do," she said. "It's fun to meet new people and travel to different places, but it can be difficult, especially when someone doesn't want to follow the program. Darryl has been an easy client which makes it very nice. Other people aren't always that committed."

"I want to make some changes," said Darryl. "I used to be in great shape and then I got involved with my show and all of my activities became centered around it. Now, it feels great to be physically active again."

"One of my best students," said Abbie, patting him on the back.

"What about you, Darryl? What made you get into comedy and then do a late-night gig on television?" said Vaughn.

Darryl gave us a sheepish look. "While Abbie was the darling of her family, I was the spoiled son in mine. My four sisters doted on me. When I was just a toddler, they used to dress me up and make me take part in their family plays. I'm told I liked it before I became aware of the fact that other kids didn't do that kind of thing. Even now, my sisters are creative in their work and with their hobbies."

"Rhonda and I watched a program of yours before you came to the hotel. You seemed almost embarrassed when a young actress talked about her sexy new love affair," I said and then wondered if I'd gone too far.

Darryl's face grew red, and his lip curled before he drew a deep breath and gazed at the horizon. He turned back.

"That's one reason I've decided to try and get out of my contract. The network is pushing me to be more provocative with my guests without crossing a line. But the truth is, I'm tired of trying to do what the network thinks is going to sell the show. I want to be real, with some good laughs, and not worry about their crazy ideas. And I have another issue my agent is trying to handle. I'm here to stay out of the limelight, and to consider what I want to do next. My agent is dealing with the network and any other problems. That's what he gets paid to do."

"Whoa! I heard your show was very lucrative," said Vaughn. "You're giving it up?"

Darryl gazed at him and nodded. "Remember those four sisters of mine? They taught me to respect women. The network wants me to have more titillating conversations with my guests, to goad them into saying things they might regret. I've finally decided I've had enough. That's not how I've been taught to live. In my stand-up routines, I mostly talk about funny things happening in a family or with kids. Good humor that's not destroying anyone."

"I admire him for that," said Abbie. "We've talked about it."

"I support you," said Ann. "People have become cruel, intrusive."

"It's not necessary," said Vaughn. "Humor that works is based on the unexpected ending. It doesn't have to be crude or hurtful."

"I don't want to be seen on television in any way that depicts me in a bad way. I think of my sisters and what they'd do and say to me if I treated other people in a hurtful way or tore someone down just to get a laugh. I'm tired of fighting to do things my way. I want to be just me."

"What will you do?" I asked.

"I'm not sure. I've got an idea for a project. And relieving the pressure to compete and continually being forced to watch my ratings will make life much better. I want to do something helpful with the money I've earned."

My thoughts spinning, I served more drinks and prepared to dish out the dinners. Rhonda had several charities she worked with. I wondered if she could come up with some ideas for Darryl.

The sun had gone down and the wind had eased a bit, making it pleasant for eating our meal. The boat rocked softly as we quietly dined, and I imagined we all were thinking of Darryl's dilemma.

After dinner, I rinsed the dishes below and chatted with Abbie as the men talked.

"I admire Darryl's decision," I told her.

"Me, too," she said. "He's a wonderful man. We've done a lot of talking. About everything. I'm not sure where it's going, but we both want to see if our relationship can grow. We've only met recently, but I'm hoping he'll come to California for a visit."

"Rhonda will be thrilled," I said. "In her mind, she had the two of you paired off from the beginning."

Abbie laughed. "Really?"

"Oh, yes. Rhonda considers herself a talented matchmaker. Just so you know."

"I love it," said Abbie. "I'm going to believe this relationship of Darryl's and mine can work out because of her."

We smiled together, and I realized how much I liked her.

"How about some nightcaps?" Vaughn said. "It's been a great evening, and it would be nice to sit and talk and enjoy a dessert wine."

"Sounds fine with me," said Darryl glancing at Abbie.

"Thanks. That would be enjoyable," Abbie said. "Tomorrow, we'll work doubly hard to work off these calories."

Darryl groaned, and we all laughed.

CHAPTER SEVENTEEN

THAT NIGHT, LYING IN BED WITH VAUGN, I TOLD HIM about my conversation with Abbie.

"I like them both. Darryl seems like a super guy, not like some other self-absorbed comedians I've met," said Vaughn. "And I admire his decision to quit the show. It takes guts and faith to walk away from a successful career."

"They'll be staying with us for a few more days," I said. "Then they'll go back to the hotel. Tina should be arriving soon to complete her stay. She had to go home to take care of some personal things."

"It's not a problem to have Darryl and Abbie here as guests."

"While I'm at work, do you mind entertaining them?"

"No problem. Darryl and I have already made plans to go sailing again tomorrow. He wants to learn what he can, and I figure nobody will bother us on the water. Abbie told us she might take time to do a little shopping. I shouldn't have to worry about her."

"I'll talk to her in the morning and ask if she'd like to meet Rhonda and me for lunch." I nestled up against Vaughn, pleased to have him home. Life always seemed much better with him around.

He wrapped his arms around me and gazed down at me with a tender smile. "This, you, are why I can't wait to come home."

He lowered his lips to mine and a familiar longing filled me. Soon, we were able to show each other how important it was for both of us.

The next morning at the hotel, Rhonda was already at her desk when I walked into the office. "I can always tell when Vaughn is home," she said to me. "You look so happy."

I chuckled. "It makes life better when he's around. How about a walk on the beach? I want to tell you about a conversation I had with Abbie. And I've invited her to have lunch with us today. We need to decide when and where."

"Okay. I want to tell you something I heard about Brock," she said. "And the best place to do that is on the beach where no one can hear us."

We headed out. I loved early morning walks with Rhonda. We did our best thinking there.

After wiggling our toes in the sand, we walked to the edge of the water and stood a moment breathing in the salt air. The soothing sound of the waves kissing the shore and pulling away in a shy dance filled my ears and I couldn't help smiling. If only running the hotel was as peaceful. But then, the business remained interesting by having different guests arriving and departing like the waves in front of me.

"Feels nice, huh?" said Rhonda, wrapping an arm around me as we stood in the frothy edge of the water.

"It certainly does," I said, hugging her before stepping away from the water. "I think you're going to be very pleased when I tell you that Abbie and Darryl are talking about seeing where their relationship will take them. I told Abbie you considered yourself a talented matchmaker, and she said she hopes you're right."

"That's great. I can always tell. Think how right I've been about so many couples, Annie. You either got it or you don't. And, Annie, I've got it."

I looked at Rhonda and didn't say a word. I couldn't ruin her moment of triumph.

"I've got news for you," said Rhonda. "I heard from Dorothy that Brock told Everly that if she wanted some action she should go down to the public docks where all the touristy stuff is. How do you like that?"

I blinked in surprise. "Surely, he wouldn't say something like that."

"That's the funny thing. I believe when Brock said 'action', he meant some local activities, not drugs. But it doesn't sound good for him, does it?" Rhonda shook his head. "If he would just learn to mind his own business."

"But his ego won't allow him to do just that," I said. "He's a nuisance to us, but I don't wish he'd go to jail or prison for this. Where is he now?"

"Dorothy said he's at home facing being removed as president of the Neighborhood Association." Rhonda smiled and I couldn't help joining her. Having hm lose that position would benefit quite a few people, including us.

We faced the water and stood quietly for a few moments. Brock's dilemma was a lot to take in.

"There you are," growled a male voice.

"Speak of the devil," I said.

We turned to see Brock pounding his feet on the sand as he headed toward us.

"Good morning, Brock," I said as I normally would. I wasn't going to accept any blame for the trouble he was in.

"It's all your fault, this mess of mine," he said, shaking a finger at us.

"Brock, you know that's not true," I said. "We did nothing to make your situation worse than it is by your own doing."

"It's your own fuckin' fault, you know," said Rhonda. "You try to interfere with our guests even after we've asked you not to. In this case, you've gotten into trouble for it. When will you learn?"

Brock drew himself up and glared at us. "This is *my* neighborhood. You'd do best to remember it."

"I heard it might not be under your influence any longer," said Rhonda. "I heard the association wants a president who's not an embarrassment."

Brock's face grew bright red. "Nothing will ever come of it. Nobody can do a better job than I can. Everyone knows it."

Rhonda was about to say something when I sent her a warning look. Arguing with Brock only led to more problems.

"Have a nice walk," I said, taking Rhonda's arm and turning away from Brock.

"You two are going to pay for talking to the police about me," Brock said.

I turned around. "We simply answered questions that we were asked. Nothing more. Don't make this worse for yourself than it already is. And don't hang around the hotel."

"You can't tell me what to do," pouted Brock.

I shrugged and walked away.

"I'd like to shut him up once and for all," said Rhonda, fisting her hands.

I patted her back. "You're not the only one. Let's go inside and see what's happening. Another VIP wedding is about to take place, and I want to make sure Lorraine and Laura are ready to handle it."

Inside, I spoke to Lorraine, who was sitting in her office going over her checklist for the wedding. A congressman from California was marrying a woman who used to work for him. It was a second marriage for both, and we wanted to make sure it was everything they wanted.

"All is in order," said Lorraine. "We had a last-minute request for a room. When I told her we were booked, the woman agreed to use the Presidential Suite as long as she got a break in the rate. She said she knew you and Vaughn very well, Ann."

"Really? Who is she?"

Lorraine looked down at her paperwork and said, "Lily Dorio. Her name sounded familiar, but I couldn't place it."

Rhonda looked as surprised as I felt. "That woman is no friend of Ann's."

Lorraine gave me an apologetic look. "I'm sorry; I didn't realize. But what could I have done? She told me she was best friends with the bride."

"You did nothing wrong," I said. "It's just that she was behind bad publicity for Vaughn, claiming they were lovers and that he'd fathered a child with her. It's a long complicated story, and I detest her. Vaughn isn't a fan either. But there's no reason either one of us must deal with her here."

"I'll make sure of it," said Lorraine.

"And I'll help too," said Rhonda.

"Thanks," I said, wondering why our troublesome guests seemed to be the most well-known ones. I was glad Vaughn would be busy with Darryl and away from the hotel. I didn't want Lily to see either one of them.

We spoke with Lorraine about arrangements and went to our office after a quick stop in the kitchen.

Sitting in a chair facing me, Rhonda looked solemn.

"What's wrong?" I asked her.

"I don't like Lily Dorio being here. She causes trouble no matter where she is. We've got enough to handle with Darryl and Abbie hiding out here. Tina arrives here today."

"Tina can take care of herself with Lily, though working with her new husband makes it a bit touchy," I said. "It's Darryl I'm worried about. He needs this time to himself to finalize arrangements for leaving the network."

My cellphone chimed and I saw I had a message from Tina:

'Guess who's on the plane with me? Lily Dorio says she's coming to The Beach House Hotel for the Brooks wedding and insisted I ride in her limo to the hotel. I thought you'd want to know. Please don't greet us when we arrive. She wants to get a selfie with you two.'

I sighed and handed the phone to Rhonda.

Rhonda's eyes widened as she read it. "That bitch! She's never going to leave you alone."

"We'll ask Bernie to meet the limo, but I know there will come a time when I'll be forced to face her," I said.

"I'll take care of being with the guests during the wedding reception," said Rhonda. "We don't want anything to disrupt the celebration."

"Thank you. That would be nice," I said, wishing I didn't feel unsettled by the idea of Lily staying at the hotel. More than that, I didn't want any pictures of me with her. She'd almost destroyed my marriage. Or tried to.

We went over the financials for the wedding, adding staff where we thought we needed, and then we went to see Bernie.

We discussed costs and staffing for the wedding, and then I told him Darryl wanted to stay at the house on the hotel property indefinitely.

"I understand you gave Lily Dorio a special rate for the Presidential Suite."

"Yes. It's a good idea to have it rented out again," said Bernie. "Everything is in excellent condition. We wouldn't want anyone staying there if it wasn't so. But if I remember correctly, Ms. Dorio isn't a favorite of yours."

I shook my head. "Even though she's still using her business name, she's newly married. Some might think that will have changed her, but I doubt it. I want as little to do with her as possible."

"I'm taking over for the two of us at the wedding reception," said Rhonda. "And Annette will be there too."

Bernie bobbed his head. "Oh, yes. I'll post a note on the VIP board to let the staff know all of Lily Dorio's needs should be taken care of promptly. She claims she's a friend of the bride." In the "back of the house" near the staff room, Bernie had hung a VIP bulletin board with pictures and requirements, if any, of our in-house VIPs. It was helpful for the staff to know who might need extra attention, even though we expected each guest to feel important.

"Thanks," I said. "I don't want her to make trouble for the hotel."

"Anything else we should know about?" Rhonda asked.

"Nothing out of the ordinary. I haven't seen Brock at the hotel recently, but I suppose he doesn't want to return to the scene of the crime, so to speak." Bernie's eyes twinkled with humor. "I hope he's learned to stay away from our guests. I've spoken to him many times about his intrusions, but this might be the best message of all."

"He's made a lot of enemies along the way," said Rhonda. "We can't keep him off the beach, but we can make sure he doesn't intrude upon our guests' stays."

"If only," I muttered, not feeling confident at all.

CHAPTER EIGHTEEN

RHONDA AND I DROVE INTO TOWN TO MEET ABBIE FOR lunch. IT was a pleasant diversion after a worrisome morning. And lunch at Andre's was always a delicious treat. Margot and Andre Durand were friends of Jean-Luc's and welcomed us with open arms and a kiss on each cheek.

I parked the car, and we hurried down the little alley to reach the restaurant. Abbie was already there, sitting at an outside table waiting for us.

"Hello," Abbie said. "Or should I say "*Bonjour*"? The owners here are so friendly."

Just then Margot stepped outside. "Ann, Rhonda, *Bienvenue*! We have a fresh asparagus quiche today plus a grilled vegetable salad."

"That sounds delicious," I said, accepting her kisses. "Abbie, outside or in?"

'I'm ready to go inside," said Abbie. "It's a little chilly."

We were seated at a table by the side window that gave a view of an herb garden planted next to the building.

"The smells," murmured Rhonda, sniffing the fragrant air inside the restaurant. "No matter what you order, Abbie, you'll love it. I promise."

The three of us ended up having the special of the day— quiche and vegetable salad. And when the food and a carafe of white house wine were served, we dug in with enthusiasm.

Abbie received a text on her cellphone and then said, "A note from Tina. She's wondering if I can stay a few extra days at your house. She's traveling with someone who can't be trusted to keep any information to herself, and she doesn't want this person to know about me. I won't be a bother to you, Ann. I promise."

"Of course. I'd be delighted," I said. "You're such an easy guest."

"Tina is going back to the cottage, but we'll do our training elsewhere." Abbie frowned. "Who is this person?"

"Lily Dorio," I said.

"Nobody you want to be involved with. She's a liar," said Rhonda.

Abbie raised her hand. "Stop! You don't need to say anything more. I've already heard a lot of negative things about her in Hollywood."

"I'm going to advise Darryl not to go back to the hotel until after she leaves," I said. "I don't think we'll have a problem with Brock wandering around the hotel property while he's under suspicion. But it should be okay for him to be at the hotel after the weekend."

"We have to be able to honor our guests' requests," said Rhonda.

"Yes," I agreed. "That's what we worry about."

"It's how we became known for hosting high-profile people," Rhonda said.

"It certainly makes it a pleasant stay," said Abbie. "It's important for Darryl to have that. You know, I'm impressed that he's trying to leave the network to do his own thing and become true to himself."

Rhonda perked up. "He's perfect for you," she told Abbie, smiling.

Abbie's cheeks flushed before changing the subject. "What's for dessert? I feel like splurging."

Margot cleared our plates and took orders for dessert. Abbie and I ordered a fruit tart and Rhonda ordered a slice of lemon cream pie.

After we finished, we each let out a sigh of satisfaction.

"The food here is absolutely fabulous," said Abbie. "Thank you. Now, I'll have to get back to business. I'm going to take a walk on the beach. Does anyone want to join me?"

Rhonda checked her watch. "I'm sorry. We have to return to the hotel, and then I have to take Willow to ballet lessons."

"And I'm going home to check on Vaughn and tell him and Darryl about the latest developments with Lily Dorio."

"I'll meet you there after I check out the town wharf," said Abbie.

We stood, and Abbie gave Rhonda and me hugs. Then Rhonda and I walked back to the car and into the normal routines of our days.

At the hotel, we looked at our messages.

"Before Tina and Lily get here, I want to check the Presidential Suite," said Rhonda. "I want to make sure Lily will have no complaints. Besides, like I said, I want to see for myself that everything is okay. That's where I lived before we made The Beach House into a hotel, and it means a lot to me."

"Okay, let's do it. I'll feel better about seeing it too," I said, even though I was hesitant to be there after discovering Everly dead on the floor.

As we entered the front entry, we noticed the sweet aroma of flowers. Sitting in the middle of the table in the hallway was a huge flower arrangement that would welcome any guest.

The living room and dining areas were spotless, the kitchen and bathrooms even more so.

After we'd checked everything but the master bedroom, Rhonda grabbed my arm. "What if Everly's ghost is in the bedroom? You know how sensitive I am about such things. If

I even get the hint of any kind of spirit, I'm outta there."

Discarding my fears, I pulled Rhonda into the bedroom. It had an entirely different look to it with new carpeting, bedding, and chairs to match the new green floral bedspread.

I drew a deep breath and closed my eyes to block out the memory of seeing Everly lying on the floor. A chill ran down my spine. Rhonda's grip on my arm tightened. "Do you see that?" she asked in a stage whisper.

My eyes flew open. "What?"

"There," said Rhonda. She pointed to the streak of sunlight landing on the carpet in the exact spot where we'd found Everly. It's a sign, don't you think?"

Letting my breath out with a puff of air, I shook my head. "It's just sunlight coming through the window."

"Yes, but why does it seem cold right near that spot," said Rhonda, studying me.

I forced myself to be reasonable. "The air conditioner is running. That's all it is."

"Okay, I needed to hear that," said Rhonda. "I couldn't stand the thought of the Suite being haunted. Everything looks great. Let's get out of here."

We hurried to the front door. No matter what anyone said, every time I was in that room, I'd see a dead body there. The way Rhonda's face had turned pale staring at the sunlight, I was sure she felt the same way. In time, the feeling might lessen, but right now the incident was too fresh in our minds.

At home, Vaughn brushed away my news of Lily coming to stay at the hotel. "She's a nobody in Hollywood. She's set up an agency, but the last I heard she's not succeeding. Now that she's married, that might change, but I doubt it. Not with her reputation."

"Well, I don't think Darryl should be at the hotel while Lily's there," I said to the two of them. "She has a way of making trouble." I turned to Darryl. "She threatened my marriage by pretending she and Vaughn were lovers and he'd fathered a child with her."

As Darryl's eyes widened, Vaughn shook his head. "That woman has no morals. And I'm not going to let her interfere with my life."

"If you don't mind, I'm going to accept your offer to stay here for the weekend," said Darryl. "I've heard from Abbie that she's going to be here too."

"I think it's wise," I said. "As I told her, you're both easy guests."

"And, Darryl, you're an excellent First Mate on the boat," said Vaughn.

"Aye, aye, Captain," said Darryl and I laughed with the others, content to see Vaughn with a new friend.

Abbie arrived, and we decided to relax by the pool.

Before we changed into bathing suits, Abbie wanted to show me her purchases.

"I've never really cared that much about my appearance beyond being healthy," said Abbie, laying sundresses, skirts, and blouses atop the bed in her room. "But it's fun to get excited about some of my new clothes. Though I was the only girl in the family, my brothers weren't going to let me get too frilly. Not when I was hanging around with them."

"It sounds fascinating. I was an only child, an orphan at six, who was raised by a strict grandmother. I wished for siblings but knew early on I would never have them."

"I hope you had some reliable friends," said Abbie with a note of sympathy.

"I did have one special friend when I was younger but then she moved away. I was invited to birthday parties and such, but my grandmother didn't approve of sleepovers and girl parties, so my friendships didn't develop. I adore Rhonda. She's the best friend I've ever had."

"The two of you have certainly made a success of The Beach House Hotel," said Abbie. "You're an inspiration to others. Tina thinks of you as the mother she wished she'd had. She told me how you saved and protected her."

"Rhonda and I knew we had to do something to help Tina. She's become part of what I call 'My Hotel Family'."

Abbie hesitated and then said, "Darryl, too? I've never met a man like him. He's strong and soft, determined and giving. He could be a self-important bastard like many of my male clients. But he's not. He's a truly nice man."

"I don't know him as well as you do, but I like him. And Vaughn's approval means a lot. In his business, he has to work with many egotistical jerks. He doesn't spend time with guests on his boat if he doesn't like them."

Abbie clapped a hand to her chest. "That makes me feel so good. Practically living with a client for a couple of weeks gives me an insight into what they're like as people, and I've never felt this close to any other clients of mine."

"Rhonda will be thrilled to hear this. But if you tell her, be careful about saying too much or she'll have your wedding planned before you can think about it."

"Oh, yes, I got that feeling," said Abbie chuckling. "Let me show you my purchases. I was delighted to find some unusual tropical wear that I can use in California."

Together, we looked over her new clothing.

I was delighted to share these moments with her. "I think you're going to enjoy everything you bought today, and I think a certain someone will too," I said, giving Abbie a quick hug.

"Thanks. I'll meet you at the pool," said Abbie.

I left her room and went to change, satisfied with what was

happening between two people I liked.

I was in my bedroom when I got a call from Tina. "Hi. I'm here. Are Abbie and Darryl with you?"

"Yes, they are. We're about to relax by the pool. Why don't you join us?"

"Thanks," said Tina. "I will. Traveling with Lily Dorio is a trip of its own. I need a little relaxing."

"I trust Bernie greeted you upon arrival," I said.

"Oh, yes. As usual, we got a warm welcome. Lily couldn't stop talking about staying in The Presidential Suite."

"Good," I said, meaning it. Rhonda and I didn't want anything to ruin the panache of staying there.

CHAPTER NINETEEN

I WORKED WITH ABBIE AND TINA FIXING A SIMPLE MEAL in the kitchen. My earlier conversation with Abbie prickled in my mind. My childhood had been lonely, but I'd made friends in college and during my marriage. But nothing could match the friendships I'd formed here in Sabal. Having Rhonda and other friends in the neighborhood and on the same charity committees that I served on, was even more precious because of my upbringing.

I remembered the first time I met Rhonda and how rocked I'd been by her language and her bluntness. Now, it was a part of her I loved.

Not wanting Rhonda to miss out on our unexpected party, I'd called her. She and Will and their two children were on their way to join us. Willow at almost nine and Drew at seven were thrilled to play board or computer games with Robbie. He seemed to thrive on being their leader. While we adults were going to have steak and salad, he'd already convinced me to order pizza for the kids.

Rhonda walked through the door carrying a cake. "Thought you'd like to have dessert. Rita's lemon cakes are the best." Rita had worked for Rhonda since Willow was born and was a warm woman who served as a grandmother as well as a housekeeper.

Will followed with the children. I studied him and noticed how tired he looked. I reminded myself to speak to Rhonda about taking the vacation they'd missed because of Everly staying at the hotel.

"Hi, Auntie Ann," cried Willow, running into my open arms. She looked a lot like Will with light brown hair and hazel eyes. But instead of his easy-going manner, she had Rhonda's energy and a bit of her bossiness, too. I loved her. She was special to me because she'd been born on my kitchen floor, a story we talked about often.

Andrew, or Drew as we called him, stood aside, used to Willow taking over. He had dark hair, big brown eyes, and an adorable dimpled smile. Happy to follow Willow's instructions to a point, he could demonstrate a fiery temper when pushed too far. I swept him into my arms and kissed him on the cheek while he nestled against me.

The children left to go to Robbie's room. Cindy followed, her short Dachshund legs moving fast to keep up with their running.

I poured Rhonda a glass of red wine while Vaughn took care of getting a beer for Will.

"Thanks for inviting us," said Rhonda. She turned and lifted her glass to the other two women. "My mother used to say, 'It's moments like these that make life precious.' So, what's cookin'?"

Tina launched into a story about her trip to Sabal with Lily Dorio. "I don't care for Lily after what she did to Ann and Vaughn. I didn't ever expect our paths would cross. But getting the role opposite her new husband, I've seen more of her than I've ever wanted."

"How did she finally land a husband?" Rhonda asked.

Tina sighed and shook her head. "Lily is attractive and has a way of making people believe she's sincere when she talks to them. Sinclair Smith is a nice guy who loves being married even though he has a reputation for wandering. Lily is his third wife. People in the business are placing bets as to how long this marriage will last. Lily is using her relationship with him to try to get new clients for her agency."

"How's that going?" I asked.

"Not too well, though she does get people to sign up. The problem is she's not known for being honest with them. After a while, people drop her and move on to someone else."

We made our way to the lanai while the men congregated down by the dock with Vaughn, giving us women a chance to talk.

Tina turned to Rhonda. "Will looks tired. What's going on with him?"

Rhonda told the story of Will wanting to compete with Reggie's father, Arthur. "Working with your son-in-law can be difficult anyway, but this is a lot of extra pressure for both Will and Reggie."

Tina said, "Why don't you two take a little break together? You're welcome to come stay with me in California."

Rhonda glanced at me before answering. "Thanks, but I've already made tentative reservations at the nearby Palm Island Club. It's close by, so I hope I can get Will to relax there by knowing he could get back to his office for an emergency."

"Reggie is a talented young man who has no interest in competing with his father. It's one reason he went into business with Will to begin with," I explained.

"Will is getting close enough to retirement that I think he wants to prove he's still capable," Rhonda said. "Believe me, he hasn't slowed down in other areas." She wiggled her eyebrows.

"TMI," I said, laughing with the others.

"Nicholas is happiest at home," Tina said. "It's a relief for me because he works with beautiful young actors who sometimes see him as a rich older man who could provide them with access to better roles and an easy life."

"Vaughn feels the same," I said. Looking at Abbie, I

continued. "That's something I like about Darryl. He hasn't been interested in being seen with young, flashy starlets. And won't be, with you here."

Abbie's cheeks grew pink, and I thought she looked darling.

Vaughn returned. "We need more beers, and I'm about to start the grill for the steaks. Is everything else set?"

I stood. "It will be. I'm putting together a green salad and Tina brought some grilled vegetables from Andre's restaurant."

"I'll help," said Tina. She followed me into the kitchen. "What can I do?"

"Let's eat in the dining room. You can set the table." I picked out placemats and napkins and showed her where the silverware and water glasses were.

Tina picked them up and faced me with a worried look. "Don't trust Lily. I have a feeling she's going to try to use Vaughn to get more business. She told me she was best friends with the bride, but I don't believe it. I think she pressured the groom into inviting her."

"That sounds about right," I murmured, determined not to let that woman get to me.

Later, sitting at the dining room table, glancing at the people gathered there, my heart filled with love. Having friends was important to me. I watched Darryl tell a joke and even while I was laughing, I was hoping he and Abbie would become part of my hotel family.

At the end of the meal, Vaughn said, "Let's go out to the lanai for nightcaps."

Rhonda and I exchanged glances. We'd have to get up in the morning to greet wedding guests, but nightcaps sounded perfect.

###

It was late by the time Abbie and I finished putting the last of the dishes in the dishwasher, but I was glad for the time with her. We'd learned that she came from a humble background where sports were emphasized as a way for the family to do better financially. One of her brothers played professional baseball for a few years. Two others played football but never made it to the NFL. The brother closest in age to her had become an orthopedic doctor. Abbie's career choice seemed natural. She had the same hardworking, pleasant nature as my daughter, Liz.

"Guess I'm off to bed," said Abbie. "Thanks for a nice evening."

"My pleasure. Rhonda and I have a wedding in the hotel, so I'll be coming and going from here this weekend. I hope you don't mind."

"No problem. I'll be busy with Darryl. I thought we'd go on a day trip to Sarasota to the Siesta Key beach there. It's supposed to be one of the best."

"It's gorgeous. And you'll be able to work there without Brock Goodwin or Lily Dorio around to interfere," I said.

"Yes, we need to spend a large part of the day running on the beach and doing other exercises to work off the food from these last few days."

"Remember, you can always order food from the hotel," I said, giving her a quick hug goodnight.

I tiptoed into my bedroom and gazed at Vaughn stretched out atop the sheet asleep. I came closer and studied him. He kept himself in great shape. There were more gray hairs at his temple, but it made him look more distinguished, not older. His eyes fluttered open. He took hold of my hand and pulled me down next to him.

I loved the feel of being close. But it wasn't enough.

Climbing out of bed, I stripped off my clothes, turned out the light, and lay beside him, smiling as he reached for me again.

The next morning, after making sure everyone was set for the day, I left for the hotel. Weddings were an important part of the hotel's business. Not only for the wedding itself but because the attendees spread a positive word about the food and elegant setting. But Rhonda and I believed our presence and the service from the staff is what made a well-executed wedding even better, and when guests realized, it was the success we strived for.

The staff was quietly bustling about in the hotel when I arrived. I went to Lorraine's office. She wasn't there, but her assistant Laura was on the phone talking to the florist.

"I'm sorry the lilies you ordered for us didn't arrive in the shipment, but we'll need to add something to the arrangements to replace them. Something at no extra cost to us." She listened. "Okay, that will be fine."

"Nice job," I said to Laura. "How is everything else going?"

"Hi, Ann. Things seem to be going well. No complaints so far except from the party in The Presidential Suite. That woman was trying to make sure she was placed at the head table for the wedding dinner. I told her to confer with the family."

"Ah, I know who that is. If you have any further trouble with her, please let me know."

I left her to go to my office, stopping for my usual cup of coffee in the hotel kitchen.

Consuela greeted me with a smile. "' Morning."

I gave her a quick hug. "How's breakfast going?"

"It's a fun-loving crowd. While the women are shopping

and getting ready for the afternoon wedding, the men are going golfing. The young men are full of teasing and seem to be very hungry. They've had a lot of sweet rolls."

I grinned. "I like it when our guests are enjoying them."

I took my coffee into the office.

Rhonda was already there. She looked up at me and shook her head. "Lily Dorio is making a fuss. She wants someone to fix her hair for the wedding. I told her that the wedding party is using our usual person on call but that she's welcome to find someone on her own. She didn't like that and started to tell me off. I reminded her that I was one of the owners of the hotel. I have a feeling she's going to call you next."

"She's already been a problem for Laura, wanting to be seated at the head table at the wedding dinner."

The phone rang. I picked it up. "Hello, this is Ann Sanders. How may I help you?"

"Ah, Ann, just the person I was looking for. This is Lily Dorio. Your partner is very abrupt. I couldn't deal with her. I need to talk to you about finding someone to do my hair. I have some interviews coming up and need someone to help me in a hurry."

"We have a wedding at the hotel and our usual sources are all busy with the bridal party. But I've heard that Henri's has good stylists. You might try there." I clicked off the call.

The phone rang again. Groaning, I picked it up.

"Hi, Ann. It's me, Lily. You didn't give me a chance to ask you to have Vaughn give me a call. I may have a lead on a big role coming up. I want to talk to him. He won't answer my calls."

"I'll give him the message you talked to me," I said. "Excuse me, but I'm in the middle of other things right now."

"It's a really good opportunity for him," said Lily. "Tell him not to miss out."

I ended the call and sat in my seat with a sigh. The woman irritated me no end. After what she'd done to Vaughn, I never wanted to deal with her again.

"What does she want now?" asked Rhonda.

I filled her in. "You know how you got a bad feeling about Everly? That's how I'm feeling about Lily."

"Oh my God! Do you think she's going to die at the hotel?" said Rhonda looking aghast.

"What? No. Though I bet a lot of people would be glad to have her gone. Tina warned me not to let Lily get close. As if I would!"

"The Sabal Book Club is having their big luncheon here today. Let's hope Lily doesn't want to introduce herself to them for business purposes," said Rhonda. "I'm going to talk to Bernie about it. Want to come?"

I shook my head. "No, thanks. I need to work on the financials for that event and the wedding to make sure everything is taken care of. Besides, I want to check with Lorraine to follow up on Lily's request."

Rhonda left, and I tried to focus on numbers. Instead, images of Lily interfering with the wedding plagued me. I finally got up and went to talk to Lorraine.

As I crossed the lobby to get to Lorraine's office, I heard someone call my name and turned to see Lily rushing toward me.

"Wait right there. I need to get a photo of you for my website. It will be publicity for the hotel," said Lily coming up to me.

Lily was a woman in her forties who looked as if the sun and alcohol, or maybe something worse, had taken a toll on her skin. She wasn't a pleasant person. The way her lips curled with distaste even as she tried to smile at me made me hesitate.

I held up my hand to stop her. "Hello, Lily. I'm sorry but I'm busy."

I turned to walk away.

She grabbed me by the shoulder and turned me around. "I know you didn't like the little game the producer and I were playing, but it wasn't meant to hurt you. I can help Vaughn, and you can help me."

"Vaughn can handle himself," I said. "I told you I'm busy, and I am." I looked up to see Bernie closing in on us.

"Go along, Ann. I can take care of this," he said, and I hurried away, thankful for his presence. I didn't want to make a scene in front of our guests, but I was NOT going to allow Lily to pull me into her net, like a spider capturing a morsel in its web.

I entered Lorraine's office and let out a long sigh.

"Everything alright, Ann?" Lorraine asked, giving me a look of concern.

"It's just one of our guests, Lily Dorio. She's the one I wanted to talk to you about. Did she by any chance get her seat at the head table at dinner?"

A look of distaste crossed Lorraine's face. "No, she didn't. The groom didn't like it when she asked. He's an older man who's recently been divorced and he's marrying the young woman he was seeing before his marriage ended. One reason he came to the hotel is because we're known for being discreet and he wants to keep the news of his wedding quiet. He doesn't even know Lily."

"Did you speak to Lily yourself and make that clear?" I asked her.

She nodded. "I must say, she's a very aggressive person. She's trying to turn this wedding into something about her. Even the bride is disgusted with her."

"Please talk to Annette about the situation, so she's aware,"

I said. "I'm very grateful to you, Laura, and Annette for handling these details. Rhonda and I are welcoming guests to the hotel for the bulk of people arriving this morning, but we'll leave it to you pros to handle the dinner tonight and brunch tomorrow. As usual, Rhonda and I will observe the wedding."

"We'll do what?" Rhonda said, joining us.

"I mentioned that you and I will, as usual, observe the wedding," I said.

"Oh, yes," said Rhonda. "It's very important that everything goes well, and weddings are usually so touching. We've had all kinds of weddings here. Each one is special."

"For good and bad reasons," I said, remembering a few terrible situations. "But, like Rhonda, I love weddings."

We left Lorraine and went to the front desk to check on arrivals. Several people on the bride's side were arriving in a group from New Jersey. At the sign of the two limos arriving with them, Rhonda and I stepped outside to the top of the stairs.

"How many times would you guess we've stood here like this?" said Rhonda.

"More than I can count. But I find it exciting to discover who's arriving next. Standing here, I sometimes still can't believe the hotel is ours."

Rhonda flung an arm across my shoulders. "Well, it is. Too late to back out now."

I laughed. "C'mon. Let's go say hello."

A group of twelve people emerged from the two limousines laughing and talking. I grinned at Rhonda. It looked like this was going to be a good crowd.

Rhonda and I separated to walk to each group.

"Welcome to The Beach House Hotel," I said. "It's a lovely day for a wedding."

A chorus of "Yes!" responded.

I answered their questions and saw that their luggage was being taken care of. Then, I went back inside to make sure the new arrivals weren't waiting long to be checked in. Preregistration of groups shortened that timing.

Rhonda said, "As long as things look okay here, I'm going home. I promised the kids we'd do something special this afternoon. I'm thinking of taking them to a movie."

"Have fun," I said. Satisfied that things were going well, I decided to visit Tina. We hadn't had much of a chance to talk privately last night.

CHAPTER TWENTY

TINA WAS LYING IN THE SUN ON THE POOL DECK WHEN I arrived. She jumped up when she heard my approach. "Hi, Ann. I'm glad to see you. Come on in."

I opened the door to the screened-in lanai and sat on a lounge chair next to her. "I thought I'd see how things are going with you. We didn't get much of a chance to chat last night."

"Thanks. I was hoping to talk with you. Things have been a little rough at home, and I need to get your advice." She took off her sunglasses, and I noticed her red-rimmed eyes. "Nicholas is frustrated that I'm taking on a new movie role when the kids need me so much. I understand, but we have a wonderful nanny, and Nick will be home most evenings for the next couple of months. So, I don't see why I should give up my chance to do another movie."

"I know Nicholas and respect him. What's really going on?" I asked.

"He couldn't get the funding for one of his projects, and he's depressed," Tina said. "I'm sorry it happened. The timing couldn't be worse."

"You're an excellent wife and mother," I said. "I don't want to intercede with your marriage. It's been a happy one as you've often told me. But if you're asking for my opinion, I think you have a right to have some time for yourself, to follow your own career. Especially after making sure things are being taken care of at home."

"Thanks. I needed to hear that," said Tina. "You know how

important being a good mother is to me after having one who wasn't. And I adore Nicholas."

"But to fulfill herself, a woman may want to be more than a wife and a mother if she is going to happily fill those roles. We all have the right to continue to grow and learn as individuals."

Tina hugged me. "You're the best mom I could ever wish for."

Tears stung my eyes as I remembered the broken young woman I first met.

We chatted for a while longer, then I headed home. Vaughn was going to attend Robbie's swim meet, and I wanted to see how it went. The house would be quiet with Darryl and Abbie gone for the day, and I needed some time with my family.

The three of us were swimming in the pool when my cell rang.

When I saw Lorraine's name on the call, I let out a long sigh. What now? The wedding wasn't until five o'clock and I'd been hoping for a couple of hours of free time before getting ready to attend it.

"Hello, Lorraine. How is it going?"

"Not well. I just got a call from the hospital, the groom tripped over something in the woods on the golf course and he has a badly sprained ankle. He says he's going to be fine for the wedding ceremony, but he's pretty doped up on pain meds. The bride is threatening to put off the wedding for a day or two, but the hotel is booked, and we don't have room for their guests to stay on. Also, we have a private wedding for a party of twelve Sunday evening."

"Have you seen the groom?" I asked.

"No, I've only spoken to the best man."

"Okay, let me go to the hospital and see what I can find out. You handle the bride and her party. I'll call you back as soon as I can see for myself what the situation is."

"Thanks," she said. "I tried Rhonda's number, but I couldn't reach her."

"She promised the kids they'd do something special. I don't know where she is. But no worries, I'll handle this."

"Thanks," said Lorraine and ended the call.

"Hotel problem?" Vaughn asked as I wrapped a towel around me and prepared to go inside.

I explained the situation to him and Robbie and gave them each a kiss goodbye. "I'm sorry. I'm going to go, and then I'll come back to change for the wedding, if, and that's a big IF, it goes forward."

When I got to the hospital, Robert Anderson, the groom, a handsome man in his fifties, was about to be released from the emergency room. His left ankle was in a soft, expandable cast and he was being handed crutches. Another gentleman stood by looking worried.

"I can't let Brianna down," the groom complained. He looked up and saw me. "Hello. Don't worry. I'm not about to ruin the wedding."

"I came to see how you are. I heard you took a nasty tumble at the golf course," I said.

He gave me a soulful look. "I was going after the damn golf ball in the woods. My foot got caught in a little hole I didn't see, and I twisted my ankle. Don't worry. I'm not going to do anything to stop the wedding. Brianna's upset, but I told her we could take our honeymoon another time. Believe me, I'll make it up to her."

"Okay, with your agreement, I'm going to call the hotel and

tell them to continue with your wedding plans."

"Oh, yes. Please. My divorce was finalized last week, and Brianna and I want to get married right away."

"Do you need a ride back to the hotel?" I asked. "I can take the two of you there now if you're ready."

"That would be great," said Robert, and I forced myself to stop thinking of my ex, Robert, and the way he'd moved on so quickly after dumping me.

I left them to go to my car and call Lorraine. After giving her the go-ahead for the wedding, I pulled the car up to the Emergency Room entrance and waited while a nurse oversaw Robert getting out of the wheelchair and using his crutches. "Remember, no walking on that cast. That will happen in time, but we don't want any pressure on that now."

Robert's friend and I exchanged glances. The wedding wasn't going to be what the bride wanted, but there was nothing either one of us could do about it.

I drove them to the front of the hotel, made sure that Lorraine met us there as we'd agreed, and then went home to change for the wedding. This was one wedding I was eager to have behind us.

At home, I greeted my family and Darryl and Abbie who'd returned to the house and went to change my clothes. Rhonda and I dressed appropriately for the weddings we oversaw. Even though we weren't in charge, we enjoyed observing the various ceremonies. We'd done it from the first one and continued as often as we could.

In my bedroom, I called Rhonda and gave her an update. "Lorraine was rattled at the thought of a late cancellation. I wanted to see for myself what was going on, and I'm glad I did. No matter how much effort the groom will put into it, the wedding won't be the same. We'll have to do extra work to keep the bride happy. Let's meet with Lorraine as soon as we get to the hotel."

"Okay. Sorry I couldn't take Lorraine's call earlier. I was in the movie theater with the kids. The animated films for children these days are fantastic. I think I enjoyed the despicable characters as much as they did."

I smiled at the mental image of Rhonda in the theater laughing with her children. Rhonda was the biggest kid of all.

At the hotel, Rhonda and I met with Lorraine. She was trying to decide how to handle the walk to the altar in the garden and back inside the hotel.

"A wheelchair would make it easiest but the groom refuses to use it," said Lorraine. "The bride's mother is willing to talk to him about it."

"I've talked with Robert Anderson, and he seems to be a man used to being in charge. Maybe we can convince him we can make it a unique experience acceptable to both him and the bride. We can use the wheelchair to get him to his spot by the altar, hide the wheelchair away during the ceremony, and then use it to get him to the private dining room."

"That might work without taking too much attention away from the bride," said Lorraine.

"And if we decorate the wheelchair with flowers and ribbons, it could be festive," I said.

"Maybe add some golf clubs for fun," added Rhonda, and we all beamed.

"Okay, I'll call the bride's mother and talk to her," said Lorraine. "Brianna was pretty upset earlier. This idea may ease her worries. She won't be the only bride who's had to deal with unexpected problems. It happens in different ways. Over time, it becomes a cherished reminder of the day."

"Okay, we leave this in your capable hands," I said. "If you need me, I'll be walking through the hotel, checking on things, before standing with Rhonda by the front door to welcome wedding guests."

"Okay. Laura will be meeting the in-house guests to direct them to the garden. I'll hurry and get the florist to help me with the wheelchair," said Lorraine. "She's in the dining room now."

Lorraine hurried away from us, talking on her cell to the bride's mother.

Rhonda and I looked at one another and breathed out sighs of relief. We couldn't afford to lose this wedding after all the expenses of getting ready for it.

"I want to see how things are going down at the sunset deck. There was a call for more chairs. I love having that deck available to our guests."

"It's the perfect place to watch the sunset and to relax any time of day," said Rhonda. "I'm glad we got that project done over Brock's objections."

We walked from Lorraine's office to the pool area and down the path to the beach to the deck. I was pleased to see several chairs positioned around the deck with a supply of folding chairs stacked in the corner.

Out of the corner of my eye, I could see a man strolling the sand in the distance and said to Rhonda, "C'mon, we've got to get back to the hotel."

She followed my gaze. "Let's go. I don't want to talk to Brock."

We hurried back to the safety of the building and into the lobby.

Bernie was there, talking to the front desk staff.

We waited until he was through and told him about the wheelchair situation. "That's fine. I was just reminding the staff that the wedding is supposed to be very private. A photographer has been hired to take pictures. The wedding party has asked that all other photos by guests be held off until after the dinner. And, no media."

"Let's go check the dining room," said Rhonda. "I want to see how that color scheme worked." The bride had chosen a bright, rich orange and dark green for her wedding colors.

We walked to the entrance of the private dining room. Peering inside, I let out a soft gasp of delight. The tables of six were covered in dark-green linen, the color of which was reflected in the crystal glassware and off the sparkling silverware. A small bouquet of orange lilies, and white, orange, and peach roses, accented with sprigs of spiral eucalyptus and other greenery, sat in the center of each table like a beacon.

"It's gorgeous," said Rhonda. "Who woulda thunk it? Can't wait to see the bridesmaids' dresses."

"Me, too," I said. "Let's take a quick peek at the garden."

We walked to the side garden which was a perfect spot for a wedding. Lush greenery and palm trees gave it an elegant tropical setting. A small white altar stood on the lawn. A pathway between two sets of chairs led to the altar. Thankfully, there was no attempt to place a running cloth on the grass defining the aisle. Instead, at the aisle end of each row of white cloth-covered chairs, small baskets of flowers hung. The effect was beautiful.

"The bright colors go well in this setting," said Rhonda. "Can't wait for the ceremony to begin."

As soon as all of the guests had been received at the front entry and were being directed to the side garden, Rhonda and I took our usual spot along the side at the back and waited for the bride's arrival. We could see Robert standing by his best man by the altar, hanging on to his crutches for balance. The best man was doing his best to keep Robert comfortable by helping to brace him.

The harpist the family had hired changed from soft background music to "At Last", the song made famous by Etta James. The notes shimmered in the air as caressing as the soft, onshore breeze. And when the two bridesmaids entered the garden in stunning deep orange dresses, I let out a sigh of pleasure.

The bride was an attractive young woman who wore a simple, white-silk slip dress that was perfect for her handsome figure. I turned and looked at Robert's face. When I saw his look of adoration, I felt a sting of tears. This is how a wedding should be.

As my gaze followed the bride down the aisle, I noticed the guest standing beside Lily speak to her and take the cell phone from her hand. Lily knew the rules. Why couldn't she honor the simple request?

We watched as the minister they'd hired raced through the short ceremony, aware of Robert's discomfort. Still, their pledges of love were touching and as the audience clapped their congratulations, the wheelchair was brought out. The applause grew and the moment turned tender when Brianna took control of the wheelchair and pushed it along the pathway that had been carved into the lawn for that occasion.

Rhonda wiped her eyes. "That was touching. I'm going to speak to the wedding party and then I'm going home to celebrate another wedding completed."

"That's a great idea," I said. "I'm not staying for dinner either. As soon as I've paid my respects to the families, I'm off. I don't like the idea of Lily being here, wanting to speak to Vaughn. And I don't want her knowing who's staying at my house."

As unobtrusively as I could, I congratulated the bride and groom and then, before Lily could cross the room to me, I slipped away. Vaughn was still refusing to take her calls, and I wasn't going to get caught up in any scheme of hers.

CHAPTER TWENTY-ONE

WHEN I GOT UP THE NEXT MORNING, I WENT INTO THE kitchen to find Abbie and Darryl sitting at the table sipping coffee.

"Wow! You're up early," I said, grabbing a cup for myself. "Where's Vaughn?"

"Down by the boat," said Abbie. "Robbie's still in bed."

"Have you already had a workout?" I asked Darryl as he wiped the sweat from his brow with a towel.

"Yeah, this beast doesn't let up," he teased, grinning at Abbie.

Observing the way, they were smiling at one another, I felt I was watching two people falling in love.

"C'mon. We need to jog around the neighborhood," said Abbie rising.

Groaning, Darryl got to his feet and followed Abbie out the door.

I sat and reached for my iPad to check for news stories. It was convenient that our local newspaper had online access. I usually started there.

The front page showed Lily Dorio's photograph directing readers to the social events section. I went directly to that page and stared in dismay at a photo of Lily Dorio, an old fake photo of Lily and Vaughn, and a photo of yesterday's wedding, showing the bride and groom.

I could feel my face grow hot as I studied them. By the time I got through the article, most of which was a great exaggeration on Lily's part as to her fame and connections, I was boiling mad.

As I picked up the phone to call Rhonda, my cell pinged.

"Did you see the paper?" Rhonda said. "Lily Dorio and her fake news is all over the social section. We're going to have to apologize to Robert Anderson and the bridal party. Not only did Lily break our hotel NDA rules, she also broke her pledge to them."

"What was Terri Thomas thinking? She understands the agreement we made with her about publicity of our guests without their permission." Terri was the reporter in charge of the social section of the newspaper and usually cooperated with us.

"You'd better call her, Annie," said Rhonda. "If I even tried to be nice, I'd end up telling her to fuck off." There was only so much diplomacy Rhonda could manage when she was upset.

"Okay, I'll do it. You call Bernie and explain the situation to him, and later, before Robert and Brianna leave, we'll apologize to both of them for the way Lily broke her pledge to all of us."

"Oh, boy. I knew we'd have trouble with Lily. I wish there was some way we could've refused her a room. "

"Me, too, but that wasn't going to happen. Be sure to ask Bernie to notify us when Lily is ready to check out. I intend to speak to her."

"Do you want me to join you?" asked Rhonda.

"You bet," I said, upset at both Lily and Terri. Lily was Lily and Terri knew darn well she should've cleared parts of that article with us.

I called Terri, who covered social news for the Sabal Daily News. Soon after we opened the hotel, we'd made an agreement with her. We'd share what news we could without jeopardizing our guests' confidentiality in return for her respecting our policy.

"Hello. Nice article, huh?" said Terri cheerfully when she answered the call. "I assigned a new young reporter to the interview. I'm hoping he'll eventually replace me."

"Didn't you proof the article?" I asked. "It was full of private information. I certainly didn't approve the picture of Lily with Vaughn, which you may remember caused an uproar a few years ago. And all wedding guests were asked not to take photographs of the ceremony. Someone must have rushed that through. You've broken your arrangement with The Beach House Hotel. How could you? Lily even mentions arriving at the hotel with Tina. That's confidential information."

"Hold on, hold on," said Terri. "My reporter told me that everything was cleared. Lily told him how she was friends with you, Rhonda, and Tina, and everything was okay."

"That's not true," I said. "Why didn't you check with us directly? We've built our business on assuring our guests of privacy. That article will prove otherwise."

"Oh, Ann, I'm sorry. The article was really about the life of a well-known Hollywood agent. At least that's how it was supposed to be presented. She just added in a few names and offered us photographs telling of those friendships."

"It was, in truth, a whole bunch of lies, something you would've caught yourself. Now, Rhonda and I are left with a mess because you didn't check the article before it went to press."

I drew in a deep breath and let it out slowly, trying to calm myself. "I'm angry and very disappointed. Hold on. Rhonda just walked into my house."

"Is that Terri?" asked Rhonda loudly. "If so, tell her I'm fucking furious."

Terri sighed into the phone. "I heard that. If I try to retract anything, it'll just bring more attention to the issues. I promise that it won't happen again. I'm trying to get out of the business, but I should've checked his work."

"You're right. Let's agree that no more comments about that article will be printed in the paper."

"Okay," said Terri and ended the call.

"How'd you do with Bernie?" I asked Rhonda.

"He said he'd be sure to talk to Robert Anderson. He told me that Lily left the hotel early this morning for a flight to New York."

We studied one another and then I rose. "I'm going to check on the Presidential Suite. Do you want to come?"

"Yes," said Rhonda. "I want to get there before the hotel staff to make sure nothing is stolen or messed up. At least, Lily paid her bill."

As we stood outside the Presidential Suite, I gathered my nerve to go inside.

"Ready?" asked Rhonda.

I nodded.

Inside the entry, all was quiet and in place.

We walked through the living room, dining room, and kitchen, satisfied things were in order.

"We'd better check the master bedroom suite," I said.

We walked into the room.

The bed covers were thrown back and onto the floor. An open box of trojans was sitting on the bedside table, A towel stained with something that looked like coffee was thrown on the floor.

Rhonda went to the closet. "Just as I thought, both hotel robes are gone. Lily must have taken them. We'll charge that to her credit card."

I checked the bathroom. The beautiful shell-shaped dish that would hold several days' supplies of toiletries was gone. In addition to the usual amenities by the sinks, we provided a toothbrush, toothpaste, and a comb for emergencies in one of the vanity drawers. They too were gone.

"Guess she took whatever she could," said Rhonda. She stepped into the bedroom and gazed around. "Funny thing, she's erased any idea of a ghost here."

"She took that too," I said, feeling the same way.

"Let's put her on a list of people who are banned from the hotel," said Rhonda. "She was trouble from the beginning. Thank goodness, Vaughn stayed out of her mess."

"He finally texted Lily and told her he would not deal with her again," I said. "He's going to be upset by the photo in the paper. What he does about it is up to him. I'm not going to get involved."

"Maybe it's better left alone," said Rhonda. She walked over to the window in the master bedroom of the suite and looked out at the scene below. "We can't let one person harm what we've accomplished."

"You're right," I said, coming up beside her. "I love sharing the hotel with people who appreciate it."

We went to the office, and I quickly checked the billing for the wedding party and then rose. "Vaughn told me he's going to have to return sometime this week and I want to spend as much time with him as possible."

"I get it. Rita is off, so I need to return home to take care of the kids. Will is stressed from work, and I want him to be able to relax."

"What about that vacation you had set up? Now is the right time to take it."

"We'll see," said Rhonda. "He's already grumbling about time away from the office."

A knock sounded at the door.

I got up to answer it. "Tina! What are you doing here?" I asked, waving her inside.

"It's the newspaper article this morning. I'm sorry, but I can't stay here. I've already received phone calls from several papers and magazines in the area for interviews. The reason I came here was for privacy while I lost a few pounds and got into shape for my next role."

I hugged her. "I'm sorry. We've already talked to the person responsible at the newspaper. It seems that Lily assured the new reporter that everything was okay. Even so, the reporter's boss should've known she had to call us before releasing private information about any guest here at the hotel."

"Aw, honey, we wish it hadn't happened," Rhonda said to Tina. "What are you going to do?"

"I've booked a flight to California for this afternoon. And I'm taking Abbie. She'll complete her contract with me."

"Oh, but ..." started Rhonda, quieting at a look from me. I knew she wanted to say something about Abbie and Darryl becoming more than friends, and that was none of our business.

"Apparently Darryl's had some awful news, and he's thinking of going to New York. So, it wasn't going to work out for Abbie to stay anyway. She's happy to come to California with me. The only problem is, I'm being forced to cancel my reservation for the guesthouse here."

"Don't worry about that," I said, privately cursing Lily. "The important thing is for you to have the proper space for you to prepare for your film. I'm sure that Consuela can give you some of the recipes for Abbie's favorite foods here."

"That would be wonderful," said Tina. "I was hoping to be able to spend some time with you both while I was here, but it seems as if this long visit was troubled from the beginning."

I hugged her. "You're welcome anytime you want. We just want you to be happy and successful."

Rhonda hugged Tina. "We love you, Tina."

Tina gave us a wan smile. "Sorry about all this."

She left, and Rhonda and I sighed together.

"It's amazing how everything that seemed perfect is ending so badly," said Rhonda. "I thought Darryl and Abbie might end up together. But if they're on a different coast of the country, I doubt it'll happen."

"I wonder what's happening with Darryl," I said. "If I hear any news, I'll let you know. I'd better get home."

As I pulled into the driveway, Darryl was saying goodbye to Abbie, who stood with her suitcase outside of Vaughn's car.

I hurried over to them. "Abbie, I'm very sorry you're leaving. I want you to know you're welcome anytime you want. I'm going to miss you."

"Thanks," she said. "I'm going to miss you and everyone here." She gave a meaningful look to Darryl.

"I'll leave you to yourselves," I said, understanding.

Inside the house, Vaughn was in the kitchen preparing to leave. "I'll drive Abbie to the hotel to be with Tina. Darryl is going to stay here to make a few calls. It doesn't look good for him."

I blinked with alarm. "What's the problem?"

"I'll let him tell you what's going on," said Vaughn. "I don't think it's my place to say."

My pulse jumped. I looked out the kitchen window and saw Darryl hugging Abbie.

A moment later Darryl walked inside, and Vaughn left.

"Hi," I said. "What's happening?"

"You'd better sit down. My situation has changed. I got a

call from my agent. I'm being sued for sexual harassment."

I frowned. "Even I who've known you for a short time find it hard to believe that you would do such a thing."

"This woman and I went out to dinner once. She invited me to her apartment, and I said no, I wasn't interested. She's been angry ever since."

"Have you called a lawyer? You'll need an excellent one," I said.

"Oh, yes. I'm going to New York today to meet with him. I want to get this settled as quickly as possible. People may think by charging me with something like this, I'll pay them off or make some kind of settlement. I'm not going to throw money at the problem to make it go away. That's not how I do things. She's got a fight on her hands."

"I wish you luck. You're welcome to use my home office here if you'd like."

He shook his head. "Thanks. I'm leaving for New York today, but I want to continue to rent the house at the hotel. If this news breaks, I can imagine all the smut that will be put out there, and I'll need to hide out more than ever."

"Yes, I'll make sure it's still available for you. Do you want to go back there to pack or are you set with the things you have here?"

"I can make do with what I have here, but thank you. I don't know what I'd do without the support of you and Rhonda. It means a lot."

"We're happy to help. I'm sorry Abbie had to leave for California with Tina. It seemed as if you were getting along well, working out, and becoming friends."

Darryl nodded. "It's disappointing, but I have to clear my name before I can move forward with any plans I may have."

Vaughn returned to the house, and the two of us sat on the lanai while Darryl made flight arrangements.

Darryl walked out to us. "It's arranged. An uber will pick me up in twenty minutes and I'll be on my way. I can't thank you enough for all you've done for me. Vaughn, I'll be your First Mate anytime." He shook hands with Vaughn and gave me a quick hug.

"Hurry and come back to us," I said, feeling sad at his departure. I'd grown to like him a lot and couldn't believe any claims of harassment. Not after seeing him in action and knowing he had four older sisters he loved. It didn't make sense to me.

At the sound of a car horn, Vaughn and I walked Darryl outside and watched him get into the vehicle and leave with a friendly wave.

"The poor guy," said Vaughn. "He seemed very upset. I don't blame him. Once a statement is made, it's hard for the public to forget it." Vaughn shook his head. "What a day this has been with Lily Dorio's antics and now this."

"It's sometimes difficult when you're dealing with a lot of different people at the hotel to remember that most are kind and easy to get along with," I said. "Think of how many wonderful ones we've added to our 'hotel family'."

"True," Vaughn agreed. "Let's hope we enjoy many more occasions with them. Stephanie and Randolph Willis have been fantastic substitute grandparents for Robbie. They attend all his swimming meets to cheer for him. It makes a huge difference in his life."

"Spending that one Christmas with us changed everything. I'm very grateful to them," I said. "Speaking of Robbie, where is he?"

"Next door. He and Brett are working on a special computer program they're putting together. He's very excited by it."

"I guess that leaves us alone for a while. Want to go for a

swim? It's turned out to be quite a warm day."

"Sounds great." He gave me a leering smile. "Need help getting out of your clothes?"

I chuckled, loving his playfulness. Later, I'd show him a more serious side to his suggestion.

CHAPTER TWENTY-TWO

I RACED INTO BERNIE'S OFFICE FOR OUR MONDAY morning meeting a little out of breath. With our houseguests gone and a late night of making love with Vaughn, I was behind schedule. Rhonda was already waiting with the other department heads.

"Sorry, I'm late," I said, sliding onto a chair next to Rhonda.

Bernie acknowledged me with a nod. "A lot has been going on. Would you fill us in on the two VIPs who rented the houses?"

I explained that with Lily's exposure of Tina staying here, Tina had decided to go back to California for the rest of her training, taking Abbie with her. "Darryl wants to continue renting the house he's in. He's meeting with a lawyer in New York to address a sexual harassment claim from one of his staff members on the show."

Next to me, Rhonda tensed. "What? That's ridiculous!"

"I agree," I said. "I can't believe Darryl would do anything like that. It's just not the way he's made."

"Not with four older sisters to keep him in line," said Rhonda. "He told us how much he loves and respects them."

"Does he expect to be gone long?" Bernie asked.

I shook my head. "When that news breaks, Darryl wants to continue to return here. He doesn't want anyone to know where he is."

"That brings me to another topic," said Bernie. "Lily Dorio outed some important people with her newspaper interview. Most of our guests understand our request for total seclusion for others staying in the hotel. While we can't be accountable for what she did, I feel we let down Robert Anderson and the bridal party who didn't want any publicity about their wedding."

"Lily's behavior was blatantly rude, taking photographs during the ceremony," said Lorraine. "I feel responsible, but honestly, I didn't see it happen."

"Annie and I were watching the ceremony, and neither of us saw her doing it. What a sneaky bitch," said Rhonda, huffing with anger.

"I saw someone stop her, but I thought she hadn't taken any photos," I amended.

"Robert is a well-known figure in Hollywood as a producer," said Bernie. "Following his divorce, he didn't want to make a big deal over his quick remarriage. Now, his ex is requesting to re-open their settlement case for a variety of reasons. He's not happy."

"I never want Lily Dorio to stay here at the hotel again," I said.

"I intend to have our lawyer write her a letter explaining what she's done so we have a paper trail to avoid any further problems with her," said Bernie.

"Vaughn refused to take her phone calls. Though the article claimed they were friends, nothing could be further from the truth." Even now, my lips thinned at the idea.

"Annie and I checked the Presidential Suite after Lily checked out. I was afraid she might've done some damage there, but aside from stealing both robes and little stuff like a soap dish, it was fine. I didn't even get a sense of a ghost."

"Great news," said Ana Gomez, head of housekeeping. "One of my workers was afraid to work there. I'll tell her you said it's safe, Rhonda."

"Even a ghost would be scared off by Lily," murmured

Rhonda.

"Now on to new business," said Bernie, and we heard a report from Lorraine about upcoming weddings.

An hour later, Rhonda and I moved to our own office, relieved to put that wedding behind us.

"The holidays will be here before we know it," said Rhonda. "I'm already working on ads for Thanksgiving even though we have a couple of months before that happens."

"I'm meeting with Dorothy soon to start organizing our annual Christmas party. She'll update the invitation list for us."

"She told me she has friends willing to help with the employee Christmas party," said Rhonda. "What would we ever do without her? She keeps us tied to the neighborhood."

"Maybe we should start a publicity campaign to counter any negativity from Lily's interview. I want people to believe us when we say we protect guests' privacy."

"Let's ask Angie and Liz to work on that," said Rhonda. "They love working on projects together, and we need their help."

"Perfect. They both need something creative to do after dealing with toddlers every day," I said. "Vaughn is spending some time with the kids today. Then, he'll take Liz to lunch so they can relax and talk."

"It's nice that they are close," said Rhonda. "Will and Reggie are very close, but sometimes it's too much—working and doing family things together."

"How's Will doing with the stress of the business?" I asked. "I'm concerned about him."

"I understand Reggie had a heart-to-heart talk with him about it. He's pushing to hire another employee to handle some of the smaller accounts. But you know how frugal Will is. He wants to wait and see."

"I hope he doesn't wait until it's too late," I said quietly. I knew Angie's husband, Reggie, would be more than ready to take over the business while Will was gone. He and Will worked well together, but Reggie was looking forward to the time when the business would be his after Will retired.

A few days later, I got a call from Darryl, telling me he'd arrive at the hotel that afternoon.

"How are things going?" I asked him.

"Not well. Right now, the woman is making a statement to the press, but nothing is in the court system yet. What will it matter? Once my name is linked to the scandal and the news makes a splash about it, I'll be declared guilty in the media."

"That's awful," I said, feeling sick.

"My lawyer is working on things behind the scenes and is telling me not to despair. He's working to bring suit against the woman. As you might imagine, I just want to disappear and ignore all the bad publicity."

"We'll keep you safe here. Why don't you invite your sisters to stay with you at the house? That might make it less lonely."

"I've already talked to them about it. One or two of them might be able to make it. We'll see."

I waited for him to mention Abbie, but when he didn't, I let it go. "If they want to join you, have them talk to Bernie to get them registered privately."

"Will do. Thanks for all your help."

"We're here for you, Darryl," I said before he ended the call. I told Rhonda about his plans.

"Does Abbie know about all of this?" Rhonda asked.

"I don't know. He didn't mention it."

Rhonda's eyes rounded with surprise. "Some matchmaker you are! She should be with him."

"That's not our call to make," I said, even as I agreed with her.

"Maybe Tina can help," she said.

"No, Rhonda. Darryl has enough to contend with. He doesn't need our interference."

She studied me and slowly nodded.

I talked to Bernie. "It's very important that his presence is a secret. Also, I've instructed his sisters to call you to privately register as guests at the house."

"Smart thinking," he said. "The media is going to go crazy over this. It looks bad for Darryl."

I wished I could deny it, but I knew he was right.

We were in our office when Darryl called. "I'm here," he said to me. "Bernie suggested I reregister to insure my identity doesn't leak out. I'm under a different name. Douglas Hathaway."

"I took the liberty of ordering the same groceries you requested for your earlier arrival. I'm happy to purchase anything else you might need."

"Thank you. I'll make do. The first announcement has already hit the network news station."

"I'm sorry," I said.

"Me, too. It didn't have to be this way." He abruptly ended the call, and I knew how upset he was.

Rhonda shook her head. "Let's turn on the news." We'd hung a smart TV on the wall of the office so we could keep up with the news.

The screen lit, and when we went to the ACBE TV station, we saw a picture of Darryl on the screen along with a photo of a young, dark-haired woman with a ponytail and wearing glasses. NIGHT SHOW HOST DARRYL DOUGLAS ACCUSED OF SEXUAL HARASSMENT streamed across the screen.

> "Mr. Douglas is in legal trouble for allegedly acting inappropriately with one of his staff members. We've learned that the young woman is a former network staffer, and that she made her accusations against Mr. Douglas after she was let go. A source claims Douglas denies the allegations. Who's lying and who's telling the truth?"

I sat back in my chair feeling helpless. There was nothing I could do except to help keep Darryl safe at the hotel. "One helpful thing is they keep showing old pictures of Darryl."

"Yeah. He looks entirely different today with his shaved head and new, tanned physique," said Rhonda.

"In a short time, Darryl has changed a lot, making him unrecognizable. And most of that credit goes to Abbie."

Rhonda didn't say anything, but I could see her mind working.

"Oh, go ahead and call Tina," I said. "I know you want to."

"I feel she should know what's happening in New York. What she does with the knowledge is up to her, but I wouldn't feel right about not calling." Rhonda picked up the phone and was forced to leave a message for Tina.

"We'll see what happens with that call," I said. "I hate to think of Darryl being alone at a time like this."

At that moment, Bernie phoned. "One of Darryl's sisters, Emma Strong, has arrived and is at the house."

"Nice to hear," I said. "Rhonda and I will go down and check on her."

###

Rhonda and I eagerly headed to the house Darryl was renting. I felt much better about Darryl not being alone. The situation was too terrible to be by himself.

When we got to the house and rang the bell, an attractive woman appeared. She had the same hazel eyes I'd silently admired in Darryl and similar facial features. She gave us a friendly smile. "I know who you are. Glad to meet you, Ann and Rhonda. I'm Emma Strong. The baby sister in the family."

"The one closest in age to me," said Darryl coming up behind her.

"I don't know what you've done for Darryl," Emma said. "He looks fabulous. I like his new shaved head and his stronger body."

"Stop, you're making me blush," said Darryl, giving his sister a little nudge.

"It's not us, it's Abbie who's given him this new look," said Rhonda, and I smiled to myself. She wasn't going to leave her matchmaking alone.

"So, who's this new woman in Darryl's life?" asked Emma, smiling sweetly. "I can't wait to hear about her."

"She's the best trainer anyone could have," said Rhonda.

"She's talented. But is she nice?" asked Emma, giving both Rhonda and me steady looks.

I spoke up. "Abbie has stayed at my house, along with Darryl, and I can honestly say you'd approve. She's a sweet, fun, hardworking woman."

"You'd better believe hardworking," said Darryl. "She's the one getting me in shape and changing me. I was very disappointed when she had to go back to California."

"We all were," said Rhonda. "We're hoping she comes back."

Darryl held up his hand. "I don't want her to go through any of this mess with me. She has jobs to do without my bothering her."

"Really?" said Emma. "If I'm understanding this situation with Abbie, you're falling for her and yet you're pushing her away? Hey, little bro, you've got to do better than that. At least call her. You owe her that."

"I like you," Rhonda said to Emma. "You and I think alike."

"How long do you think you'll stay?" I asked Emma.

"I'm not sure. I'm the first one here, but my other sisters will come if needed. Besides helping Darryl, it's a break for all of us."

"I promised them each a relaxing vacation," said Darryl wrapping his arm around Emma.

I warmed inside at the smiles they shared.

CHAPTER TWENTY-THREE

"**IF YOU HAVE TIME, PLEASE SIT AND ENJOY A COLD DRINK** with us," said Darryl. "I'm giving Emma an update on the situation."

"Thanks," said Rhonda. "I want to know what's going on."

"Great. I've got lemonade with or without liquor," said Darryl.

"Make mine without," I said, and Rhonda quickly agreed. We didn't drink alcohol while on the job.

Emma helped Darryl serve the drinks, and we sat together on the lanai under the umbrella of the high-top table.

"My lawyer is taking an attack role," explained Darryl. "He feels we have enough to prove that the woman's claim was all part of an effort to extort money, that she has no proof that I ever touched her or said sexual things to her. One of my other co-workers will be glad to make a statement that will prove my accuser is doing this for the attention and money."

"You will have dozens of character witnesses," said Emma.

"I appreciate that." Darryl grinned at his sister and then his expression became serious. "My lawyer is going to speak to the network to allow them to release my contract, which is what I've wanted all along."

"Wow! That's a lot for you to handle," said Rhonda.

Darryl gave her a thoughtful nod. "I trust my lawyer to do an excellent job to prevent such bullshit happening to others working for the network. Out of this bad news will come something good for me."

"Unfortunately, the news of the woman's accusation is

everywhere," I said. "It's such a shame this couldn't be handled more privately."

"Yes," Darryl said. "I agree. We knew it was coming and tried to deal with her. But she wanted to drag me through the court of public opinion, hoping I'll cave in to her demands."

"Are you going to be okay?" asked Emma.

Darryl nodded. "You know I would never do what that woman is charging me with."

"Absolutely," she responded, and I was reminded how strong his family bonds were.

"Tell us a little about yourself, Emma," I said.

"I've been working in an accounting office in our hometown in Ohio since I graduated from Ohio University. I have two high school-aged children, twins, Amy and Jeff. My husband died a few years ago. We had a nice life together." She had a way of smiling when she was speaking that made everything seem upbeat.

"She's a smart woman and a great mom," said Darryl proudly. "She's helped me with a financial plan."

"Now, I'm curious to know about you and Rhonda," said Emma. "It's great that women my age have accomplished so much. The hotel is beautiful and has an outstanding reputation."

"I met Annie when our daughters were roommates at college. I wasn't too sure of her when we first met, but I knew she was smart," said Rhonda.

"I was devastated following a divorce and didn't know where I'd live or what I'd do for a job," I explained. "Once I got to know Rhonda better, I liked her idea of taking a chance on converting her mansion into a hotel."

"We both had a lot to prove," said Rhonda. "And I couldn't have chosen a better partner."

"Amen," I said. "We're perfect partners and best of

friends."

Emma shook her head in wonder. "What a great story. I'm sorry bad news has brought me here, but I want to enjoy every minute I have with Darryl. Look what it's done for him."

I checked my watch. "It's been wonderful meeting you, Emma. And, Darryl, you know we're here to help you in any way we can. I'm sorry, but I must leave."

'Yes," said Rhonda. "We're having a meeting to discuss the upcoming holidays with one of our best volunteers."

"She's part of what we call 'the hotel family'," I explained. "She's been with us from the first day we opened."

"We could hire someone professional to do the work but she's very proud of her job," said Rhonda.

I hugged Emma and Darryl goodbye. "Something good will come of this. I just know it."

"Be sure to ask Darryl about Abbie," said Rhonda, giving him a wink.

Emma laughed. "Don't worry. I will."

Back in our office, we received a phone call from Bernie. "Thought you'd want to know that the house next to Darryl's will be rented to a friend of the governor, a man named Randall Haven. I don't think it'll be a problem to have him living close to Darryl. He wants isolation and I imagine he understands how the press works. He's been called the 'Playboy of Southern Florida,' according to what I've read."

Rhonda's smile grew wider as Bernie stopped speaking.

I held up my hand to stop her. "I see your mind spinning. No matchmaking on this. Emma has her life away from Florida."

"Wait a minute! You were thinking the same thing," said Rhonda.

"Yes, but then I allowed reason to win," I responded. "That's what I want you to do."

"What's going on?" asked Bernie.

"Nothing," I answered. "Thanks for the news. We appreciate it."

Bernie ended the call and I looked at Rhonda and laughed. He wouldn't understand by having happy marriages, we wanted everyone to have one too.

That night, as I lay in Vaughn's arms, I smiled at the memory of Rhonda thinking she was a talented matchmaker. True, some of her pairings had worked, but having Randall Haven at the hotel didn't necessarily mean he'd be a willing part of her schemes. I'd read about him online and though he was wealthy, smart, and handsome, he was elusive when it came to marriage. He was also an early-morning jogger.

"What's up, babe?" Vaughn murmured.

"Nothing much. Just thinking about how much I love you. Were you ever called a playboy?"

"No, and for a very real reason. I had a great life with my wife, Ellie, and now with you. Why would I want to screw that up?"

"I hope you never would," I said, giving him a teasing smile.

"That's my woman," he said, pulling me closer and planting his lips on mine.

I was still cuddled up next to him in the morning when my alarm went off. I'd set it so I wouldn't miss the chance of seeing Darryl on his early morning run. Or Rand.

Vaughn rolled over when I slid out of bed.

I quietly showered and dressed before going to the kitchen to put Cindy out and turn on the coffee pot. After I let Cindy back inside, I poured myself a cup of coffee and took off for the hotel.

I loved this time of day when the sun was emerging from a sleepy dawn, filling the pink and gray sky with a promise of a good day. The fronds of palm trees rustled in the onshore breeze as I got out of my car at the hotel, making distinctive music of its own.

I took off my sandals and walked onto the beach. Another pleasure of this early morning hour was the freedom from others you could find.

Shell seekers carried net bags as they searched for beautiful gifts from the sea, walking slowly in a bent position near the water's edge. Joggers and walkers used the hard-packed sand away from the edge for their exercise.

I walked to the water and allowed waves to wash over my feet. I could feel the push and pull of the water as it raced onto the shore and pulled away again, taking some of the sand beneath my feet.

I studied the joggers but didn't see Darryl, and I decided to walk north away from the hotel. As I did, I noticed three figures standing and talking in the distance. Hoping one of them wasn't Brock Goodwin, I walked forward.

As I approached, I could see Darryl, Emily, and a man I didn't know. Darryl and the man were talking while Emma had her back to them looking at the birds whirling above them.

"Hey, Ann," said Darryl. "Have you met my new neighbor here at the hotel? Rand Haven moved into the house next to me yesterday. Rand, this is one of the owners of the hotel, Ann Sanders."

Dazzling blue eyes focused on me and a smile spread across Rand's handsome face. "Hello, Ann. My pleasure. I'm glad to be here for some quiet time, away from Miami."

"We're delighted to have you. I suspect you've been told about our confidentiality policy here at the hotel."

"Indeed. That's why I chose The Beach House Hotel," Rand said, still smiling at me. He gazed at Emma who was paying us no attention.

I went over to her. "I hope you're enjoying yourself. It's such a beautiful morning."

"Oh, yes. The white wings of the birds are beautiful against the blue of the sky. They remind me of poems my kids made for me when they were writing Haiku poetry in school. Birds have always been of interest to me. My husband used to love to track them as they migrated each fall and spring."

"Well, you know what we call people who migrate here for the winter."

"Snow birds," she said, and we laughed together.

"Hey, Sis, I'm going to jog down the beach with Rand. Do you mind?"

"Not at all," said Emma. "I'm enjoying myself right here."

I felt Rand's eyes on us and noticed they settled on Emma. She turned away to lean down and pick up a shell.

I couldn't hold back a chuckle as Darryl and Rand took off. Rand was obviously used to being noticed, and Emma wasn't paying attention to him.

I caught up with Emma. "I'm glad to see Darryl is still following the workout program Abbie set up for him."

"Yes, we talked about it. He says he's never felt nor looked better. I agree with him. He wasn't fat, just a little bit pudgy. Now, he's ruggedly handsome, more like I've always known him."

"What do you think of Rand Haven?" I asked, thinking how pleased Rhonda would be to know I'd asked.

"So far, I'm not about to succumb to his charms. He's strikingly handsome and is used to being the center of attention. He's a wonderful diversion for Darryl."

"I don't know Rand. But he's known as a real playboy." I looked up. "Oh, oh, here comes someone I do know. Though he's attractive, Brock Goodwin is someone to avoid for many reasons. And for sure, don't tell him where you're staying or with whom. He'd take pleasure in exposing Darryl." I took her arm and led her away.

"Ann! Wait!" Brock called. "I need to talk to you."

Groaning, I slowed. "There's no stopping him. He'll run faster if we try to get away."

Brock jogged up to us and paused a moment to catch his breath. "I want you to know I've been cleared of all charges in the Everly Jansen case, and I want to be welcomed back at the hotel." He turned to Emma and gave her a leering look. "Who do we have here?"

"Emma is a friend of mine, visiting for a short time. As far as being welcomed back to the hotel, you know the rules about privacy and your need to stay away from any guests. That's what got you in trouble with Everly."

"I was just being pleasant and helpful. Like I always am." He turned to Emma. "I'm president of the Neighborhood Association, and I have a responsibility to make sure everything is going well under my control."

I rolled my eyes.

Emma grinned at me. "You're right. You have some very interesting neighbors."

"At your service," said Brock, giving her a little bow.

"See you later, Brock," I said, taking hold of Emma's arm as we walked away. "Brock is a pain in the butt and has done everything he can to undermine what Rhonda and I try to do. He thinks because he's a single man in a group of single women that he's a real Casanova. Rhonda and I detest him."

"What about Rand? Is he like that too?" Emma asked. She

frowned as she saw Darryl jogging toward them with Rand.

"Tell you what, why don't you come with me to the hotel? I can show you where Rhonda and I work, and we can have some of Consuela's sweet rolls."

Relief washed across Emma's face. "Let's go." She turned and waved at Darryl and then hurried away with me.

At the hotel, we walked into the busy kitchen. I introduced Emma to Consuela and explained that Consuela and her husband, Manny, were more like family than staff members.

We grabbed some cinnamon rolls and cups of coffee and went into the office.

Rhonda was there looking through some brochures. "Hi, there. Nice to see you here, Emma."

"We're escaping Brock and Rand," I said.

"Brock, I can understand, but Rand is mighty fine to look at online," said Rhonda.

"But Ann told me he has a reputation for playing around," Emma said. "Believe me, I'm not interested."

"Well, those are stories about him. We don't know the real facts," said Rhonda, ever the matchmaker unwilling to give up on a cause. "Has Darryl heard from Abbie?"

"She called last night and wanted to come to Florida to keep him company. He turned her down."

"What?" said Rhonda drawing herself up in her chair. "Why would he do that?"

Emma shook her head. "He told her that he didn't want her pulled into this mess, that when he was cleared of all charges, he'd love to see her."

"That's awful. That's pushing her away," said Rhonda.

"It's wonderful that she wants to support him," I said.

"It's that Douglas family stubbornness. He won't budge,"

said Emma. "I tried to talk to him, but he cares for Abbie and doesn't want to see her hurt by bad publicity."

"That's very honorable," I said. "I just hope it doesn't ruin a beautiful, growing relationship. Abbie works with well-known people and knows how to handle herself."

"Thanks for your concern," said Emma. "I wish you two would talk to him. I've never seen him this happy with someone. He even talked about a future that they wanted together."

"Okay," said Rhonda. "When you're ready to go back to the house, I'm going with you."

"Me, too," I said. When Rhonda got her mind made up about something, there was no use trying to talk her out of it.

We chatted for a while, answering Emma's questions about running a hotel, and then she said, "I suppose I should head back. Darryl will be wondering where I am."

"We're going with you," Rhonda said, rising to her feet.

When we arrived at the house, Darryl and Rand were sitting on the lanai talking. Both men rose as the three of us approached them.

"Hi, there," said Darryl. "Rand, I don't believe you've met Rhonda Grayson, Ann's partner.

Rand beamed at Rhonda, and as they shook hands, I noticed how her cheeks grew flushed with color.

"Nice to meet you. Welcome to The Beach House Hotel," Rhonda said.

"It's my pleasure to be here. As Darryl told me, it's a perfect place to hide out and be able to be yourself," said Rand. He glanced at Emma as she left the room.

"Darryl, can we talk?" Rhonda said.

Rand held up his hand. "Nice to meet you both. I'll leave

you to yourselves. It's time for me to return to my house."

As he left the room, my eyes weren't the only ones focused on his butt before I faced Darryl. "We don't mean to pry, Darryl, but Rhonda and I are concerned that you don't want Abbie to come here to support you."

"We and Emma know how she feels about wanting to help you, and we support you both," said Rhonda. "What's the problem?

Darryl ran a hand across his bald head and sighed. "Abbie is someone very special to me. I don't want her name dragged into the mud along with mine. It's going to get nasty. I want to protect her."

"That's sweet," I said. "But we and your sister are concerned you're pushing her away when you should be together."

"I appreciate your concern," he said. "Now, I'm ready for something to eat."

He left, and Rhonda and I faced one another.

"That's it," I said. "We've done what Emma asked us to do. Now, we have to let it go."

"Okay, but I hope he hasn't ruined the match," sighed Rhonda. "I could even envision a beach wedding for them."

"That, my friend, is out of our hands," I said, throwing an arm around Rhonda. "Time to get back to work."

CHAPTER TWENTY-FOUR

THAT EVENING AS VAUGHN AND I WATCHED THE NEWS ON television I was astounded by how quickly many people either defended or trashed Darryl. Some from years back when he was just a kid. The ones who claimed he wasn't as nice, as funny, or as kind as others said, seemed to have an agenda of their own.

The person I was most interested in was Darryl's accuser. She was someone who others at the network didn't like. The network had fired her before Darryl made his decision not to renew his contract. Some claimed she was after the money; others claimed she wanted her job and reputation back.

It hurt me to see this. I just couldn't believe this claim to be true. And if it was judged to be false, this untrue claim hurt all women, not just one.

My cell phone rang.

"Hi, Tina, what's up?" I asked her.

"What's going on with Darryl and Abbie? She's very upset that he won't allow her to come to Florida. What happened? I thought they were much more than friends."

I told her what Darryl had explained to us. "He has his sister staying with him now, so he's not alone. But both Rhonda and I tried to tell him in protecting Abbie, it seemed as if he was pushing her away."

"I'm relieved to understand his side of things. I'll let Abbie know, and she can take it from there. I realize how much she cares for him. I've never seen her so unhappy."

"I'll tell Darryl's sister, Emma, about our call, and she can do with it what she wants," I said. "I think it's only fair for those involved to have as much information as possible."

"I agree. I really hope this all works out," said Tina. "In the meantime, Lily Dorio's new husband told me that Lily claims you've banned her from the hotel because you were jealous of her."

I shook my head. "I can't even respond to that."

"You don't have to," said Tina. "No one listens to Lily anymore. What few clients she had have dumped her. That's why she's so desperate. Her new husband isn't happy with her. She's damaging his reputation."

"I'm not sure she even knows what that is," I said, unexpectedly feeling sorry for her. "How are the boys? I hope you can come back to The Beach House Hotel as a family. The pictures you send show them growing way too fast."

Tina sighed. "They really are. I keep wondering if we should try for another baby. Working on this movie may help me decide."

"You'll know if it's the right decision," I said. "Please tell us if you need any help with Abbie. Rhonda and I want a relationship with Darryl to work out for her. She's a wonderful woman."

"I think so, too," said Tina. "I'll talk to you later."

After I ended the call, Vaughn looked at me. "Everything all right?"

"Just relaying information that I hope will help both Abbie and Darryl."

He wrapped his arm around me. "It makes me realize how lucky we are."

Cindy jumped up on the couch and wiggled between us.

Laughing, we leaned over her and kissed.

###

The next morning, I decided to take an early walk on the beach. With Vaughn at home to take care of Robbie getting ready for school, I could quietly slip out of the house. There was something healing about being on the sand, enjoying nature there.

I drove to the hotel, slipped off my sandals, and headed out to the sand. The tang of the salty air made me sigh with pleasure. As usual, sandpipers and sanderlings marched along the water's edge in a line, stopping to scoop up a tasty morsel from time to time.

A trio of pelicans flew in formation, like navy pilots, skimming the water's surface looking for food. When one of them dove headfirst into the water to retrieve a fish, I gazed at the way its pouch stretched to scoop the fish into its mouth and swallow the catch. Nature was interesting, so complex. Like people.

"Ann!"

I looked up to see Emma trotting toward me, and I walked forward to greet her. "Hi. Another nice day."

"Yes. Darryl is jogging with Rand again this morning, so I have some time to myself. But I know you're a morning beach person like me, and I wonder if I can ask you to join me. I'd love the company and a chance to talk to another woman."

"Sure. I can arrange to meet you," I said, pleased by the invitation. "Is there something you want to talk about now?"

"There is. Rand has invited me out to dinner tonight, and I've told him I'd think about it. My sisters would tell me to go ahead and do it, but I know you and Rhonda have some reservations about him, and I wondered what you thought about it."

I studied her. She was a beautiful woman but not as young as some of the women I'd seen Rand photographed with. "Why do you want to go out with Rand?"

"I'm attracted to him, and I don't mean his looks. It's been a long time since I've dated and, I admit it, I'd be using him to see if I can get back into the dating scene. The last date I had at home thought because I said I'd have coffee with him that I automatically wanted to go to bed with him when I saw him again. I can't think of anything worse."

"You're only going to be here a short while?"

"I have several weeks' vacation owed to me, so I have flexibility," said Emma. "You told me that Rand is known as a playboy."

"I don't know him. I've only read a couple of stories about him in some of the Florida social magazines. So, please don't take what's been said about him to heart. That's like believing some of the stories about Darryl because someone said so."

"I don't want to do that."

"I want only the best for you," I said. "So, like your sisters, I'd probably say go and have fun. Let's exchange information on our phones in case you need to call for some reason."

"Okay, I'm going to tell Rand yes, but I'm not going to be someone who throws herself at him. I just want to try dating again. With my twins going off to college next year, I know it's going to be lonely."

"It's smart to plan ahead. It was a real shock to have Liz leave me to go to college at the same time her father dumped me for his receptionist."

"I'm sorry. It must have been awful," said Emma, giving me a look of understanding.

"Thank goodness for Rhonda," I said, remembering her persistence in getting me to help her with her plans to open The Beach House Hotel.

Darryl and Rand jogged up to us.

"Glad to see you here," said Darryl. "Come join us for something cool to drink. Or coffee, if you wish."

"Thanks, I will," I said, eager to get a better idea about what kind of person Rand was.

We walked back to the house, and I liked how Rand held the door open to his house for us. I expected to find the house messy, but everything was in place as we walked through the living room to get to his pool lanai.

Rand took drink orders, and then he and Darryl went to the kitchen to get them.

"He seems very nice," I murmured to Emma.

She gazed at him in the kitchen and shrugged her shoulders. "Hard to tell right now."

My cell rang. *Rhonda.*

"Where are you?" she asked.

"I'm at the house Rand is renting, having coffee."

"Do me a favor, will ya?" said Rhonda. "Invite all three of them to come to my house for dinner tomorrow night at six o'clock. I'm following through on some of my instincts. And you know everyone loves my food. I'll go easy because Darryl is watching his weight."

"Okay, hold on, and I'll ask," I told the others and all three accepted the invitation.

"Okay, you're set for tomorrow," I said. "I'll be back to the office soon."

"See you then," she said. "I'm going to grab a coffee and a sweet roll and look at what our girls came up with for some PR graphics."

We loved having our daughters involved to the extent they could. The day would come when they would run the hotel. But with all our grandchildren so young, that wouldn't happen for a while.

I sipped my coffee and listened as Darryl gave us an update on his situation. "My lawyer has addressed the media, telling them the claim has no truth."

"It's a shame the accusation became public right away because most of the negotiations take place behind the scenes," said Rand. "Believe me, I know how damaging so-called 'truths' can be."

We all turned to him.

"It's true. I bet each of you has no idea who I really am," said Rand.

"I'm about to find out a little about you," said Emma. "That is, if we're going out to dinner tonight."

Rand's startling blue eyes sparkled. "Is that a yes?"

Emma nodded and gave him a tentative smile.

"Okay. Thanks," said Rand, as Darryl's cell phone rang.

Darryl looked at the screen and got to his feet. "I'm leaving to take this call. See everyone later."

I checked my watch. "I've got to get back to the office. Thanks for the coffee, Rand."

Emma made no move to leave, and I gave her a wink before I turned and walked away.

In the office, I told Rhonda what was going on with the three of them and grinned. "I think your dinner party is going to be very revealing. It'll be interesting to see how Rand and Emma do together tonight and with a follow-up social situation."

"I've got a strong feeling about it," said Rhonda.

CHAPTER TWENTY-FIVE

THE NEXT EVENING AFTER WORK, I SHOWERED AND dressed for dinner at Rhonda's. Vaughn was looking forward to an evening out of the house and eating Rhonda's excellent cooking. Growing up in an Italian neighborhood, Rhonda had learned recipes and cooking from the best.

I was looking forward to seeing how the date between Emma and Rand went. I'd been unable to get away for our scheduled early morning walk because Robbie wasn't feeling well. He was much better now and loved having Liana stay with him while we were gone, claiming she was a great game player.

When Vaughn came into the room, I was putting on my earrings. He came up behind me and gave me a squeeze. "You look extra beautiful tonight. I like that blue dress. It matches your eyes."

I turned around and kissed him. "Thanks. You're looking handsome yourself."

"Anything I should know before we arrive at Rhonda's?"

"Rand and Emma went on a date last night. I have no idea how things went. I've heard nothing more about Darryl's situation. Rhonda's hoping that we all can relax and enjoy ourselves."

Vaughn gave me a little salute. "Okay. Got it. Let's go."

I grabbed my purse and walked out to the kitchen to say goodbye to Robbie. After making sure he had some healthy food for dinner, I kissed him and left with Vaughn, stopping to give Cindy a pat on the head.

###

When we arrived at Rhonda's, the house was lit up from the inside. She and Will lived in a gorgeous, expansive two-story home with white-painted stucco walls and a red tile roof.

Vaughn and I got out of the car and were walking toward the front entrance when Darryl, Emma, and Rand arrived. We stopped to greet them and then went to the front door.

The door opened and Willow and Drew stood there smiling. Willow wore a pretty flowery dress and Drew looked spiffy in a clean T-shirt and shorts.

"Hi, Auntie Ann and Uncle V," said Willow. "Please come inside."

I smiled and leaned down to kiss her.

"Mommy says we can greet the guests," said Willow proudly.

"How do you do?" Drew said to the trio behind us.

I stood aside to listen.

Willow said, "Welcome." She stared at Emma. "You're pretty."

"Thank you," said Emma politely.

Willow stared up at Rand and I waited to hear what she had to say. "You're ... nice."

Rand blinked in surprise. "I appreciate that very much."

Willow's gaze swept over Darryl. "I like your bare head."

Darryl chuckled. "An honest compliment."

Rhonda rushed up to the doorway. "Hello, everyone. Please come in." She turned to Willow and Drew. "Thank you both for greeting our guests. Now we'll show them inside like a good host and hostess."

Will was in the den, standing at the bar. "Good evening, everyone. What can I offer you to drink? We're serving a red Italian wine, a Barolo, with dinner. I can offer you something lighter, perhaps a pinot noir, beer, or any cocktail."

Emma and I went with pinot noir. Vaughn, Darryl, and Rand went with vodka on the rocks, while Will chose his favorite scotch. Rhonda joined us holding a glass of red wine.

Rita followed behind carrying a tray of stuffed mushroom appetizers.

"Please sit everyone. It will be a short while before dinner," said Rhonda. "Will, I want to introduce you to our hotel guests."

Will, who was a true gentleman, shook hands all around and kept the conversation going while Rhonda disappeared into the kitchen.

The subject of sailing came up and Darryl proudly told the group that he was Vaughn's First Mate.

"I've got a motorboat, but I always thought I'd like sailing," said Rand. "Do you allow for more than one First Mate?" he asked Vaughn.

As the conversation continued about sailing, I found it interesting to see Emma and Rand interact with one another now and then. Their dinner date must have gone well.

When Will's business came up, Rand reacted. "I'm interested in finding a new financial manager. We'll have to chat sometime."

Will beamed at him. "Certainly. My pleasure."

It did my heart good to see Will so pleased. He'd been my financial advisor when I was trying to come up with my share of funds to invest in the hotel. That's how he and Rhonda met. I'd never forget how kind he was to me or how he and Rhonda had quickly fallen in love.

Rhonda appeared. "Dinner is ready."

She led us into the dining room.

A place card sat in front of each chair, and I was pleased to be seated between Rand and Darryl. Rhonda caught my eye and winked. She, no doubt, was hoping to collect a lot of information from me.

Rhonda was a marvelous cook, and even though she'd promised to make a simple meal, we started with a large antipasti platter fit for a meal. It was loaded with veggies, meats, cheese, olives, peppers, and every other item usually found in the dish. Accompanying it was fresh, warm Italian bread and a seasoned olive oil mixture for dipping the bread.

"This is delicious," said Emma. "What a delightful dinner."

"Uh, this is just the beginning," I murmured. "Rhonda's maiden name is DelMonte. Be prepared for a lot of excellent food."

Emma covered her mouth with her hand, stifling a laugh. "Of course." She gazed at Rand, and he grinned at her.

"She's adorable," I quietly said to him.

He continued staring at Emma and nodded.

While Rhonda talked to Rand, I turned to Darryl. "How did the day go?"

He let out a long sigh. "It's hard to sit and hear all kinds of things being said about you while having to remain quiet. But my lawyer has been digging up information. He tells me it'll be just a matter of time before my accuser is forced to recant her statement."

"I'm sorry this has happened to you," I said.

"I got a call from Abbie. She's upset with me. She thinks I'm pushing her away."

"Isn't that what you're doing?" I asked.

"Emma thinks so, but what if the newspeople find out we've been training together? They'll make it something it's not. Something cheap. And our relationship is not that way at all. I've fallen for her, and I don't want to mess that up."

"I understand what you're trying to do," I said, "but if you both are in love with one another, then you must unite to face your troubles if you're going to have a true relationship."

Rhonda entered the room carrying a platter and announced, "We're serving family style tonight."

"We can talk later," I said to Darryl. "I know how delicious this is. You won't want to spend a minute chatting instead of eating."

Darryl grinned. "I already know I'll have to do twice as much jogging tomorrow."

Rhonda placed a platter filled with Chicken Parmesan on the table. A bowl of freshly made pasta and a bowl of what Rhonda called "gravy" or red sauce was placed near the pasta.

Rita filled our water glasses, and Will poured more wine. We took what we wanted as the dishes were passed around, and then Rhonda and Will helped themselves. When Rhonda lifted her fork, we all took bites of our meal. Silence followed, then murmurs of pleasure surrounded the table.

"Rhonda, this is delicious," said Rand. "Are you sure you don't want to run a restaurant too?"

"I was the first chef at the hotel before we got Jean-Luc," she said. "It almost took a battle to get me out of the kitchen, but I'm glad to leave the cooking up to him."

With tasty food and wine, everyone relaxed. Will told a few stories about the town of Sabal before it grew from a fishing village into the upscale city it was today. Emma told about Darryl growing up with four sisters, teasing him and making us all laugh.

"How about you, Rand?" I asked. "Where did you grow up?"

"I grew up in Pennsylvania, but after I came to Florida on spring break from college, I decided I wanted to live year-round in warmth. I've done well with some real estate ventures and live and work here in the state." He put a hand through his silvery hair. "I intend to keep on working and playing for as long as I can."

"Are you a playboy like some articles have said about you?" Rhonda asked bluntly after having a couple of glasses of wine.

Rand frowned. "Me? Not a chance. I simply haven't found the right woman yet." He gazed at Emma and away, and I noticed how Emma's cheeks flushed. Something was going on between them.

The next morning, I couldn't wait to get to the beach to meet Emma for a walk. I was brimming with curiosity about her date with Rand. They certainly seemed to have hit it off last night. Besides, after the scrumptious dinner Rhonda served us, I was ready for a nice, long walk before getting ready for work at the hotel.

I dressed, grabbed a cup of coffee, and headed out.

The hotel was quiet as I drove through the gates. I stopped the car to admire the pink stucco building that meant so much to me. It was, in one word, beautiful. The landscaping, under Manny's supervision, was stunning with natural-looking trees, bushes, and flowers. A huge ceramic pot stood beside each carved wooden door held open by them for visitors. Sliding glass doors led to the lobby and living area beyond it. Rhonda and I had wanted to keep the sense of guests arriving home when they entered the hotel, and the Oriental rugs and plush furnishings in the lobby added to that effect.

Even from my car, I had a sense of the hotel welcoming me.

Satisfied, I drove on, going behind the hotel to the "back of the house" parking lot. Most staff members were able to ride one of the hotel vans to and from work. A mutual benefit.

I waved to a member of the kitchen crew having a smoke on the loading dock, got out of the car, and headed onto the sand.

When I arrived, I saw some shellers and joggers but no

Emma. I waded into the water and stood as I usually did, staring up at the sky, and breathing in the clean air. I loved the sense of being part of nature.

I remained still as a white cattle egret walked along the shallow water searching for food. When it darted its head into the water and pulled out a small fish, I wanted to applaud. Nature's cycle was as constant as the push and pull of the water at my feet.

I felt rather than heard someone approach and turned to see Emma.

She'd put a baseball cap over her brown waves of hair. Beneath the brim of the cap, I could see the sparkle in her hazel eyes.

"' Morning! How are you?" I asked.

"Fine," she answered. "Still full from the marvelous dinner Rhonda served last night. It's time to work off some of those calories."

"I agree," I said, holding back questions. I wanted our conversation to flow naturally, not be an inquisition by me.

We moved together, matching paces, as we headed down the beach away from the houses.

Unwilling to wait a moment longer, I introduced the subject of Rand. "I liked listening to Rand talk about his businesses last night. He's a very interesting man."

Emma smiled. "I agree. Not at all what I expected."

"And what did you expect?"

"I thought a handsome, successful man like that would be full of himself, uninterested in what I had to say. Funny thing is I learned he's a bit shy beneath the image he projects. We had a long talk about anything and everything. It was very nice."

"Aren't you glad your sisters and I encouraged you to date and have fun?" I said to her.

Emma stopped and threw her arms around me. "Who am I fooling? I'm hopelessly in love with the man. He's everything I've wanted all my life. Don't get me wrong. I loved my husband, and we had a wonderful life. But being with Rand, talking business or water sports or whatever we wanted filled me with a sense of awe."

With Rhonda's silent blessing, I said, "And beyond the talking?

Emma hugged herself. "Wow! That's all I'll say."

I laughed and clapped my hands. "Wait until Rhonda hears this. She'll be as delighted as I am for you."

Emma held up a hand. "We can't get too carried away. Rand told me he wants to see me every night he's here, but that's as far as it's gone. I'm staying with Darryl, and that's how it's going to be unless Rand and I both decide to do something different. I know younger people hop into and out of bed, but that's not me. We may have kissed and all, but we haven't gone to bed."

"There's no rush," I said. "But you either have chemistry or you don't, and it sounds as if the two of you do."

"Yes," said Emma as a satisfied smile crossed her face.

"It's magic when it happens and everything else is right. I hope this is the case for you."

"Me, too. I feel absolutely giddy with the possibility," said Emma.

"Let's enjoy the walk. It's a beautiful day." I gave her an excited hug before we resumed our walk.

Emma kept up with my brisk pace. I let her talk as she told me more about Rand and the harsh childhood he had growing up. "He is by nature a cautious man because of the stringent expectations placed upon him by his father. He told me he's always wanted a family but was afraid that he might be difficult like his father."

"That's very honest of him," I commented.

"Yes, after I answered his questions honestly, he began to open up to me. He's been hurt by other women who didn't care about him as a person but wanted his money and to be seen with him."

"Whew! That's degrading," I said. I'd married Vaughn who had both the looks and the money, but those were not the qualities I measured him by or ever would. The man himself is what I loved. I remembered him first touching my hand, how his fingers wound around it, signaling strength and gentleness at the same time.

Emma stopped, looked at me, and shook her head. "Is this thing between Rand and me crazy? A fairytale?"

"No, I don't think it is. But because it's happening this fast, you have to give it the test of time," I said. "If it's real, you'll both know it here." I tapped my chest over my heart.

We walked farther before I stopped. "How's Darryl this morning? I told him I thought he was pushing Abbie away. I know he wants to protect her, but ..."

"He and I had an argument about it, and this morning he's going to call her," Emma said, breaking into my conversation with a thumbs-up signal. "I think you helped him see that this is what he should do."

"I'm glad," I said and looked up to find Darryl and Rand jogging toward us.

We waited for them to approach.

"Two lovelies on a lovely day," said Rand, beaming at us.

"Hi, guys," said Emma. "How many miles have you done today?"

"I figured it was about six up and back," said Darryl. "I think Abbie is going to be pleased when she hears."

"You're going to ask her to come to Florida?" I asked him.

"Yes. I'll protect her as much as possible, but it'll be a test to see if what we have can work. Her clients consist of many high-profile people. She's used to the idea of publicity because of them."

"I'm really happy she'll be here," I said.

"She knows about the plan I have for my future and has already agreed to help me organize it," said Darryl.

"It pays to have a smart woman beside you," said Rand, settling a gaze on Emma. "I've been thinking about your suggestion for a charitable opportunity."

"That makes me happy," said Emma.

"Well, I guess I'd better head back to the hotel. It's great to see everyone. Let me know if the hotel can do anything for you," I said, wanting to give them their time alone.

"See you tomorrow," said Emma. "Tell Rhonda hello and thank her again for dinner last night."

"It was delicious," said Rand.

"Fantastic," agreed Darryl.

I gave them a wave and walked into another busy day at the hotel.

CHAPTER TWENTY-SIX

I WALKED INTO THE OFFICE, CARRYING A CUP OF COFFEE and a sweet roll. "Good morning, chef!" I teased. "Dinner last night was spectacular as always and Darryl, Emma, and Rand wanted me to thank you again for it."

"You're just who I wanted to see," said Rhonda. "I want the complete lowdown on everyone. Are Emma and Rand hitting it off as well as I think? Is Abbie coming back here? What's going on?"

I took a seat at my desk, sipped my coffee, and said, "Abbie is returning, and Emma and Rand really like one another."

Rhonda leaned forward. "Okay, they were the headlines. Now I need details."

"Coming up." I filled Rhonda in on my conversation with Darryl at dinner and then told her, "He's calling Abbie today and inviting her to come and stay at the house with him."

"You're right," said Rhonda. "If they're going to make a relationship work, they have to be together through thick and thin."

I gave her a thoughtful nod as I took a bite of the cinnamon roll." "Ah, this is just what I needed."

"Okay, now tell me about Emma and Rand," said Rhonda.

I reiterated what Emma had told me, allowing myself to think about the two of them realistically. "It could work. They're both at a time in their lives when they know what they want and need. If you had seen the looks they gave each other this morning, you'd not doubt their attraction."

Rhonda rested her head in her hand. "You know, I'm really

amazing. I somehow know when a relationship can work. I've pegged both of these latest ones."

I tried not to roll my eyes. It made Rhonda happy to think she had arranged for these growing relationships to happen. If she helped things along by giving dinner parties and such, all the better.

"We have a small, VIP dinner party for the governor of Florida and three other governors from neighboring states tonight," said Rhonda. "Annette and Bernie are both off today, and Lorraine is going to help make sure everything is set the way we want. I'll handle the cocktail hour and you'd already agreed to be present for their private dinner. Are you still okay with those plans?"

"Sure. It'll be like the old days when we did everything ourselves. Let's see what Lorraine has written down for the event."

"They're flying in today and leaving late tomorrow. Room reservations are all set for them," said Rhonda, rising and following me to Lorraine's office.

"Hello," said Lorraine cheerfully. Since marrying Arthur Smythe, Reggie's father, thanks to Rhonda's pressure, she seemed to glow with happiness.

"We're here to check on the private arrangements for the governor's group," I said.

Lorraine lifted a folder off her desk. "I've got the details here. I understand you, Rhonda, will be overseeing the cocktail party, and you, Ann, will handle the private dinner."

Rhonda and I nodded.

"Jean-Luc is already prepping part of their meal. The department heads have been notified, and the VIP pictures posted on the staff bulletin board," said Lorraine.

"Have you assigned someone to give the governors a tour of the property?" I asked. Our state governor and his wife were well-acquainted with the hotel. Their daughter had even been married here. But we always liked for special guests to be shown the property. It was not only a good PR move, but it made them feel especially welcome.

"Yes, Laura is going to do that," said Lorraine. "She's such an asset to my staff."

"Great," said Rhonda. "Thanks for handling this for us."

"Anything we should know about these guests?" I asked. "Any food allergies, dislikes, etc. for dinner?"

"Nothing that hasn't been cleared with Jean-Luc," said Lorraine.

Satisfied that things were under control, Rhonda and I returned to our office to discuss the PR advertising program Liz and Angie had set up for social media. Having had a person die at the hotel and another guest "outed" for his private marriage, we needed to keep the "positives" before the public.

We sat waiting for our daughters to arrive. The day would come when our roles would be reversed, but for now, having them do small projects for us was satisfying for us all.

Liz and Angie arrived together, looking like healthy, young, active mothers in their short skirts and knit tops. A closer look allowed me to see how tired they were from handling their toddlers. But their spirits were high as they took seats at the small conference table in our office.

Liz, tall, with blonde hair, and Angie, short, with dark curly hair, were best of friends. I found it interesting that as far as personalities went, Liz was more outgoing like Rhonda, while Angie was more like me, taking care of details.

"Okay, we liked the graphics and videos you came up with. Now, tell us about the marketing plan," I said.

"Well, as you suggested, we wanted to attack the privacy issue and the positives of staying at the hotel," said Angie, pulling out a folder from her small computer carrying case.

"We also had to identify different markets for your guests," said Liz.

Angie gave Rhonda and me a sheet of paper listing the type of guests we had. Among them were those taking advantage of the young mother's retreat, the spa specials, weddings, anniversaries, etc.

"Then we listed the social media sites most would use," said Angie. "Because many of your guests are older, we knew they wouldn't use TikTok, X, and other sites younger guests might use. So, we came up with a few news releases for travel bloggers."

"Those will do especially well as the weather changes up north," Liz said. "But we can handle the social media sites ourselves for a very reasonable cost."

"The PR company we use will be able to take care of advertising with your input," said Rhonda, sitting back as Angie demonstrated the various posts they'd created.

"They're great," I said with genuine enthusiasm. "Let's get started."

"Yes," said Rhonda. "We don't want to wait."

"Okay," said Angie, sliding a contract across the table for us to sign.

Seeing it, I was pleased by how professional these two women were. When the time came to do it, I think they'd be excellent taking over for us. But neither they nor we were ready.

"Shall we have some lunch?" I said, after signing the contract.

"I'd love to," said Angie.

"And while I have someone watching the T's, I want time to do some shopping," Liz said. "Maybe we can have a quick bite here?"

"Sounds fine with me," I said, and Rhonda agreed.

"Let's take our food up to the balcony in the Presidential Suite," I said. "It's private and beautiful."

"Wait! Isn't that where that woman died?" asked Liz.

"Yes, but any weird feelings about that have disappeared after Lily Dorio stayed there," I said. "Let's give that space some of our love to make ourselves comfortable about renting it out."

"Annie's right. It's too beautiful to let a bad memory take over," said Rhonda. "Luckily, no other guests were aware of what happened there." She chuckled. "If I feel safe, you should too. You know how sensitive I am about those things."

"I do know," said Angie. "Remember when you thought you saw a ghost in the hotel right after you bought it, and it turned out to be a bird?"

I joined in the laughter, pleased that we'd make the Presidential Suite right again.

Sitting with our daughters on the balcony overlooking the side garden, I breathed in the sweet air and studied the scene below. It was a perfect spot for a wedding. One we often used. It had taken a few growing seasons to turn it from a simple lawn into the garden it was today.

"Mom, you should hear the T's say their alphabets. It's adorable," said Liz.

I focused on the conversation as it turned to talking about the six grandchildren Rhonda and I had. It was such a joy to have our families close by.

When the girls got up to leave, I turned to Rhonda, "I'm going to go home. I'll be back in time for the dinner tonight at seven."

"I'll check on a couple of things and then I'm out of here

until five."

I called Housekeeping to take care of the suite and headed to my house, ready for a break. Vaughn understood when I had to work in the evening, but I always tried to balance that commitment with extra time for him.

That evening, I stood aside as the specially selected staff members served the four men in the small reserved dining room. Allowing political guests to meet in private had helped grow the hotel's business. In the beginning, I'd been the one to oversee the dinners, assuring the diners that any information overheard would remain privileged.

It had amazed me what was taking place behind the scenes—the maneuvering, compromises, and deals. But I soon learned that even that information turned out not to be true. In any case, I could never discuss it with anyone else.

Governor Horne from Florida thanked me as three men and one woman rose after dinner. "It's always a pleasure to be here at The Beach House Hotel. Lorna and I want to come for a restful stay before the holidays."

"It's our pleasure for Rhonda and me to have you here," I responded as the other members of the group gathered around us to thank me.

They left, and after seeing that the staff would take care of cleaning up, I drove home, lost in memories of such dinners in the past. Never would I have imagined having such a glamorous life. I thought of my blessings and hurried home.

CHAPTER TWENTY-SEVEN

THE NEXT MORNING, I MET EMMA ON THE BEACH.
Seeing her smiling face as she approached me, I knew things
must be going well with Rand and her, and I was happy for
her.

"That's fantastic, huh?" I teased.

She laughed. "Well, we've done a lot of talking. And getting
to know Rand is very satisfying. He is a fascinating man with
a lot of interesting experiences. But the real man, the
somewhat shy and introspective person I'm beginning to
know is the one who intrigues me."

"And the chemistry?"

She giggled softly. "Out of sight."

I gave her an impulsive hug. "It sounds perfect."

She hugged me back. "I can't believe I'm so lucky. We've
even talked about my coming to Florida after the twins
graduate high school."

I saw Darryl jogging toward us with purpose and turned
toward him.

"' Morning! What's up?"

Darryl ran up to us and paused to get his breath. "Emma,
you won't believe what's happening. I got a call from Kim. She,
Jessie, and Alex will be here this afternoon. Kim said they're
staying with me to make sure I'm all right. But I know better.
Our sisters are coming here to check out Abbie and Rand."

"Oh, dear," said Emma. "I think you're right. They can stay
with you, and I'll ask Rand if I can move to his house to give
them space."

"They said not to worry about the kids. Joe is staying with them." Darryl stood with his hands on his hips and faced me. "Kim is my oldest sister and has been married to her husband, Joe, for years. They're both very protective of me, especially after my mother died when I was still in Middle School. My other two sisters used to like to boss me around, but since we've grown up, they, too, want to make sure I'm okay."

I remembered the many times I'd wished for siblings. "You're a very lucky man."

"I guess. Well, Emma, this is it. The family test."

"Nothing anybody says is going to interfere with the relationship I'm building with Rand," she said. She noticed Rand jogging toward us and waved.

"My sisters don't know Abbie. She's one tough lady," said Darryl.

"Where is she?" I asked.

"Sleeping in," said Darryl. "We stayed up late. I told her I'd go ahead without her."

Silence followed, but we all thought the same thing. They'd had a very sexy reunion.

"Hey, there," said Rand. "What's going on?"

"Can I move in with you?" Emma asked.

Rand blinked rapidly and then grinned. "Yes, but do you want to tell me why."

Emma told him about her sisters' visit. "They're great and you'll love them, but it's best if I give them the space at Darryl's house."

"Best for you," grumped Darryl and then elbowed her. "Kidding. Go ahead and stay with Rand. That way, it might be less confusing. Abbie will have a better chance to get to know them."

"Are you sure it's okay?" Emma asked Rand.

"Of course," said Rand, and winked at her.

"Do you still have time for a walk?" I asked Emma.

"Sure, everything else can wait. Let's go."

We walked side by side down the beach. As we moved, I could sense Emma's excitement.

"Do you think there will be any problems with your sisters?" I asked her.

"Honestly, all three of them will be surprised at the way things are between Rand and me. They'll be happy for me, of course, but I think they might object to my falling for him so quickly. It's not like me."

"Maybe they, like others, won't see the man you know beyond his appearance and manner."

"His money and looks will mean little to them. They're all happily married to decent men. They will want to make sure he's worthy of me."

"I like that," I said, thinking some interesting days were ahead. "If there's anything Rhonda and I can do for you or them, please let us know." I checked my watch. "I'd better go."

"Thanks," said Emma. "Maybe you and Rhonda can stop by after work for a quick drink. I'd love my sisters to meet you both."

"We'll do that," I said, knowing full well that Rhonda would never be left out of such an opportunity to keep an active role in her matchmaking plans.

Before going into the office, I raced home to change my clothes. I'd hoped to see Vaughn but realized he was meeting that morning with the board of cultural affairs in Sabal. He liked helping out where he could to keep theater alive in town.

As I showered and dressed, my mind kept comparing Rand and Vaughn. Both men were very handsome and successful. And more alike than some might suspect. Beneath their smooth manner and appearance were men who were quiet and introspective when alone or with someone they trusted.

Late afternoon, at a call from Emma, Rhonda and I headed to Darryl's house anxious to meet the Douglas sisters. And we couldn't wait to see Abbie again.

I carried a tray of appetizers from the hotel kitchen and Rhonda held two bottles of chilled, sparkling rosé wine.

Before we could even knock, Emma opened the door. "Hi, I'm glad you're here. Come inside." She accepted the tray from me and came back from the kitchen to take the wine from Rhonda. "Thanks for the treats."

We stepped into the living room. A group of women were sitting together, talking.

"Hey, everyone!" said Emma. "Let me introduce Ann Sanders and Rhonda Grayson, the owners of the hotel."

As one, they turned to face us.

Abbie waved, and I studied the other three women as Emma introduced them.

Kim, the oldest, was an attractive woman who wore her blond hair pulled back into a bun, had brown eyes, and wore round horn-rimmed glasses. Stylish, almost regal-looking, she smiled warmly at us.

Jessie was introduced as next in age to Kim. She was a little shorter and was pleasantly plump. Her facial features were similar to Darryl's. She moved forward and hugged both Rhonda and me.

Alex, closest in age to Emma, looked a lot like her with frosted brown hair and bright hazel eyes. She wore a two-piece bathing suit showing off her trim, curvy figure. Her grin was impish, and I suspected she and Emma got into trouble as children.

Darryl came over to Rhonda and me and took the bottles of wine from Emma. "Here, let me open these, and we can toast being together. Rand should be here soon."

I followed him into the kitchen to see if I could help.

"How's it going? Any news from your lawyer?" I asked him.

"He called to tell me that he and the woman's lawyer are working out a deal whereby we can announce that there's been a misunderstanding and the woman no longer wants to proceed. We all feel that gives her an out without our suing her and ruining her life more than she's done for herself."

"That sounds promising," I said. "It's terrible to have someone's life ripped apart by statements that aren't true."

Rand arrived, and Darryl went to greet him while I walked into the living room to chat with Abbie and Darryl's sisters.

Abbie came over to me and gave me a hug. "I'm grateful you helped Darryl realize that we needed to be together. It made such a difference to him to hear it from you."

"I'm glad I could help," I said. "It's true. You must be able to go through the ups and downs together."

"It sounds as if things are going to be settled fairly quickly," Abbie said. "But knowing Darryl, it will have a long-term effect on him. Such a shame."

Darryl came over to us and wrapped an arm around Abbie. "My tormentor is back," he said, grinning at Abbie. "But I've worked hard, even after she left. Tell her, Ann."

"He did. I swear it," I said.

Rhonda joined us, and while she talked to Darryl and Abbie, I left them to chat with Darryl's sister, Kim.

Kim was clearly upset that Darryl had to go through the public humiliation of being accused of inappropriate behavior. "Anyone who knows my brother would realize that wasn't true. But how many others were quick to judge him? It doesn't seem fair."

Jessie, the sister I picked to be the most easy-going, patted Kim on the back. "We know Darryl is an honorable man. It'll all turn out in the end."

Alex closest in age to Emma nudged me. "What do you think of Emma and Rand?"

"They are quickly falling for one another, and I'm happy for them. It happened that way for me and my husband."

"Vaughn Sanders is your husband?" she said. "I loved watching him in *The Sins of the Children*."

"He's making movies now and does some ads," I said. "It's best when he's home and being a dad and granddad."

"Because my sisters live within easy driving distance of one another, it makes it nice for us and our kids," said Alex. "I think the idea of Emma moving away is something that scares us all. It won't be the same without her."

"Just look around you," I teased. "Where else could you be having cocktails in the afternoon in such a beautiful setting?"

Alex chuckled. "You're right about that."

"About what?" asked Emma, bringing Rand over to us.

"Nothing, just girl talk," said Alex, gazing up at Rand.

I went to the kitchen to make sure there were plenty of appetizers left on the tray to pass. Keeping busy made me happy when others talked of such strong family connections.

Rhonda was telling them about running a hotel, and I smiled as others laughed at her stories.

"Okay, everyone!" said Darryl, carrying a tray of drinks. "Take a glass of wine, and let's make a toast to becoming new friends!"

We each took one and lifted it to salute one another. It was a sweet moment that I hoped would bring happy results.

Later, walking back to the hotel, Rhonda and I exchanged

tidbits of information. One thing was clear. No way did Darryl act in a way that would anger and disappoint his sisters. The case against him seemed as clear as the lawyer declared.

"I'm glad Abbie returned," said Rhonda. "The way she and Darryl are with one another is adorable. Even Kim, the oldest sister, was amused."

"Rhonda, you have an older brother who protected you in the neighborhood. What must it be like to have someone like that growing up?"

Rhonda threw an arm around my shoulder. "You may have had a lonely childhood, but remember, I'm here now. No one is going to get away with hurting you without me fighting back."

Tears stung my eyes. What had I done to ever deserve her friendship? It was priceless.

CHAPTER TWENTY-EIGHT

THE NEXT DAY, RAND, DARRYL, AND VAUGHN DECIDED TO go sailing while Emma organized a shopping trip for her sisters and Abbie. Rhonda and I opted out of their plans to give attention to projects at work. I'd learned that if I didn't keep up with my administrative duties, I paid for it in the end by having to work long extra hours. We did, however, decide to meet them for lunch at André's.

With another wedding about to take place over the weekend, Rhonda and I met with Lorraine, Laura, and Annette to ensure that all were ready and able to take care of the many details and be able to pamper the wedding party. Rhonda and I would stop by for the ceremony and for a few minutes during the celebration to greet the wedding party.

Next, we set up a meeting with the reservations department to discuss the media advertising being done by Liz and Angela. If the people in the department were doing their job, they'd act as salespeople to requests for information.

Later, when it was time for lunch, I was more than ready to take a break. Besides, I wanted to see how the women had gotten along. I hoped Emma's sisters would be supportive of her attraction to Rand and had grown to like Abbie.

At André's, the women were seated at a large round table.

"We've just started," said Abbie, waving us over. "Margot has opened a bottle of Champagne for us. We're here to celebrate." The excitement in her voice rang out.

"What's going on?" I slid into a chair next to her.

Abbie raised her fist triumphantly. "Darryl just called to tell us that the woman who accused him of sexual harassment has recanted her words. She's saying that it was a huge, emotional mistake due to financial stress over the loss of her job."

"Wow! That's a big admission," I said.

"It is," agreed Abbie, "but it's better than going to trial and exposing herself for additional bad behavior. I'm just glad it's over."

Margot quickly filled tulip glasses with champagne for Rhonda and me and stood aside.

Kim tapped against her glass with a fork for attention. "Let's toast Darryl and wish him more success!"

"Hear! Hear!" We cried together and lifted our glasses in a group salute.

I was touched to be part of this. As often happened to Rhonda and me, we'd become friends with people who'd started as guests.

Alex, sitting next to Emma, raised her glass again. "And here's to Abbie for being so supportive of Darryl."

Smiling, we turned to her.

Abbie, who was fit and strong, seemed to crumble. She covered her eyes for a moment and then lifted her face. "Thank you," she said quietly as we all saluted her with our bubbly wine.

Watching Abbie compose herself again, I was amazed to discover her vulnerability. We humans are a very complicated lot with needs that often surprise us.

Later, during lunch, I spoke to Abbie. "Having four older brothers, are you finding it fun to be part of Darryl's sister group?"

Abbie nodded and grinned. "It's interesting. They're all

very different, but very kind. It makes me think that what Darryl and I share is as special as they think."

I gave Abbie a quick squeeze and studied the women at the table. Women supporting women made all the difference in how we lived.

When I returned home that evening, Vaughn, Darryl, and Rand were lying in lounge chairs by the pool, their hair damp from swimming.

"Hello," I said to Vaughn. "Did you have a good sail?"

All three men sat up in their chairs.

Vaughn said, "It was terrific. We had some brisk wind, and now I've got two First Mates, not one."

Rand gave me a boyish smile full of pride. "I may have to buy a boat."

"You heard my good news?" said Darryl.

"Yes, I did. Abbie, your sisters, Rhonda, and I all toasted you with champagne at lunch. I'm so happy for you."

"That's not the only news I have," said Darryl. "Vaughn, why don't you explain it because you're the one who made it happen."

I lowered myself onto the chair next to Vaughn. "Okay, spill."

Vaughn grinned. "Darryl has a wonderful idea for a comedy show that he's going to pitch to Tina's husband. It's a family situation—two men, one older, one younger, meet at a grief counseling group. The older man has three daughters. The younger one has three sons who are all teenagers. The older man has a big house and has invited the younger family to move in with him when he learns his new friend spent all his savings and mortgaged his house for his wife's medical treatment."

"I like the idea," I said.

"There's a part for Vaughn," Darryl said.

"And I'm interested in helping to finance it," said Rand, "if Tina's husband will produce it."

I studied the excitement on all three of their faces and hugged myself. It was moments like this that made me believe in miracles. Wait until the others learned the news! It would take more than a tiny glass of champagne to celebrate appropriately. We'd have dinner and end the evening with nightcaps at The Beach House Hotel. I couldn't think of a better way to bring this group of people into the hotel family.

CHAPTER TWENTY-NINE

IT HAD BEEN SIX MONTHS SINCE DARRYL'S SISTERS HAD visited the hotel. Now, they and their husbands and children had come to Florida to celebrate Darryl's wedding to Abbie. This was a wedding Rhonda and I wanted to be part of.

Darryl had rented a house at the hotel for himself, Kim, and her husband, and two of their three children. Tina, Nicholas, and their two boys were in the other house on the hotel property. Abbie was staying in the bridal suite, while Rand and Emma were staying in another suite here at the hotel. The rest of Darryl's family and all of Abbie's family were scattered between the Sanderling Cove Inn and the Salty Key Inn within a doable range. A couple of grandchildren were among the mix of family members. All in all, the small, family wedding included almost fifty people.

Darryl and Abbie had opted for a beach wedding, declaring that's where a lot of their early courtship had taken place.

On this April morning, I walked on the beach with Emma, delighted to be able to catch up with her. We were going to meet Rhonda for coffee as soon as we finished our walk, and then the wedding party would be busy getting ready for the day. Fortunately, the weather was cooperating, and it promised to be perfect for a late afternoon wedding.

"I can't believe I have only two more months in Ohio before moving to Star Island to be with Rand." She held out her left hand and gazed at the sparkling diamond on her ring finger. "It's been such a blessing for me to find Rand. My kids adore him, and I can't wait to be here in Florida permanently with him."

"How are the wedding plans coming along?" I asked. They'd booked the hotel for a September wedding.

"We both want to keep our wedding low-key, like this," said Emma. "Rand isn't close to his family, but we'll include his parents, of course, and a couple of his friends. The rest will look pretty much like this. Maybe with fewer kids because of school." She turned and shrugged. "We'd prefer simply to elope, but I can't let my sisters down. They'd never forgive me if I did."

"It can get distressing, trying to keep everyone happy. I thought it was sweet that Abbie asked Tina to be her matron of honor. She didn't want to hurt any feelings between you and your sisters."

"I'm very pleased Darryl is marrying Abbie, and he's having such success pulling together his idea for a television series. It's made us all one big family."

"I agree. Vaughn is thrilled about working on it with Tina's husband, Nicholas, and it's nice to see Rand be part of the project. Life has a way of shuffling things around making unexpected changes."

Emma grinned and nodded. "Yes, from the bad news that Darryl was going to have to face criminal charges to what our lives are like now is dramatic and so very satisfying."

We picked up our pace when we saw others coming onto the beach. "Time to meet Rhonda," I said, hoping to avoid seeing Brock Goodwin.

Inside the hotel, we went to the kitchen, grabbed cups of coffee, and went into the office. Rhonda was there, talking on the phone with Angela. "Okay, see you later. Great job on the promo stuff we asked for."

Rhonda turned to us with a smile. "Our daughters are a great help to us."

"I'm glad for the opportunity to see you," said Emma, giving Rhonda a hug.

"Let me get a gander," said Rhonda, and Emma proudly held out her left hand.

Rhonda studied it. "It's gorgeous. I wish the best to you and Rand. I can't wait to see your wedding here in the fall."

"It's going to be pretty similar in attendance to this one," said Emma. "But we'll make it our own."

"For all the weddings that Annie and I have overseen, each one is very special for its own reasons. Yours will be extra special because you found love here at the hotel."

"Thanks," said Emma. "I'd better join the other women. We're getting our hair and nails done this morning."

Emma left, and Rhonda and I sat and faced one another. "Another wedding. Let's hope this one happens without any problems."

That afternoon, Rhonda and I stood on the sand with our husbands and the other wedding guests. A few chairs formed a circle around the small altar for those who couldn't stand for long.

To the soft music of the guitar player, Darryl's sisters walked down the boardwalk one by one and onto the sand. Then it was Tina's turn to make her way toward us.

Her face was glowing with happiness as she approached Nicholas and the rest of us in the wedding circle.

Then everyone focused on Abbie walking with her father.

Wearing a stunning slip-like mid-calf white silk dress, Abbie's gaze remained focused on Darryl who was trying not to cry as he stared at her. His father, who was acting as best man, patted Darryl on the back.

As Abbie came closer, I could see tears welling in her eyes

and felt her happiness at reaching this very special moment with the man she loved. I glanced up at Vaughn standing beside me, and he squeezed my hand to let me know he was remembering our beach wedding.

Knowing the hotel had played a role, I glanced at Rhonda, who winked at me. The Beach House Hotel was much more than a place to sleep, eat, and play. It brought out the best, sometimes the worst, in people because it was run by us with our wish for each person to find joy here.

After the ceremony, we'd celebrate with excellent food, stunning accommodations, and a toast or two. We might even end the celebration with nightcaps. One thing was for certain, there would be many more celebrations at The Beach House Hotel.

# # # # #

Thank you for reading *Nightcaps at The Beach House Hotel*. If you enjoyed this book, please help other readers discover it by leaving a review on your favorite site. It's such a nice thing to do.

For your further enjoyment, the other books in The Beach House Hotel Series are available on all sites. Here are the Universal links:

Breakfast at The Beach House Hotel:
https://books2read.com/u/bpkoq4

Lunch at The Beach House Hotel:
https://books2read.com/u/3GWvp3

Dinner at The Beach House Hotel:
https://books2read.com/u/4N1yDW

Christmas at The Beach House Hotel:
https://books2read.com/u/38gZvd

Margaritas at The Beach House Hotel:
https://books2read.com/u/bMRrP7

Dessert at The Beach House Hotel:
https://books2read.com/u/mV6kX6

Coffee at The Beach House Hotel:
https://books2read.com/u/bOnE7A

High Tea at The Beach House Hotel:
https://books2read.com/u/mgN9AK

Bubbles at The Beach House Hotel:
https://books2read.com/u/meGgRV

Sign up for my newsletter and get a free story. I keep my newsletters short and fun with giveaways, recipes, and the latest must-have news about me and my books. Welcome! Here's the link:

https://BookHip.com/RRGJKGN

Enjoy the first chapter of *Bubbles at The Beach House Hotel,* Book 10 in The Beach House Hotel Series, which will be released in 2025:

CHAPTER ONE

"Annie, take a look at this," said Rhonda DelMonte Grayson, my best friend and fellow owner of The Beach House Hotel. She waved me over to her desk in our office.

I leaned over her shoulder to read the message we'd received from our reservations department. When I was through, I sat down in my desk chair and felt the sting of tears.

Five women, members of a book club in a small town outside Pittsburg, had reserved one of our guesthouses on the property for ten days. Each had confessed that they'd all had to save for some time to be able to do it, and all five had asked for champagne to be delivered to the house on a different evening as a surprise to the others.

"That's so sweet," I said. "We've got to do something nice for them."

"One of the women, Jane Sweeney, said she wants to include packages of bubbles from our spa with her gift so they can take bubble baths," said Rhonda. "She said they wanted bubbles, bubbles, bubbles to celebrate being here. Isn't that adorable?"

"What could we do to help them make their time here more special? Give them spa packages?" I asked.

Rhonda looked at me and nodded. "Perfect."

My mind spun. "Maybe they'd allow us to interview them for our special 'Pamper Package Program'." Even with the stellar reputation our upscale hotel on the Gulf Coast of Florida enjoyed, we were always trying to find ways to put "heads in beds", as they say in the business.

Two days later, on a balmy October morning, Rhonda and I stood at the top of the front stairs of the hotel to greet our book club guests.

When we saw the white stretch limo pull through the gates, Rhonda nudged me. "Guess they decided to go all the way for their ride. I freakin' love it."

I laughed. "I can't remember when we've been so excited about new guests."

As the limo pulled to a stop, Rhonda and I hurried down the steps to greet them. I couldn't wait to meet these women. They sounded like people I'd want as friends.

The back doors of the limo opened, and a group of women laughing and talking got out of the car and faced us. They looked as different as could be. But one, a woman with dark hair and a streak of gray across the front, seemed to be in charge.

She stepped forward. "Hello, I'm Jane Sweeney. You must be Ann and Rhonda. We've read all about you."

"Welcome to The Beach House Hotel," I said.

Rhonda smiled. "We're so happy you're here."

One of our valets rolled a luggage cart over to the limo driver to help with the luggage.

"Your luggage will be taken to your house," I said. "Come into the hotel to check in, and then Rhonda and I will escort you to your house."

"Okay," said another woman with auburn hair. "First, I want to get a photo of the entrance to the hotel. It's gorgeous!" She turned to the others. "Just think! We get to live here in the lap of luxury for ten whole days."

One woman, a pleasantly plump woman with blond hair, clapped and the others joined in, smiling at one another.

"May I take a photo of the two of you right here?" asked a woman with dark curly hair and pretty dark eyes.

I hesitated and then said, "Certainly." Normally, I hated to have photos taken of me but for this friendly group, I couldn't resist.

Rhonda gave me a nod of acceptance, and we stood together for the group.

At the entrance to the hotel, Rhonda and I introduced Bernie to them.

He bobbed his head. "Welcome to The Beach House Hotel. Let us know if we can do anything for you. We're here to see that your stay with us is everything you want."

A woman with brown hair and pink color flowing through it smiled at Bernie. "Glad to hear it. We investigated several properties but chose this hotel because of the reputation you have for excellent service."

Bernie looked surprised at the no-nonsense way the woman spoke but nodded politely. "Compliments like that are always appreciated. We work hard for them. Have a good stay."

He turned and walked away.

"He sounds so European," gushed one of the women.

"I believe with a name like Bernhard Bruner, he's of German descent," said Jane. She turned to Rhonda and me. "I'm a librarian and love facts of all kinds."

"Jane is the one who got this group together some years ago. She even came up with the name of our book club, The

Book Circle," said the blonde. "And that's what we've become—a circle of friends."

"Best friends," said the woman with curly dark hair.

"You're very lucky," I said. "Women being together, listening to one another, supporting one another is a precious gift."

"Women helping women is something we all need," said Rhonda. "Right, Annie?"

"Yes. We never could have created this hotel if we weren't best of friends. So, we want you to enjoy being together here. "Let's get you registered, and then we'll go over to the house."

Thanks to pre-registration information, we quickly got everyone signed in, and then Rhonda and I walked the group over to the guesthouse they'd rented. With three bedrooms, a nice-size kitchen and living space, plus a private pool, there was plenty of room for them.

As the women entered the house, the first thing they saw was the huge bouquet of fresh flowers we had placed in the living room. Beyond that, the pool and the palm trees outside the pool cage beckoned.

"Wow! This is even more beautiful than I thought it would be," said one of the women.

"We've put bottles of water, and a small charcuterie plate in the refrigerator. The dining room is open and I'm sure you've made reservations for dinner tonight," said Rhonda. She didn't mention the bottle of champagne one of the women had ordered and was now hiding in the refrigerator.

"Oh, yes. We've read all about Jean-Luc and his delicious meals," said Jane.

A valet was waiting in the kitchen. "I need to know where to put the luggage. If you'll show me which room you each are in, I'll be happy to carry the bags there."

After some commotion, the valet was able to get all the

luggage into the right rooms. Jane was taking the master bedroom suite, while the others were settled in the other two rooms.

"It seems right that Jane was given the master suite because she's the one who organized all of this for us," said the pink-haired woman, returning to the living room.

"Now that you're all getting settled, Rhonda and I will leave you," I said.

"Enjoy your stay," said Rhonda.

As we left the house, Rhonda said, "I'm so glad we're friends."

"The best of friends," I said, laughing when she pulled me into a bosomy hug. I'd grown up with a strict grandmother who wasn't open to many displays of affection. It had taken me a while to get used to Rhonda and her openness to others.

"Those women are bound to have a good time," said Rhonda. "They seem very different, but they've been friends for years."

"Go ahead and make fun of me, but I get a little nervous when things seem too perfect," I said, wishing I didn't sound like my grandmother who became suspicious of happy times.

"Well, no matter what happens with them, we can handle anything together," said Rhonda.

My spirits lifted. "You're right. The two of us together. Let's hit the beach for a few minutes. We have plenty of time before we're to meet with Lorraine." Lorraine Grace handled weddings for the hotel through her business, Wedding Perfection. She'd become a very valued member of our team.

We walked to the edge of the beach, removed our shoes, and walked onto the warm sand. The salty tang of the air filled my nose, and I inhaled it gratefully as I moved toward the water. I felt part of a different world whenever I stood in the water feeling the push and pull of the waves at my feet. I looked up as a trio of pelicans flew in formation close to the water's surface looking for food to fill their pouches.

Close by, seagulls circling in the air caught my attention, and I listened to their high-pitched cries with a sense of rightness. All seemed as it was supposed to be in my world and my worries about the group of women in one of the guesthouses disappeared. After all, what could go wrong? It was a group of long-time friends in one of the most beautiful spots in the country.

I was so lost in my thoughts that when Rhonda elbowed me, I jumped with surprise.

"Here comes Brock Goodwin," she said with annoyance. "I thought he was an early morning walker. There must be some reasons he's so late."

"He's heading right toward us. I wonder what he wants now," I said. Brock Goodwin was the president of the Neighborhood Association and thought he could tell us how to run our hotel. He'd fought us at every step when we'd tried to open it.

"Ah, you're just the two I was looking for," said Brock, coming up to us and giving us a fake smile that made my blood boil.

By the looks of it, Rhonda was as irritated as I was by his condescending tone.

"Hello, Brock," I said.

"I heard you had a whole bunch of women arriving at the hotel and staying in one of the guest houses. I bet you didn't know that the neighborhood has regulations about how many people can stay in a rental house."

"I bet you didn't know I don't give a rat's ass about that and what you're trying to do," said Rhonda.

"Your neighborhood rules don't apply to the hotel," I said, trying to calm Rhonda while talking straight to Brock. "I'm sure you're aware of that. If not, read the bylaws of the association again."

Brock made a face and slammed his hands on his hips. "You two think you can do anything you want, but as president of the Neighborhood Association, I'm here to keep watch on you. You are part of the neighborhood whether I like it or not."

"You've made that point too often," I said. "We're not the only ones who think you constantly try to make your position more than it is for your own self-importance."

"Yeah," said Rhonda. "Eff off."

I knew Rhonda was just getting started on telling Brock what else he could do, so I took hold of her arm, and we turned away from Brock.

Brock ran around us and blocked our way. "You may think you have the last word on this and other problems at the hotel, but I promise I'll keep my eye on you."

"Brock, you know what I told you," said Rhonda. Having grown up in a tough neighborhood, Rhonda was no stranger to speaking her mind or facing an enemy.

Afraid the situation was just going to become worse, I said, "See you later, Brock. And this time, please have the courtesy to step out of our way." I could see Brock trying to control his emotions as if deciding whether to stay or move. Finally, he stepped back and Rhonda and I went on our way.

"That bastard is going to make me do it," said Rhonda.

"Do what?" I asked.

"Wring his fuckin' neck," said Rhonda, her dark eyes flashing. "He has no right telling us how many guests can stay in one of our guesthouses."

"Of course not," I said. "He just keeps trying to push his position on us. He's done it from the beginning. If he'd had his way, the hotel would never have opened. And to have it be the success it is really irritates him."

"I don't like thinking he has some inside source talking about our guests. Let's tell Bernie what has happened. The staff needs to know they can't talk about our guests and who's staying where," said Rhonda.

"I agree," I said, and we headed inside to see Bernie.

Bernhard Bruner or Bernie was a superb hotel manager. His presence and manner were noticeably autocratic, but he was a nice man determined to do a good job. If you gave him the respect he deserved, he was a loyal friend and an excellent person to run our hotel for us. We adored him and his wife, Annette, who worked in hospitality for us.

When we knocked on Bernie's door, he waved us inside his office.

"We just saw Brock Goodwin on the beach," I began.

"That's enough to ruin anyone's day," said Bernie. "What now?"

"He thinks he can tell us how many people we must limit to either of our guesthouses," said Rhonda.

"We all know he can't. What else did he say?"

"He's going to be keeping his eye on us, which is nothing new," I said. "But we're unhappy that he knew there was a group of women staying in one of the houses. Do we need to talk to staff again about not saying anything about the people staying here?"

"It's always good to remind staff of that, especially if new people come on board. I'll add that to the agenda for the upcoming staff meeting," said Bernie. "It seemed like an enthusiastic group of women. I don't want to do anything to make them think less of the hotel."

"My feeling exactly," I said. "Brock tries to make things difficult for us. Even after the episode of being under suspicion for aiding one of our guest's deaths."

"We can't let that ... jerk stop us from doing well," said Rhonda, struggling not to swear in front of Bernie.

"On another note," said Bernie. "I heard from vice-president, Amelia Swanson. She has a favor to ask."

"Another one?" groaned Rhonda. "What now?"

"Two of her staffers, good men, need a break. They've been traveling out of the country with her and need time to write up a few reports and to relax. I've agreed to put them in the vacant guest house for two weeks, full price."

"When are they arriving?" I asked. "I don't think anyone will interfere with the fun the women are planning."

"They're arriving late tonight," Bernie said. "I'll make sure the night staff is aware."

"That will be great. I'm glad for the income," I said. "This isn't our busiest time."

"Let's hope the weather holds," said Rhonda. "The last hurricane threat died when the system weakened and headed away from the coast."

"We can't let weather forecasts take away the pleasure of Florida at this time of year," said Bernie. "We certainly don't want to ruin any vacations with threats of bad weather. I like autumn here."

"Me, too," I said. "A few more weeks and we'll be into Christmas holiday planning."

Having my triplet grandchildren around made each holiday special. This year they'd be four years old and more fun than ever.

"Hold on, let's not get ahead of ourselves," said Rhonda, sounding panicky. "We need to take it day by day. Who knows what can happen here at The Beach House Hotel?"

A shiver traveled down my back. I glanced at Rhonda knowing she was right. Every day was full of surprises.

About the Author

A **USA Today Best-Selling Author,** Judith Keim is a hybrid author who both has a publisher and self-publishes. Ms. Keim writes heart-warming novels about women who face unexpected challenges, meet them with strength, and find love and happiness along the way—stories with heart. Her best-selling books are based, in part, on many of the places she's lived or visited, and on the interesting people she's met, creating believable characters and realistic settings her many loyal readers love.

She enjoyed her childhood and young adult years in Elmira, New York, and now makes her home in Boise, Idaho, with her husband, Peter, and their lovable miniature Dachshund, Wally, and other members of her family.

While growing up, she was drawn to the idea of writing stories from a young age. Books were always present, being read, ready to go back to the library, or about to be discovered. All in her family shared information from the books in general conversation, giving them a wealth of knowledge and vivid imaginations.

Ms. Keim loves to hear from her readers and appreciates their enthusiasm for her stories.

"I hope you've enjoyed this book. If you have, please help other readers discover it by leaving a review on the site of your choice. And please check out my other books and series:

The Hartwell Women Series
The Beach House Hotel Series
The Fat Fridays Group
The Salty Key Inn Series
The Chandler Hill Inn Series
Seashell Cottage Books
The Desert Sage Inn Series
Soul Sisters at Cedar Mountain Lodge
The Sanderling Cove Inn Series
The Lilac Lake Inn Series

"ALL THE BOOKS ARE NOW AVAILABLE IN AUDIO on iTunes! So fun to have these characters come alive!"

Ms. Keim can be reached at **www.judithkeim.com**

"To like my author page on Facebook and keep up with the news, go to: **http://bit.ly/2pZWDgA**

"To receive notices about new books, follow me on Book Bub:

https://www.bookbub.com/authors/judith-keim

"Sign up for my newsletter and get a free story. I keep my newsletters short and fun with giveaways, recipes, and the latest must-have news about me and my books. Welcome! Here's the link:

https://BookHip.com/RRGJKGN

"I am also on Twitter @judithkeim, LinkedIn, and Goodreads. Come say hello!"

Acknowledgments

As always, I am eternally grateful to my team of editors, Peter Keim and Lynn Mapp, my book cover designer, Lou Harper, and my narrator for Audible and iTunes, Angela Dawe. They are the people who take what I've written and help turn it into the book I proudly present to you, my readers! I also wish to thank my coffee group of writers who listen and encourage me to keep on going. Thank you, Peggy Staggs, Lynn Mapp, Cate Cobb, Nikki Jean Triska, Joanne Pence, Melanie Olsen, and Megan Bryce. And to you, my fabulous readers, I thank you for your continued support and encouragement. Without you, this book would not exist. You are the wind beneath my wings.